DEATH STALKS the RANGERS

Center Point
Large Print

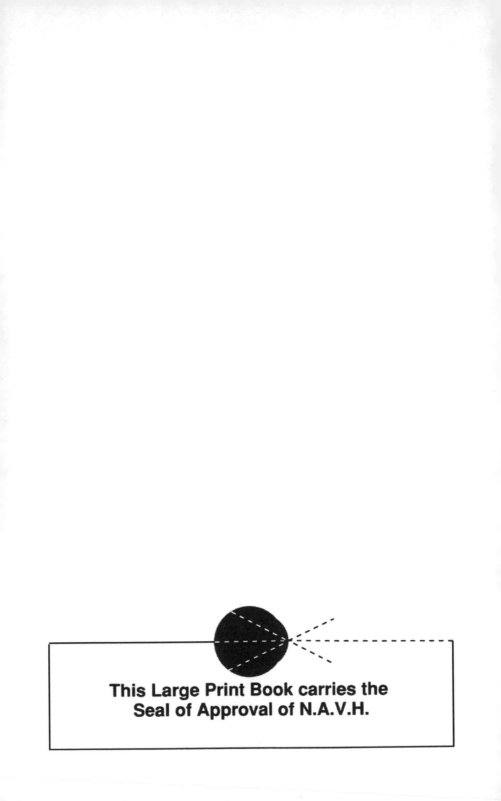

This Large Print Book carries the Seal of Approval of N.A.V.H.

DEATH STALKS *the* RANGERS

A Texas Ranger Sean Kennedy Story

JAMES J. GRIFFIN

CENTER POINT LARGE PRINT
THORNDIKE, MAINE

The text of this Large Print edition is unabridged.
In other aspects, this book may vary
from the original edition.
Printed in the United States of America
on permanent paper.
Set in 16-point Times New Roman type.

ISBN: 978-1-68324-316-8

Library of Congress Cataloging-in-Publication Data

Names: Griffin, James J., 1949– author.
Title: Death stalks the Rangers : a Texas Ranger Sean Kennedy story / James J. Griffin.
Description: Center Point Large Print edition. | Thorndike, Maine : Center Point Large Print, 2017.
Identifiers: LCCN 2016056206 | ISBN 9781683243168
   (hardcover : alk. paper)
Subjects: LCSH: Texas Rangers—Fiction. | Western stories. | Large type books.
Classification: LCC PS3607.R5477 D43 2017 | DDC 813/.6—dc23
LC record available at https://lccn.loc.gov/2016056206

Dedication

In memory of my friend Gale Buffum, a great lady, and a wonderfully talented illustrator. God needed an artist in Heaven.

Thanks to Paul Dellinger for his invaluable suggestions and editing.

As always, thanks to Texas Ranger Sergeant Jim Huggins of Company A, Houston, and Karl Rehn and Penny Riggs of KR Training, Mannhcim, Texas, for their help with technical information.

Chapter 1

Texas Ranger Sean Kennedy awoke just before sunup, while the other members of his Ranger Company were still snoring in their bunks. It was his morning to feed the horses and start the breakfast fire.

Sean swung his legs over the edge of his mattress and sat up. He pulled on his jeans, boots, and then ran a hand through the thatch of unruly dark hair covering his head. He stood, yawned and stretched, rubbed his beard-stubbled jaw and scratched his belly. Sean lifted his shirt from the peg behind his bunk and shrugged into it, tied a blue bandanna around his neck, then jammed his battered gray Stetson on his head. Finally, he buckled his gun belt around his waist and headed outside.

Sean stepped from the bunkhouse on the abandoned ranch just northwest of Laredo, which his company had been using as a headquarters for the past six weeks.

His blocky blue roan gelding, Ghost, nickered a greeting when the Ranger headed for the corral. The mount, which had been named not only for his coloring but also for his uncanny ability to move almost silently through the brush, was a big horse, which was necessary to support his rider's size. Kennedy was a large man, just about six feet tall, lantern-jawed, barrel-chested, and thickly built. His bulk belied his quickness, for he could out-draw most men, and had catlike agility in a fistfight.

"Mornin', boy," Sean called to his mount. The horse whinnied again, more urgently this time. He and the other horses in the corral had their heads lifted and ears pricked sharply forward, gazing at something in the distance.

"What's botherin' you, Ghost?" Sean asked.

Sean turned to follow the horse's gaze, his \ dark eyes narrowing against the glare of the rising sun, now gilding the eastern sky blazing yellow and orange. He could barely discern an approaching object off to the east.

Sean squinted, trying to ascertain exactly what he was watching. He finally realized it was an approaching horse.

"Somethin's wrong, though," he muttered. "That horse doesn't appear to be movin' right. I don't see a rider, either."

The horse broke into a trot as it drew nearer the ranch.

"That's Thad Dutton's horse!" Sean exclaimed, recognizing the blaze-faced chestnut. When he started toward the animal, it stopped, whickered nervously.

"Thad!" Sean shouted.

Ranger Thad Dutton, his left foot caught in the

stirrup, hung upside down from his saddle. His six-gun was gripped tightly in his hand, which dragged the ground; his eyes were wide open in the unseeing stare of death. Dried blood stained his shirtfront and covered his face. It coated Thad's Stetson, still held tightly on his head by its chinstrap.

"Lieutenant Blawcyzk!" Sean called. "Sergeant Huggins! Get out here, quick!"

He stepped carefully toward the animal. "Easy, Toby, easy," Sean attempted to sooth the nervous horse. He lunged, and grabbed the gelding's reins before it could trot off.

Lieutenant Jim Blawcyzk emerged from the bunkhouse, closely followed by Sergeant Jim Huggins and several other members of the company.

"What is it, Sean?" Blawcyzk called.

"It's Thad Dutton. His horse just brought him back. Thad's dead."

"What?" Blawcyzk exclaimed.

"Appears like he was gut-shot," Sean answered. "And maybe took a bullet in his head. Can't tell for certain until we get him off his bronc."

"Johnston, Mallory, help Kennedy get Dutton off Toby," Blawcyzk ordered two of the Rangers assembled around their dead comrade.

"Right away, Lieutenant."

While Sean held Dutton's horse steady, the two men attempted to remove him from the saddle.

9

"Thad's pretty stiff, Lieutenant," Rick Johnston noted. "We're gonna have trouble gettin' him off this horse."

"Seems he's been dead for some time," Levi Mallory added. Mallory was a young Ranger, in his early twenties. In contrast to the blocky built, darkly-featured Kennedy, he had a slim build, hazel eyes, and light brown hair. Mallory's rugged good looks were accentuated by his wind and sun darkened skin.

"We'll let Sergeant Huggins figure out when he was killed. That's his area of expertise. You just get Thad down," Blawcyzk replied.

After struggling to bend the muscles and joints of Dutton's rigor mortis stiffened limbs, the two men were finally able to free him from the saddle and lay him on the ground.

"Jim . . ." Blawcyzk said to Huggins.

"Yep," the veteran sergeant answered. He glanced at Sean.

"Kennedy, get someone to handle that horse. Now's your chance to show you've learned some of what I've been teachin' you."

"Sure, Sergeant," Sean agreed. After he handed Toby's reins to Mallory, he and Huggins knelt beside Dutton's body. By now the entire company of Rangers had gathered around them.

"What's the first thing you notice?" Huggins asked.

Kennedy swallowed hard to help get his

emotions in check. He and Dutton had ridden together for two years. He resolutely put aside his distress over the loss of his friend and fellow Ranger, to concentrate on the task at hand.

"Thad was shot with his gun in his hand. His grip tightened on it when the bullet hit him. Cadaveric spasm happens immediately."

Sean lifted Dutton's arm to sniff the gun barrel.

"This gun's been fired, too. Thad got off at least one shot."

"That's correct. What else?"

"I was right sayin' he was shot through the head. I believe Thad took the bullet in his belly first. Despite the slug in his guts he was still able to shoot back at whoever killed him, but then they shot him in his head and finished him off."

"You're doing fine," Huggins assured him. "Go on."

"I'd guess Thad was killed sometime less than twenty-four hours ago. His body hasn't begun to decompose all that much. Rigor mortis is still present, which means he's been dead less'n thirty-six hours or so. Judging by the condition of his horse, which isn't all that gaunt, I came up with a twenty-four hour guess."

"That's reasonable," Huggins agreed. "Anything else?"

"That's about it," Sean answered.

"What about the livor mortis?"

"We didn't talk all that much about that, Sergeant. Maybe you'd better explain."

"All right," Huggins agreed. He opened Dutton's shirt and removed his hat. He then pointed out several purplish-red areas on Dutton's body.

"See these discolored spots? That's livor mortis. Gravity causes the blood to pool once the heart stops pumping. Since Thad was hung up in his saddle, most of the blood settled in his upper chest, neck and shoulders. Look here."

Huggins indicated the large splotch of dried blood running from the bullet hole in Dutton's lower abdomen, over his stomach and chest, and the dried blood matting down his dark hair.

"This much blood on the outside of the body indicates Thad was alive for a while after he was shot. His heart would have had to keep working for this much blood to flow from the wounds. Sean, you were right, up to a point. Thad was shot in the gut first, then the head, but he didn't die right off. I'd say his heart didn't give out for ten or fifteen minutes after he took the second slug. Not that he ever had a chance with two bullets in vital spots. His heart just didn't know he was already dead."

Huggins pulled his Bowie from the sheath on his belt and used the heavy bladed knife to slice open Dutton's abdomen for several inches, from the navel toward the breastbone.

Dennis Knapp, one of the new recruits, turned away, retching violently.

"Guess he's never seen anyone dig for a slug," Huggins offhandedly remarked. He shoved the knife's blade deeper into the dead Ranger's belly, searching for the bullet.

"Got it," Huggins grunted in satisfaction when the blade hit a solid object. He twisted the Bowie to deftly remove the chunk of lead.

"Appears to be a .45 slug by lookin' at it. Once I weigh it I'll know for certain," Huggins noted. "So I'd say Dutton was most likely killed with a pistol, not a rifle. The fact he apparently shot back before he died indicates that, too. He wasn't shot from long range."

Huggins wiped the blade of his knife on Dutton's jeans before shoving it back in its sheath.

"What about the time of death? Was Sean right about that?" Blawcyzk asked.

"Close as anyone can come," Huggins shrugged.

"So we can figure out about how far off Thad was killed, backtrack, and hope we come up with something," Blawcyzk stated.

"It'll be a pretty wide area, but sure, we can narrow it down some," Huggins agreed.

"Fine. Go through Dutton's clothes and see if there might be any clue as to where he was or who might have killed him. I'll check his saddle-bags and gear. Once that's done we can get Thad buried and start searching for that lowdown skunk," Blawcyzk ordered.

"It'll be a job gettin' his limbs straight," Mallory observed.

"They'll bend. Just keep workin' at it," Huggins said.

"Sure, Sergeant."

"Wait a minute! I just noticed somethin' else," Sean exclaimed.

"What?" Blawcyzk asked.

"Thad's belt's missin'. You know, the one he had custom made in San Antonio, with the fancy buckle and all."

"That's right," Johnston agreed. "Thad had a Ranger badge engraved on the buckle and his initials on the keepers. He was right proud of that belt. He wouldn't take it off for anything."

"Except a good-lookin' señorita," Sean said.

"Well, whoever shot Thad didn't take his belt, that's for certain," Huggins observed. "His horse took off with him soon as he was plugged. Thad's killer didn't have the chance to remove that belt."

"Whoever does have Thad's belt might just lead us to his killer," Sean replied. "We are goin' after him, ain't we, Lieutenant?"

"We'll settle that once we lay Thad to rest," Blawcyzk answered.

Chapter 2

"Eternal rest grant unto him O Lord, and may perpetual light shine upon him. May Thad's soul and the souls of all the faithful departed, through the mercy of God, rest in peace. Amen." With the traditional words from the Catholic funeral service for the repose of the soul of the departed, which he used whenever he presided over a service for one of his deceased men, no matter what their faith, Lieutenant Blawcyzk concluded the brief interment ceremony for Ranger Thaddeus Charles Dutton.

"You were a good man, Thad," Blawcyzk murmured as he threw the first clods onto Dutton's coffin. "We'll get whoever murdered you. Bet a hat on it."

Blawcyzk stood silently for a few moments while some of the men filled in Dutton's grave. The Ranger had been laid to rest in a far corner of the ranch, his final resting place overlooking a small stream. A wooden cross would be carved by Ranger Charlie Moses and placed on the grave.

"Jim, Sean, come with me," Blawcyzk ordered once the grave was completely covered. "The rest of you men, finish the jobs you were assigned yesterday. Make sure your tack's in good repair and your horses are ready for a long ride. Be certain none of 'em have loose shoes. If there's any doubt about one, replace that shoe rather'n chancin' it bein' thrown on the trail. We'll be ridin' out tomorrow."

Kennedy and Huggins followed the lieutenant into the ranch house. Blawcyzk led them into the bedroom he was using as sleeping quarters and office.

"Have a seat, men," he invited.

Sean settled on a worn leather chair in the corner, while Huggins reversed a ladder-back chair and straddled it, his arms resting on its backrest.

Blawcyzk sat in the chair behind his battered desk. He took a piece of licorice from a jar on the desk, popped it in his mouth, and shoved the jar across the desk.

"Candy?" he asked.

"Sure." Sean took a piece of the licorice. "Thanks, Lieutenant."

"You sure you don't need these for your Sam horse, Jim?" Huggins laughed as he also took a candy. Blawcyzk's paint gelding was as well known among the Rangers for his insatiable sweet tooth as his bad temper.

"Nope. Peppermints only for him." Blawcyzk chuckled. The lieutenant grew serious when he continued, "Sean, Jim, you know we can't let the murder of a Ranger go unanswered. We've got to try and track down Thad's killer, no matter how long the odds are of finding him."

"So we're goin' after him?" Sean asked.

"Just rein in a minute," Blawcyzk answered. "First, there was absolutely nothing in Thad's gear or pockets to give us a hint as to why he was shot. Second, we don't really have any idea where to start lookin'. You said Thad's horse came in from the east, right Sean?"

"That's right, Lieutenant."

"Then there's a problem already. Thad was supposed to be on his way back from San Antonio. There's no reason he'd have headed any direction from there but straight south for Laredo. Except for a couple of Mexican villages and a few scattered ranches there's nothing between Laredo and Falfurrias. His horse comin' in from that direction makes no sense."

"A cayuse without a rider guidin' it is liable to wander in any direction. You know that, Jim," Huggins pointed out.

"Of course, but we've been stationed here for nearly two months, so Toby would know where to head for oats. There's not much grazin' around this time of year, especially considerin' the dry spell we've been havin'. My guess is that horse headed straight here from wherever Thad got shot."

"That's not one hundred percent guaranteed."

"Of course not. Only thing I'd say for certain is

17

Thad didn't get killed in Laredo. Too many people there. Someone would have grabbed his horse before he got too far."

"No one saw him after that, either, or they would have stopped Toby," Huggins pointed out.

"Any possibility the killin' might've happened in Mexico?" Sean asked.

"It's possible, but I doubt it," Blawcyzk explained. "Thad had no reason to cross the Border. Even with the Rio runnin' low, it'd be hard for a horse to swim the river with a rider hangin' off his side. I also didn't notice any dried mud on Thad's clothing. Did either of you?"

"No," Huggins replied.

"Me neither," Sean conceded.

"So apparently his horse didn't take him into any muddy water, like the Rio. No, Thad was murdered on Texas soil," Blawcyzk concluded.

"But where?" Sean asked.

"That's what I'm assigning you to find out, Ranger Kennedy," Blawcyzk answered.

"Me?"

"That's right. You, Sean," the lieutenant confirmed.

"Beggin' your pardon, but there's plenty of others with more experience than me, Lieutenant," Sean protested.

"I know that, but I think you're the man for this job," Blawcyzk replied. "You've been with the Rangers for nearly four years now, and you've done a fine job. Don't forget the training Jim Huggins has given you. That's invaluable, and none of the other men have taken lessons from him. Not even me, for that matter, so you have an edge no other member of this company has. Much as I'd like to, I can't take this entire troop ridin' all over south Texas searchin' for Thad's killer. That wouldn't work anyway. A whole company of Rangers would just scare him off. Besides, our orders are to patrol the Rio from here to Eagle Pass, mebbe up to Del Rio if necessary, to try and stop the rustlin' and smugglin' plaguing the entire border region. Cap'n Trumbull would have my head if I disobeyed those orders. We ride out tomorrow as planned."

"What about Sergeant Huggins himself?"

"I can't spare him. If anything should happen to me, he'll be in charge of the company. In fact, he's the reason I'm giving you this assignment. You've learned a lot from him, and I figure with that knowledge you're the only man in this company, except for Sergeant Huggins, who can track down Thad's killer. Do you agree, Jim?"

Huggins thumbed back his Stetson and scratched his jaw before replying.

"I sure do. Sean, like the lieutenant says, you've been a good student, and you've got fine instincts. There's not much more you can learn from me. What you need now is experience, and you have to get that on your own. I've got confidence in you. You'll find the hombre who plugged Thad."

"I'm not askin' you to do this all by yourself, Sean," Blawcyzk added. "Pick a man to ride with you."

"Anyone in particular?"

"He's gonna be your pardner, so it's your choice."

"Levi Mallory."

"You've got him. Tell Dundee to give you all the supplies you need. How soon will you be ready to leave?"

"Soon as Levi and I can get our horses saddled."

"Good. Anything else you'll require?"

"Just one thing. I want to take Thad's horse along."

"Dutton's horse? Why?" Huggins asked.

"He might be able to help us. If Toby was really spooked by whoever shot Thad, he might react if he sees him again," Sean explained.

"That's not a bad idea, Sean," Blawcyzk agreed. "Toby also might act up when you reach the place where Thad was killed. That could give you something to go on—only not much, but at least something. Take him with you. Give him a good feed and waterin' first, then let him rest a while. Leavin' an hour or so later won't make any difference."

"Thanks. I'll find Levi and tell him to get ready to ride."

"Good. Sean, don't worry about how long it takes you to find the man who killed Thad Dutton. Just find him."

"I'll do my best, Lieutenant," Sean promised.

"That's all I ask. We'll be patrolling along the Rio for the next several weeks, so if you need to reach me, get a wire to Laredo. Try to do that every couple of weeks in any event, so I know where to get in touch with you if necessary," Blawcyzk requested.

"I'll do that," Sean assured him. "When I catch up to Thad's killer, you want him brought in alive . . . or belly-down over a saddle?"

"Whichever way you have to," the captain replied.

"Yessir." Sean got to his feet.

"Good luck, Sean. Vaya con Dios," Blawcyzk said.

"Thanks, Lieutenant."

Ninety minutes later, Sean and Levi started on the trail of Thad Dutton's murderer.

Chapter 3

"Levi, we won't have a hard time following this trail, long as the weather doesn't turn against us," Sean remarked when they were about two miles from the Ranger post. "It's plenty clear."

Toby's hoof prints were plainly visible in the sandy soil. More importantly, as far as tracking was concerned, were the marks made by Thad Dutton's hand and pistol. As his horse carried him along, the dead Ranger's Colt, clamped in his fist, had left a clear line where it dragged in the dirt, Dutton's hand occasionally brushing a wider mark in the soil.

"Or until the track crosses a rocky arroyo or stream," Levi answered. "Those wouldn't show any prints. And if Dutton's cayuse followed a well-used road, we'll have a hard time distinguishin' his hoof prints from all the others."

"I doubt Toby traveled along any kind of road. Someone would have picked him up if he had. We should be able to find his trail again without too much trouble if he did cross any rocky ground or forded a creek," Sean explained.

"How long do you think we'll have to follow these tracks until we come up with something?" Levi asked.

"Not all that long," Sean answered. "I doubt

Toby traveled very far, carryin' a dead man half-out of the saddle. Right now these tracks show he kept pretty much to a straight line, but I'd say that's 'cause he knew he was gettin' close to his stable. As Lieutenant Blawcyzk would say, I'd bet a hat Toby's hoof prints are gonna start wandering all over the place shortly. I think we'll find he got spooked when Thad was shot, took off at a run for a ways, and then moseyed around once he calmed down. He undoubtedly stopped to graze or rest more'n once. I figure Thad was killed no more than ten or fifteen miles from the post."

The two men rode steadily for the next three miles, until Sean pulled Ghost to a halt. He pointed to the hoof prints left by Toby. They were now deviating from the straight line they'd maintained toward the Ranger post. The gelding's tracks led to a small grove of mesquite.

"See there, Levi. Like I figured, Toby wandered for a spell and it looks like he headed for that water hole over there. We'll have to move a bit slower so we don't lose the trail. With any luck we'll still find where Thad was killed before nightfall. Let's take five minutes and give the horses a breather."

Sean climbed from his saddle, loosened his cinches, and led Ghost and Toby to the small spring. Levi did the same for his sorrel gelding, Monte. Once the horses drank their fill and were cropping the grass surrounding the water hole, the

Rangers dropped to their bellies to dip their sun and wind burned faces in the cool water, then took a drink. Sean settled against the trunk of a large mesquite, while Levi hunkered on his haunches, took out the makings, and rolled a quirly. He lit the smoke and took a long drag.

"Sean, I know Lieutenant Blawcyzk told us not to quit until we found Thad's killer, but do you really figure we've got a chance?" he asked. "Seems to me it's a real long shot."

Sean thumbed back his Stetson and scratched his head before replying.

"We're gonna find that S.O.B.," he snapped, "if we have to follow him across all of Texas, into Mexico, and even to Hell and back if necessary. It's not gonna be easy, but we will find him. I'm not quittin' until we do."

"That's fine. Mind if I ask you another question?"

"Boy howdy, you're just full of 'em today, ain't you?" Sean chuckled. "Sure, go ahead."

"Why'd you ask the Lieutenant to send me with you?"

"Couple of reasons. You've got a level head and you're real good with a gun. I figure you're a man to ride the river with. I have a feelin' before all this is done we'll find out for sure."

Sean pushed himself to his feet.

"Time to get movin'."

They retrieved the horses and tightened their

24

cinches. Sean retied Toby's lead to his saddle horn, and then both men mounted to resume their trek.

Six hours later, Sean once again called a halt, next to a narrow creek. For the past several hours the Rangers had been forced to slow their pace, following Toby's meandering hoof prints. Sean glanced up at the sky. Clouds were blotting out the sun, which was now well past its zenith.

"Gotta admit I'm surprised we've gone this far without any sign of where Thad was killed," he said. "Toby traveled further than I figured. We're gonna run out of daylight soon. There's a new moon tonight, so we can't count on any moonlight even if those clouds do clear. Reckon we might as well camp here for the night and start out fresh in the morning. Tell you what. I'll try'n hunt down a jackrabbit or mebbe a couple of quail for supper while you take care of the horses."

"Sure," Levi agreed.

After they dismounted, Sean took his Winchester from its boot and disappeared into the brush.

Levi cared for their horses, rubbing them down, and then picketing them to graze. Once the mounts were settled, he started a small campfire and settled down with a smoke to await his partner's return. Twenty minutes later the sound of two rifle shots indicated Sean had flushed his quarry.

"Reckon there'll be somethin' besides bacon and beans on the menu tonight, Monte," he remarked to his horse.

A short while later Sean emerged from the scrub, holding up two plump quail.

"Fresh meat tonight," he called.

For supper that night, instead of the usual bacon with their beans, and biscuits, the Rangers enjoyed freshly roasted quail. When they were done eating and the dishes scrubbed, they lingered over a final cup of thick black coffee. Levi built and smoked another cigarette.

"Sure hope those clouds don't bring rain," he remarked when a cool breeze, heavy with moisture, drifted over their camp.

"I doubt they will," Sean responded. "Looks like some breaks in 'em already."

He tossed the dregs from his mug to the ground.

"Time to turn in. G'night, Levi."

" 'Night."

Heads pillowed on their saddles, rolled in their blankets, both men were soon asleep.

Chapter 4

Sean and Levi awoke before sunup. As Sean expected, the clouds of the previous evening had not produced any rain; however, they had brought in cool, moist air. Dew covered the ground and coated the Rangers' blankets. A thin fog swirled on the slight breeze, blurring the horizon and dimming the gray of false dawn.

"Bit nippy this mornin'," Levi remarked when he slid out of his bedroll. He pulled on his boots, and then began building a smoke.

"Sure is," Sean agreed, "but once this mist burns off it'll warm up right quick. Let's rustle up some grub. Soon as we're finished with breakfast it'll be light enough to travel."

"I'll get more firewood while you feed the horses," Levi answered.

"Sounds fair."

By the time Sean had retricved the sack of oats from his saddle horn and poured out a measure for each mount, Levi had a fire started and bacon sizzling in the pan. They ate quickly, saddled their horses, and broke camp. The sun topped the eastern horizon, gilding the fog a brilliant hue.

"Sorry, pardner, nearly forgot," Sean apologized to his horse when Ghost nuzzled insistently at his hip pocket. Sean produced a piece of licorice, which the gelding greedily snatched from his hand.

"Still can't believe your horse eats that stuff. I never heard of a cayuse who eats licorice," Levi noted.

"What about Lieutenant Blawcyzk's horse?" Sean replied, referring to Blawcyzk's ill-tempered paint.

"Sam? That ornery critter? Yeah, he eats candy, but peppermints, not licorice. He also likes to take a bite out of anyone who gets too near him, except the lieutenant," Levi answered.

"Boy howdy, that's for certain," Sean chuckled. He swung into his saddle. "Let's go."

They heeled the horses into a walk until they warmed up, before increasing their pace to an easy lope.

Four miles along, Sean reined in, dismounted, and then knelt to study the hoof prints of Dutton's horse more closely.

"What'd you find?" Levi asked.

Sean came to his feet and brushed dirt from his knees.

"We're gettin' closer to where Thad got plugged," he answered. "See those prints? They're deeper'n they were, and spaced farther apart. Toby ran this far."

He turned to Dutton's chestnut and patted his nose.

"Sure wish you could talk, Toby."

The gelding nuzzled his shoulder and nickered.

"Not quite the same, boy," Sean said. "I reckon you're missin' Thad."

Sean remounted.

"Let's go, Ghost. Slow and easy."

He put the blue roan into a walk.

Half a mile later, at the edge of a deep arroyo, Toby began prancing anxiously, snorting and pulling back on his lead.

"It's all right, boy." Sean reassured the nervous horse, "Nothin's gonna hurt you."

"Look down there, Sean."

Levi pointed to the floor of the arroyo, where the tracks they'd been following dissolved into a jumble of hoof prints.

"Yep, this is the spot we've been lookin' for. Toby's tellin' us that as loud and clear as if he could speak," Sean replied. He and Levi eased their horses carefully down the steep side of the ravine. Once they reached the bottom, Sean again dismounted.

"Hold still, Ghost," he told his horse, then slipped him a licorice. Thad's anxious horse pulled hard on his lead.

"Easy, Toby." Sean stroked the gelding's neck, again attempting to reassure the frantic horse. Toby's eyes were wide with fright, his nostrils flaring. He trumpeted his fear and pawed the dirt.

Sean hunkered to study the ground, his gaze following Toby's hoof prints.

"Toby came over the rim there, after Thad was shot," he noted. "Looks like whoever was followin' him lost control of his horse and it fell, so that's why he couldn't retrieve Thad's body and get rid of him. Let's get outta this arroyo. I'll bet we'll find where Thad was plugged just beyond the opposite rim."

Sean climbed back into his saddle, urging Ghost and Toby up the sandy slope and out of the arroyo, Levi on Monte close behind. Once they climbed out of the defile, they could see where Toby had come to a sudden stop. The chestnut's tracks, and those of Thad's killer's horse, were a confusing muddle. Sean again dismounted to examine the prints.

"Get down and take a look here, Levi," he ordered.

Levi swung off Monte's back to join his partner.

"See this faded brown patch. That's dried blood. Hard to see after the time that's passed, but it's plain if you know what to look for."

"Thad's blood?"

"I'd say so. We know he got off one shot, but there's nobody here, and no sign of anything the coyotes and buzzards were workin' on. So even if Thad winged whoever plugged him, the hombre wasn't hurt so bad he couldn't ride away. That means he wasn't losin' all that much blood."

"If any."

"That's right. Now let's try'n pick up his trail. Hold the horses for a minute."

After Levi took the reins of Ghost and Toby, Sean circled the area, studying sign.

"Find anything?" Levi asked after a few moments.

"Yep, I've got him. Whoever killed Thad was trailin' him." He pointed toward the northeast. "Two sets of hoof prints comin' from that direction, then one headin' back the same way. Thad's killer caught up with him here. He shot him, and then rode back to wherever they were comin' from."

"I'm kinda surprised he didn't just backshoot Thad," Levi remarked.

"Thad was a pretty clever hombre," Sean answered. "It wouldn't be easy to bushwhack him. Besides, I have a feelin' whoever shot Thad wanted him to know who it was. I'd guess he didn't really want to drill him through the head. I'm thinkin' he wanted only to gut-shoot Thad and let him die slow and painful. He didn't figure on Thad bein' able to get out his gun and shootin' back after takin' a bullet in the belly. When Thad did, his killer didn't have any choice but to finish him off."

"Why do you think he didn't keep after Toby, since it appears he was able to get back on his horse after it fell?"

"Dunno," Sean shrugged. "Mebbe he was hurt

when he took that spill, or even afraid someone had heard the shots. He also could've figured if he kept after Toby for too far he might run into someone who'd realize what happened."

"Out here?"

"I reckon you're right. It's unlikely. We have no way of knowing what that gunman was thinkin'. Mebbe he still wanted to catch Toby, but his own horse was worn out so he gave up. He also probably figured Thad would fall out of the saddle eventually. In any event, I'm certain he didn't expect Toby to bring Thad all the way back to the Ranger post. Mighty few horses would've done that."

"So now all we've gotta do is find the sidewinder."

"Which we won't do standin' here jawin'. Let's go."

Sean picked up Ghost's reins and climbed back into the saddle. He put the gelding into a long-striding lope.

They rode for nearly three more hours, following a trail that showed little sign of fading.

"That hombre sure didn't bother hidin' his tracks," Levi observed. "Reckon he figured no one'd find Thad for quite a spell and he'd be long gone by then."

"Well, he figured wrong." Sean answered. "So far we've caught a break with the weather, and let's hope this dry spell lasts a bit longer. Rain doesn't wash out hoof prints as quick as most people think, so I've been able to follow a trail even after a downright gullywasher. I can't figure where this hombre's headed, or for that matter where Thad was comin' from. Falfurrias is the only town of any size in this direction. It's southeast of here, but this trail's headin' northeast. There's nothing this way for a hundred miles. Makes no sense, unless this hombre's gonna double back."

"Well, Thad must've had a reason for wherever he went," Levi replied. "You been wonderin' who might've killed him, and why?"

"He was a Ranger, just like us. Plenty of renegades would give their eye teeth for the chance to put a slug in our backs or sink a knife in our guts," Sean explained. "It could've been any of a few dozen hombres, with just as many reasons for wantin' Thad dead. Tell you what. When we catch up to this one, you can ask him . . . before I plug him."

"That's right generous of you, pardner," Levi chuckled. He squinted into the distance.

"Looks like a ranch ahead."

Sean followed Levi's gaze, attempting to ascertain exactly what the structures were on the horizon.

"Appears like it. Mebbe they can tell us something."

"It's just about dinnertime too, so with a little

luck they'll feed us. My belly's been rumblin' for the past hour," Levi complained.

"Let's find out."

Sean pushed Ghost and Toby into a gallop with Levi and Monte hard on their heels. Fifteen minutes later they were riding up to the gate of a small, well-tended ranch. The house and barn were in good repair, the buildings sporting a fresh coat of whitewash. Chickens pecked busily in the front yard, while the corral held several fine horses. Fat steers grazed in a fenced-in pasture.

A gray-haired woman was on the front porch, sitting in a rocking chair, and shelling peas. She was humming the old hymn, "Farther Along." Hearing the Rangers' horses' hoof beats, she glanced up at the approaching riders.

"Ezekiel! Company comin'!" she called.

A man of approximately the same age emerged from the barn and picked up the rifle leaning next to the door, holding it at the ready.

"Howdy, strangers," he greeted the newcomers.

"Howdy yourself," Sean replied, smiling. "Mind if we light and rest a spell? We need to water our horses and give 'em a breather."

"Long as you ain't lookin' for trouble, you're welcome," came the reply.

"We're not searchin' for any," Sean grinned. "Just been travelin' quite a ways and could use a break. I'm Sean Kennedy. This here's my pard, Levi Mallory."

"Ezekiel Daniels. My wife, Martha."

Sean and Levi touched two fingers to the brims of their Stetsons in greeting.

"Ma'am."

Martha looked the two young men up and down and smiled.

"You boys must be hungry. I'll whip up some ham and eggs while you settle your horses."

"That sure sounds good, ma'am," Levi said. "But please don't go to any trouble."

"Oh, hush. It's no bother at all. I'm glad to have company. We don't get many visitors way out here. My name's Martha."

"Yes, ma'am, I mean Martha," Levi grinned.

"Well, don't just sit on those saddles. Let's get your horses settled," Ezekiel ordered.

"All right."

Sean and Levi dismounted. The elderly rancher led them into his bright, airy stable.

"Put your horses in those first three stalls," he said. "I'll toss some hay and grain to 'em while you unsaddle and rub 'em down, only I'll let you water 'em. Trough's outside the back door and buckets are stacked at the end of the aisle. Once you're finished with the horses you can clean up there. I'll see you back at the house."

Sean and Levi led their mounts into the indicated stalls. Sean noticed that Ezekiel studied Thad Dutton's horse closely when they walked by.

He's seen Toby before, Sean thought.

The sweat-streaked and dust-caked horses were thoroughly rubbed down.

"Another licorice? You just had three," Sean laughed, when Ghost lifted his nose from his ration of oats to nuzzle his rider's hip pocket. "All right, but this is the last one today."

He dug a candy from his pocket and slipped it to the gelding.

"Now you finish your dinner," Sean ordered, with a fond slap to Ghost's shoulder.

Levi had finished caring for Monte.

"You about done there, Sean?" he asked.

"I'm set. Let's wash up," Sean replied.

They headed for the trough back of the barn, where Martha had set out a bar of yellow soap, two washcloths, and towels. They stripped to their waists, ducking their heads in the cool, refreshing water. Both men scrubbed themselves thoroughly and then toweled off. They shrugged back into their shirts, retied their bandannas around their necks, and jammed their Stetsons back on their heads.

"Let's go eat," Sean said.

"I was beginnin' to think you were gonna starve me to death," Levi retorted.

They headed for the house, climbed the porch stairs, and knocked on the door.

"C'mon in," Ezekiel called.

They stepped into a spotlessly clean kitchen. Lace curtains hung at the window, and a checked cloth covered the table, which was laden with platters heaped full of ham, eggs, and biscuits. There were thick slices of cheese and bread, freshly churned butter, crocks of molasses, and a pot of coffee.

"Sit down boys, and make yourselves at home," Martha invited.

Sean and Levi hung their hats from pegs near the door and took seats at the table.

"We always take a moment to give thanks to the Lord," Ezekiel said. When he bowed his head the others followed suit.

"Dear Lord, we thank Thee for Thy bounty, and for the food of which we are about to partake. We ask Thee to bless this table, and the men who have come to visit us today. Amen."

"Amen."

"You boys are guests. Please, take what you wish first," Martha requested.

"Sure thing," Levi answered. He and Sean dug into the platters of food, piling their plates high with the piping hot meal. As badly as Sean wanted to question the rancher and his wife about Thad Dutton, he realized it would be impolite to press the issue during dinner. His questions could wait until the meal was finished.

When they had just about eaten their fill, Martha brought a buttermilk pie from the pie safe.

"You'll surely want some dessert, won't you?" she asked.

"I reckon I could squeeze in a bit more before I bust," Sean grinned.

"Same here," Levi added.

"Good." Martha cut two huge slabs of the pie and placed them in front of the Rangers.

Once he had finished his pie, Sean pushed back from the table.

"Martha, that was the best meal I've had since leavin' Austin," he declared.

"You sure you wouldn't want another slice of pie?" she asked.

"I'd explode if I ate another bite," Sean laughed. "I'll just have another cup of coffee."

"Of course."

Martha refilled all their cups. Ezekiel dug his pipe from his pocket and filled it.

"You can smoke if you want," he told the Rangers.

"Thanks," Levi responded. He took his sack of tobacco and the cigarette papers from his vest pocket to roll a quirly.

Ezekiel lit his pipe and took several puffs. He eyed his guests closely and then requested, "You mind if I ask you something?"

"You've got the right," Sean replied, "long as your question ain't too personal."

"Fair enough. What brings you two by here? This is a pretty out of the way spot. You two ain't on the run from the law by any chance?"

"Ezekiel! What kind of question is that?"

Martha scolded. "It's plain these men aren't outlaws."

"It's all right," Sean assured her. "I was about to explain who we are and what brought us here, since you may be able to help us. We're Texas Rangers, and we're looking for a man who might've come by here."

"Rangers? I might've guessed," Ezekiel said.

"We are," Sean confirmed. "We've been trailin' a man who came this way."

"You mean the man riding that chestnut horse you've got with you?"

"Not exactly. Did his rider stop here?"

"Yes," Martha answered. "He was a very polite young man. He told me his name was Thaddeus . . . Dutton, I believe."

"That would be correct," Sean told her. "However, we're searching for another man, one who might also have stopped by at about the same time, or shortly after."

"There was one other man," Ezekiel said. "A Mexican fella who said he was tryin' to catch up to his friend. Asked if he'd been by and described Dutton. We told him he had been, of course. No reason not to, was there?"

"Mexican?" Sean echoed.

"Well, not exactly Mexican. He spoke American plain as you and me, except he was of Mexican blood, sure as we're sittin' at this table. He stopped a few hours after Dutton. Watered his horse, but said he couldn't stay to supper, because he was in a hurry to meet up with his friend."

"That's right, so I gave him a sandwich to take with him," Martha added.

"He's gotta be the man we're after," Levi exclaimed.

"So it seems," Sean agreed. "Martha, Ezekiel, did that Mexican-lookin' hombre happen to give you his name?"

"No."

"Can you describe him?"

"Sure," Ezekiel said. "He was a young fella, early twenties at the most, probably younger. He was of average height, kind of wiry, with a beard framin' his jaw, and his hair was close-cropped. Black."

"He was a handsome man," Martha added. "He had very dark eyes, but they weren't shifty at all and he would look you straight in the eye. Why are you looking for him?"

"Because we're pretty certain he murdered Thad Dutton, who was also a Ranger. His horse brought Thad's body back to our post two days ago and the man had been shot. We followed his horse's tracks to where it happened. Another set of hoof prints came to the spot and then turned back. We followed those prints and they led us here. It appears your visitor trailed Thad, killed him, and then returned this way."

"He shot that nice young man?" Martha

exclaimed, horrified, as tears welled in her eyes.

"It appears so, ma'am," Sean softly replied. "So if you and Ezekiel will tell us everything you can about him, it'd sure help."

"Dunno how much more we can give you," Ezekiel said. "He was ridin' a big bay gelding. No markings on that horse."

"He wasn't dressed like a Mexican either," Martha added. "He wore the usual cowboy duds, a dark red shirt, jeans, tan hat, and a black leather vest."

"How about his belt?" Sean asked.

"Nothing out of the ordinary, just a plain brown belt."

"His gun belt wasn't fancy either," Ezekiel stated. "Plain dark brown leather, like all of his gear, only it was well-kept and serviceable. No silver trimmin' or anything like that."

"Wait, there is one thing. He had a fancy feathered band on his hat," Martha recalled. "Perhaps that will help."

"It surely might," Sean answered. "One more thing, did either of you happen to notice Thad's belt?"

"No," Ezekiel answered. "Why?"

"Thad wore a real fancy belt. It was hand-tooled brown leather, with a big silver buckle. There was a Texas Ranger badge engraved on that buckle and his initials on the keepers."

"He wasn't wearing a belt like that," Martha said.

"You're certain?"

"Absolutely."

"I'm positive he wasn't wearing a belt like that, Ranger," Ezekiel confirmed. "Elaborate rig like that'd be hard to miss."

"I reckon you're right," Sean conceded. "It's just that Thad rarely took his belt off. It's unusual he wasn't wearin' it."

"I can't believe he's dead and that man who claimed to be his friend shot him," Martha said, her voice still shaky. "They both seemed like fine boys."

"Thad certainly was, I can vouch for that," Levi answered. "Far as the Mexican, mebbe he didn't kill Thad, except it sure looks like it."

"Martha, Ezekiel, thank you for the meal, and the information. You've both been a great help. We've got to be on our way," Sean said. "Levi."

"Yep."

They rose from their chairs.

"If you boys will wait a few minutes I'll wrap some food for you to take along," Martha said.

"It'll take us a little while to ready our horses," Levi grinned.

"Then I'll have it ready in a jiffy," Martha promised.

"I'll give you a hand with your mounts," Ezekiel offered.

It only took a few moments for the Rangers to saddle their horses. When they led them from the stable, Martha was already waiting in the yard, a large wrapped packet in her hands.

"There's ham, some hard-boiled eggs, and bread in there, along with some green beans you can cook," she told them. "I slipped in some carrots for your horses."

"Good thing we're not staying here. We'd be too fat to climb into the saddle before long," Sean chuckled.

"He's right, and my pardner's horse is spoiled enough. Last thing he needs is Sean givin' him carrots," Levi laughed. "We're sure grateful for the grub."

"As well as your hospitality," Sean added.

"It was nothing, we enjoyed your company," Martha replied.

"You boys be sure'n stop by whenever you ride this way," Ezekiel ordered.

"We'll do that," Sean replied and then added, "Muchas gracias for your assistance."

"Sure hope you find whoever killed your Ranger friend," Ezekiel answered.

"Your information might help us do just that."

"You boys be careful," Martha said. "Good luck. I'll pray for you."

"We appreciate that," Sean responded. "Adios."

"Vaya con Dios."

Once again Sean and Levi resumed their

northward trek. They had only traveled for little over an hour when the tracks they'd been following met a well-used trail. The hoof prints disappeared into all the others dug into the dusty road.

Sean rode Ghost back and forth for a quarter mile in each direction, struggling in vain to pick out the prints they'd been following. He finally gave up in frustration.

"There's no way to tell which way this hombre headed, Levi," he muttered.

"So what do we do now? We're not givin' up, are we?" Levi questioned.

"Heck no, we ain't givin' up," Sean snapped.

"Then what's our next move?"

"Only one thing we can try. We know Thad was in San Antonio," Sean explained. "We'll head there and see what we can find out."

He turned Ghost northward and put him into the big horse's mile-eating lope.

Chapter 5

Late in the afternoon five days later, the pair rode into the bustling city of San Antonio, the city which would forever live in the annals of Texas history. San Antonio was home to the Alamo, where a small band of Texans, vastly out-numbered, held off the army of Mexican general Santa Anna for days. "Remember the Alamo" became the rallying cry for Texas independence.

However the ancient Mission San Antonio de Valero, cradle of Texas freedom, now stood forlorn and virtually abandoned, used as a storehouse. Most folks went right on past without giving the building a second glance.

Sean and Levi paused for a moment to contemplate the structure, with its adobe walls burnished rich ochre by the late afternoon sun, then continued past the plaza and the San Fernando Cathedral.

"We'll put up the horses at a good livery stable I know, wire Lieutenant Blawcyzk letting him know where we are, and what we've learned so far. Then we'll get ourselves a hotel room. We'll probably be here a few days, so we might as well be comfortable," Sean told his partner.

"That sure sounds good, I'm real tired of sittin' this saddle," Levi answered. "I wouldn't mind spending some time in one of the cantinas washin' the trail dust from my throat. I'd also like to get a good meal in my belly. A man gets plenty tired of bacon, beans, and biscuits."

"I think we can manage both those things," Sean grinned.

No one gave the two men a glance as they rode through town. Rangers didn't wear uniforms and like most of the force, Sean and Levi wore no badges. They were dressed in ordinary range garb, faded shirts, leather vests, jeans, scuffed boots, bandannas tied loosely around their necks, and sweat-stained Stetsons. The Colts at their hips were plain and serviceable, as were their gun belts and holsters. While the three horses were superior animals and would attract some attention, their saddles and bridles were basic working gear, unadorned with any ornamenta-tion. With themselves and their mounts coated with the dust of days on the trail, the two lawmen resembled any of the hundreds of grubline riding cowpunchers wandering through the Southwest.

"Stable's just down this alley," Sean announced. He turned Ghost left, into a narrow passageway between a mercantile store and a millinery shop. At the end of the alley stood a large barn, with 'Hector's Livery Stable—Horses for Rent, Traded, and Sold. The Finest in Boarding Services' painted in large, flowing red and green script over the main doors. The San Antonio River ran just behind the corrals.

Sean reined to a halt in front of the stable and dismounted.

"Hola, Hector. You in there?" he called.

A moment later the door slid open to reveal a young Mexican, his hair and beard neatly trimmed under a huge sombrero. An extremely small black and white pinto horse, no taller than twenty-eight inches at the withers, walked at his side.

"Ranger Sean? I'd know that voice anywhere. Buenas tardes, Ranger. When did you arrive in San Antonio?"

He shook the Ranger's hand with a firm grip.

"Just now," Sean replied. "I'd like you to meet my pardner, Ranger Levi Mallory. Levi, Hector Melendez. He runs the best livery in San Antone and that miniature horse with him is Amigo."

"Howdy, Hector," Levi said.

"Of course. The pleasure is mine, Ranger Levi," Melendez responded, shaking Levi's hand.

"How's Amigo doin'?" Sean asked. He scratched the little pinto's ears. Amigo nickered his approval.

"He's doing just fine," Hector answered.

"Hector, we need stalls for our horses," Sean requested. "I want a real good rubdown for 'em, some extra grain in their bins and plenty of hay."

"Certainly. Will you be leaving some licorice for Espiritu, as usual?" Melendez questioned.

"Reckon I'd best," Sean laughed.

"How long will you be staying in town?"

"I'm not quite sure," Sean replied. "Probably a few days, but keep our horses ready in case we need to leave sooner."

"I'll do that," Melendez promised. "If you'll put them in the middle three stalls on the right and unsaddle them I'll get to work grooming them."

"All right," Sean agreed. He led Ghost and Toby into the neatly kept stable.

"Ranger Sean, isn't that Ranger Thad's horse you're leading?" Melendez suddenly asked, recognizing Thad Dutton's chestnut.

"It sure is Toby," Sean confirmed.

"Why do you have his horse? Where is Thad?"

"He was killed, shot down outside of Laredo. We're trying to find his murderer," Sean explained.

"Madre de Dios!" Melendez crossed himself. "Ranger Thad, murdered! He was a good man."

"That he was," Sean agreed. "So far we haven't had much luck trailin' the hombre who plugged him. That's why we're in San Antonio, because the last we knew Thad was on his way back to the post from here. His horse brought him back dead. We're hopin' to find some clue as to who might've killed him and why. Did Thad stable his horse with you?"

"Si, he did, as always," Melendez responded, "and I did see Thad several times during his stay in San Antonio."

"Did you see anyone with him, or did he mention anyone in particular who might've roused his suspicions?"

"No, Sean, not at all. The only persons Thad spoke of were the señoritas. As you know, he had quite the way with the ladies. I was very envious of him."

"That's a fact," Sean agreed. "Did he happen to speak of any señorita in particular?"

"No, he did not. He rode out alone, to anticipate your next question. Almost three weeks ago."

"Three weeks!" Levi exclaimed. "It shouldn't have taken him that long to reach Laredo."

"No, it sure shouldn't have," Sean concurred. "It certainly wasn't a couple of weeks after he was killed that Toby brought his body back, so we need to puzzle out where he was durin' those missin' days. Hector, did Thad happen to mention anything at all that might give us a hint where he headed after he left San Antonio?"

"Not a word, Sean," Hector answered and immediately continued, "I certainly wish he had, so I could be of more help."

"Don't worry about that. I realize you'd tell us if you knew what Thad was up to," Sean assured the hostler. "I reckon our next move is to check around in the saloons and cantinas to see if anyone might have somethin' we can use."

"You might try the Gilded Cage first," Hector suggested. "That was one of Thad's favorites."

"You read my mind, Hector," Sean chuckled. "If we don't have any luck there we'll try the Casa D'Plata."

"Buena suerte," Hector answered. "Your caballos will be well cared for until you return."

"I know they will," Sean responded. "Buenas noches, Hector."

"Buenas noches and be careful," Hector advised.

"Always try to be," Sean laughed.

The Rangers shouldered their saddlebags and then carrying their Winchesters, headed into the lengthening shadows of the hour just before sunset.

"The Alhambra's a few blocks east of here. It's not expensive, and as it's as clean as any of the hotels in this town. We'll bunk there," Sean explained, turning right from the livery stable.

"Anyplace with a soft mattress'll do just fine," Levi answered.

A few minutes later they reached the Alhambra Hotel. The clerk recognized Sean when he neared the desk and said, "Ranger Kennedy. I didn't expect to see you back so soon. I assume you want a room?"

"Howdy, Juan." Sean returned the clerk's greeting. "Yep, the usual one, and this is my partner, Levi Mallory. I dunno how long we'll be in town, so I'll pay a week in advance."

"I'm very pleased to meet you, Ranger Mallory," the clerk stated.

"Same here," Levi rejoined.

Sean spun a gold eagle onto the counter and then signed the register. The clerk handed him a key.

"Room sixteen, as always."

"Gracias, Juan. If you could have some hot water sent up that would be much appreciated," Sean requested.

"Of course and right away," the clerk agreed.

"Let's go, Levi."

The Rangers climbed the stairs and walked the length of the corridor, to a far corner room, where they entered, tossed their saddlebags over a chair, and leaned their rifles against the wall.

"This isn't bad," Levi noted as he stretched out on his bed. The chamber, while small, was clean, the furniture in good repair.

"That's why I stay here," Sean answered. "This room has a view of both the front and side streets. Reason I chose it."

"Makes sense," Levi agreed. "So what's our next move?"

"We're gonna clean up a bit and grab some chuck. Then we'll start askin' around the saloons to see if anyone can give us a lead as to what Thad might've gotten himself into that earned him a couple of bullets. I . . . ."

Sean stopped talking at a soft knock at the door. He eased his Colt out of the holster.

"Who is it?" he called.

"Miguel, with your hot water, Señor," a quick response was heard.

"C'mon in." Sean slid his gun back in place when the door opened to reveal a boy of no more than ten, carrying two steaming pitchers. He had several towels draped over his arm. The urchin placed those on the washstand and removed a bar of yellow soap from his pocket, placing it on top of the towels.

"Muchas gracias, Miguel." Sean tossed the boy a dime.

"Gracias, Señor. Will you need anything else?"

"No, Miguel."

"If you should need something later, just let me know, por favor."

"Of course. Buenas noches, Miguel."

"Buenas noches, Señores."

"You want to wash up first, or should I?" Sean asked Levi once the boy had left.

"You go ahead. I'm right comfortable," Levi answered, yawning.

Sean stripped out of his clothes, and then stood over the washstand, pouring water from one of the pitchers over his head. As the water fell into the basin, it soaked his thatch of dark hair. He took the soap and scrubbed himself thoroughly from head to foot, rinsed, then vigorously toweled off. Once he was done, he stood in front of the mirror and took his razor to the several days growth of dark whiskers stubbling his jaw. His ablutions completed, he dug in his saddlebags for clean underwear, socks, and his spare shirt. He redressed, using the damp towel to wipe dust from his Stetson, jeans, and boots. Finally, he tied a clean blue bandanna around his neck.

"Your turn," he told Levi.

"Reckon so," Levi grunted. He swung his legs over the edge of his mattress and pulled off his boots.

Levi repeated Sean's actions, also washing himself completely. He now stood at the mirror combing down his unruly hair.

"Not as nice as a long soak in a barbershop tub, but it sure feels good, gettin' some of that trail grime off," he remarked.

"Sure does," Sean agreed. "Once you're satisfied you won't scare off the ladies it's time we headed out, I'm starved."

"I'm just about ready."

Levi hurriedly redressed.

After a meal of beefsteak, potatoes, black-eyed peas, and apple pie washed down with strong black coffee at the nearest café, the Rangers headed for the Gilded Cage Saloon.

"We gonna see some good lookin' gals in this

here Gilded Cage?" Levi asked as they climbed the stairs.

"Not exactly," Sean replied.

"What d'ya mean by that?"

"You'll find out in a minute, pardner."

Sean pushed open the batwings and stepped inside.

One of the most popular drinking and gambling establishments in San Antonio, the Gilded Cage was always mobbed, and this night was no exception. Sean and Levi had to elbow their way through the crowd, then squeeze between other drinkers, to find a place at the bar.

"What the devil . . . ?" Levi exclaimed.

"That's why this place is named the Gilded Cage," Sean chuckled. On the center of the room-length bar was a large bird cage, its wires coated with gold leaf. The cage held two jet-black squawking ravens.

Sean signaled to one of the bartenders, a burly man with a huge handlebar mustache. His hair, carefully pomaded in place, was as black as the ravens. A once-white, now dull-gray apron was stretched to its limit in a vain attempt to cover the man's huge paunch.

"Sean Kennedy!" the saloon man exclaimed, hustling to greet the new arrivals. "Sure didn't expect to see you here. The last I'd heard your company was down on the Rio."

"You heard right, Bart, and the company is still

down there. I hadn't planned on makin' it back to town for quite a spell. This is my ridin' pard, Levi Mallory. Levi, this is Bart Mitchell, owner of this fine establishment."

"Pleasure to make your acquaintance, Levi."

"Same here."

"What're you boys havin'?" Mitchell asked.

"Beer," Sean answered.

"Make that two," Levi added.

"Comin' right up."

Mitchell drew two beers and placed them in front of the Rangers as he said, "That'll be four bits."

Instantly, one of the ravens began croaking, "Four bits. Four bits."

"Pay for the beers, Levi," Sean ordered.

"Sure."

Levi dug in his pocket and came up with a silver dollar.

He started to hand it to Mitchell, but Scan said, "No Levi. You pay the birds." Sean laughed.

"Huh? What're you talkin' about, Sean. You gone plumb loco?" Levi retorted.

"I'd better explain, or Sean'll have you goin' all night," Mitchell grinned. "You see, those ravens are my pets. Their names are 'Nevermore' and 'Poe.' They get the coins from the bar, so just slip that silver piece through the wires."

"Sure," Levi dubiously answered. He took the coin, held it between two fingers, and gingerly slid it into the ravens' cage. One of the birds hopped from its perch, snatched the dollar, and then deposited it in a metal box hanging inside the cage.

"Thanks, pardner. Thanks, pardner," the bird rasped.

"Well, I'll be, I've never seen the like," Levi exclaimed. "Except, what about my change?"

"You're also buyin' the next beers, so don't worry about that," Sean answered.

"Since Nevermore got the dollar, one of you'll have to give Poe the next one," Mitchell added.

"I still don't believe what I just saw," Levi said, shaking his head. "Poe and Nevermore are strange names."

"Bart here's a big fan of Edgar Allan Poe," Sean stated.

"Never heard of him."

"Edgar Allan Poe's a well-known writer from back east, Baltimore, Maryland to be exact. He wrote poetry and some really hair-raising stories," Mitchell explained and then added, "One of those poems has as its main character a raven. The raven speaks to the narrator several times, but says only one word, 'Nevermore.' The line reads 'Quoth the raven, Nevermore!' So when a peddler offered me these two birds in exchange for a bottle of whiskey I jumped at the chance and named them after Poe and his poem."

"Poe sounds like a character I'd like to meet," Levi noted.

"I would've liked that too, but Poe died back in eighteen forty-nine," Mitchell answered. "Tell you what though, if you're gonna be in town a few days I'll let you borrow the book which contains that poem."

"Sure, I'd like to read it," Levi replied. He took a long swallow of his beer.

"This beer is real good, nice and cool."

"Thanks." Mitchell turned to Sean.

"So what brings the Rangers to town? You're not here just for pleasure, are you?"

"I wish we were, but no," Sean replied. "We're on the trail of a murderer. We're lookin' for the hombre who shot down Thad Dutton."

Mitchell gasped as if he'd been punched in his huge gut.

"Thad Dutton's dead?"

"He is," Sean confirmed. "Somebody put two bullets in him. We were able to follow the sidewinder's trail for a spell, but finally lost it. Since Thad was in San Antone last, we're hopin' someone here might be able to help us. With any luck maybe even you, Bart. Did Thad stop in here?"

"Of course, he always did," Mitchell replied. "However, he didn't mention anything out of the ordinary. Thad stopped by a couple of times, had a few drinks, played some faro, and then left."

"You didn't see anyone with him?"

"Nope, I don't think so. He visited with some of the regulars, but that's about all."

"How about any women?" Levi asked. "Thad did like the ladies."

"As Sean can tell you, Levi, I don't have any women at The Gilded Cage. This is strictly a saloon and gambling hall. When Thad wanted any female company he'd go next door to Hattie's place."

"We'll check there next," Sean said. He drained the remainder of his beer.

"You want another?" Mitchell asked.

"Sure do." Even though Levi had paid for two rounds, Sean dug in his pocket and produced a half-dollar. When he slid the coin into the ravens' cage, the bird called Poe hopped from its perch, took the money in its beak, and then deposited it in the box.

"Thanks, pardner," he squawked.

"I still can't believe that," Levi muttered. "Bart, how do you get the money from these birds?"

"After I close up and turn down the lights, I cover their cage with a towel. Once they settle down, I open the cage and take out the box, then replace it the next day. No one's ever tried to steal the cash from my birds," Mitchell concluded.

"Let's get back to Thad," Sean requested. "How about gambling? Did Thad have any trouble during a faro game? Or did he have an argument with anyone?"

Mitchell shook his head and replied, "Nope, he had no trouble at all. As I recall, he lost some money, but not a whole lot."

Mitchell paused and then added, "Speakin' of cards, there's a couple open spots at Ambrose's table. You interested in a game?"

"Not tonight," Sean replied. "Mebbe if we're in town a few days we'll take you up on the offer."

"You'll want another beer though, won't you?"

"Sure. We've paid for it," Sean agreed.

"Fair enough."

Mitchell placed two more beers in front of the Rangers. Just as he did, Nevermore squawked.

"Gun! Gun!"

Sean whirled, dropping his hand to his Colt. He began to yank the pistol, but stopped with the gun half out of leather. The tall, lean, and steely-eyed man he had started to draw on wore a city marshal's star and carried a double-barreled shotgun.

"Sorry, Larry." Sean grinned sheepishly and dropped his gun back in its holster.

"Nevermore got ya again, huh Sean?" Larry Kane, the marshal, chuckled.

"Reckon he did. I plumb forgot he yells whenever he sees a gun in someone's hand. Buy you a beer?"

"Sure," Kane agreed. He placed the shotgun on the bar.

"Larry, this is my pardner, Levi Mallory. Levi, Larry Kane."

"Pleased to meet you, Marshal."

"Likewise."

The two men shook hands.

"Sean, what're you doin' in San Antone?" Kane asked. "You're about the last person I expected to run across."

Kane took a swallow from the mug Mitchell placed in front of him.

"Thad Dutton was killed, gunned down. We're tryin' to backtrack his killer, only so far we haven't had much luck, so we came up here. Thad was supposed to be headed back to the post after leavin' your town. He never made it alive."

Kane inhaled sharply. "Thad's dead? I'm sure sorry to hear that. He was a good man."

He took a long drink of his beer.

"He was that," Sean agreed. "Did you run across him while he was in town?"

"Our paths didn't cross," Kane admitted. "I was off work for a couple of weeks. My wife was ill, so I stayed home to help with the kids. Wish I could be more help."

"Don't worry about that," Sean answered. "How's Liddy feelin' now?"

"She's just fine. Thanks for asking," Kane replied. He drained the last of his beer and picked up his shotgun.

60

"Thanks for the drink, Sean. I'd better get back to my rounds."

"Don't mention it," Sean replied. "If you should happen to hear anything about Thad, either find me or Levi, or else get a wire to Lieutenant Blawcyzk in care of Western Union in Laredo."

"I'll do that," Kane promised. "Good luck, Sean, Levi. You two be careful."

"You do the same," Sean said. Kane stepped through the batwings and into the night.

"You boys gonna want another beer?" Mitchell asked.

"No thanks, Bart, it's time to head next door," Sean answered. "Mebbe Hattie or one of her girls can help us."

Mitchell grinned knowingly.

"You mean with information, or something else?"

"Just information," Sean shot back. "For me, anyway, although I can't speak for Levi. Don't forget I'm engaged to be married."

"That's right," Mitchell replied. "Still, it can't hurt a man to play once in a while. Hattie's got some mighty fine merchandise to sample."

"I'm not that kind," Sean retorted. "It just wouldn't be right. I sure couldn't let Amy down like that, because she's too fine a gal, in fact, she's the best thing that ever happened to me. Bart, we'll stop by again before we leave town."

Like most of the Rangers, until he'd met Amy Sean had been a hard-drinking, rough and tumble lady's man. He'd enjoyed nothing so much as a night of gambling and liquor, topped off by a visit to one of the women always readily available for a man with the cash. Amy had changed all that. She was brunette, petite, and soft-spoken, but with a will of iron. Sean had fallen for her hard the minute he'd laid eyes on her. Now, while he still enjoyed a few drinks and a game of cards, he rarely drank to excess. He'd even sworn off other women entirely.

"Make sure you do," Mitchell ordered. "Levi, you're welcome here anytime."

"Appreciate that, Bart."

"Hasta la Vista, Bart," Sean said.

"Mañana, Sean."

The Rangers headed for Hattie's.

Sean hesitated before knocking on the door of Hattie's Parlor House, a large two story building which adjoined The Gilded Cage.

"Amy'd kill me if she ever saw me goin' in here," he fretted.

"You're just after information that might lead to Thad's killer," Levi reminded him. "Your fiancée would understand that."

"I guess you're right," Sean shrugged. He knocked twice.

The heavy oak door opened to reveal a well-endowed woman in her late forties. Her auburn hair was piled high on her head, and she wore a deep green silk gown which matched her eyes of the same hue. The dress was cut extremely low to emphasize her full bosom, which threatened to spill from its confinement at any moment. A large diamond and emerald necklace nestled in her cleavage.

"Sean Kennedy!" She exclaimed, recognizing the Ranger. "It's been ages. I never expected to see you set foot inside my place again. You said as much when you told me you'd gotten engaged."

"Hello, Hattie," Sean replied. "Mind if we come in?"

"Of course not, darlin', come on in," Hattie replied. She swung the door wide.

"Who's your handsome friend?"

"This is Ranger Levi Mallory. Levi, this is Hattie O'Rourke."

Levi touched two fingers to the brim of his Stetson in greeting.

"I'm very pleased to meet you, Miz O'Rourke."

"Miz O'Rourke? I'm Hattie, and don't you forget it, Ranger. C'mon in, the night air's a mite nippy."

"I don't doubt you're getting a chill with that dress," Sean laughed.

"Don't tell me you're not enjoying it . . . engaged or not, Mister!" Hattie retorted. "Now get inside."

"All right."

Sean and Levi stepped into a room decorated with heavy red velvet drapes and ornate wallpaper. Several sofas, upholstered in the same material as the drapes, lined the walls. At the bottom of a wide staircase was a large birds-eye maple desk.

Several women of various ages, sizes, complexions, and hair color lounged on the sofas. They stirred at the sight of the ruggedly handsome Rangers.

"Just take it easy, girls," Hattie advised. "These men will be ready for the pleasure of your company soon enough. First, would either of you Rangers like a drink?"

"I wouldn't mind a whiskey," Sean admitted. "How about you, Levi? Levi?"

The younger Ranger was staring unabashedly at the ladies.

"Uh, yeah, that'd be good," he spluttered.

Hattie gestured to a willowy blonde.

"Jacqueline, would you get the gentlemen their drinks?"

"Certainly, Miss Hattie," the tall blonde said. She then walked from the room.

"You boys come with me," Hattie ordered. She led them to a corner sofa where she said, "Have a seat."

A moment later Jacqueline reappeared, carrying a silver tray which held three cut crystal tumblers and a cut crystal decanter filled with a dark amber liquid. She placed the tray on a bright red Chinese carved table in front of the sofa.

"Thank you, Jacqueline, that will be all," Hattie said.

"You're welcome, Miss Hattie." Jacqueline gazed boldly at the Rangers before she departed.

"I believe Jacqueline would like to better make your acquaintances; however, it's her day off. I never allow my girls to work seven days a week."

"That's too bad," Levi murmured.

"If you're in town for more than tonight, you'll have a chance to get to know Jacqueline better," Hattie noted.

She pulled the stopper from the decanter and filled the tumblers, passing two to the Rangers.

She lifted her glass and said, "To the Texas Rangers."

"To the Texas Rangers," Sean and Levi answered and then took a sip of whiskey.

"That's mighty smooth red-eye, Hattie," Sean praised.

"It should be. I have it brought down special from Kentucky," Hattie replied.

Sean took another swallow before continuing, "Hattie, I'm afraid we're not here for pleasure. This visit is strictly business."

"I surmised as much, because you haven't stopped by since you told me you were engaged, Sean. So what business brings the Texas Rangers to my door?"

"Thad Dutton was in San Antonio a few weeks back. Did he come here?"

"Of course, Thaddeus always made it a point to visit me. Why?"

"I have some bad news, Thad's dead. He was murdered, so we're hoping you or one of your girls might be able to help us. We don't have much to go on."

Tears welled in Hattie's eyes.

"Thaddeus is dead? He was always such a gentleman. I don't see how any of us can help, because he never discussed his business in here. He came strictly to relax."

"I suspected as much. Perhaps Thad mentioned something in passing, or maybe someone came looking for him. Even the slightest thing might help us," Sean urged. "Which girl entertained him?"

"He saw Martine, she's a new girl. You haven't met her."

"Can we speak to her?"

"She's upstairs. I'll get her."

Hattie disappeared up the staircase.

"That gal is somethin' else," Levi stated. "She wouldn't keep anything from us, would she?"

"Hattie? Not on your life," Sean replied. "She might be a madam, but she's honest as the day is long and a lot more respectable than some of those so-called 'proper' women, too. Hattie'll help us if she can."

A moment later, Hattie reappeared, and with her was one of the most spectacularly beautiful women either of the Rangers had ever seen.

"Gentlemen, this is Martine Dubois. Martine, meet Rangers Sean Kennedy and Levi Mallory."

Martine extended a slender hand, which Levi grasped.

"It's a pleasure to meet you," he said.

"Charmed, I'm sure," Martine purred, with a seductive Southern accent dripping with honeysuckle and magnolia.

The blood of the white, African, and Spanish flowed through Martine's veins, with perhaps a touch of Indian and Creole mixed in. The result was an exotic beauty, the epitome of womanhood. Martine was slender with a full bosom and gently curved hips. Her flawless complexion was the color of café au lait. Long ebony hair, as black as a crow's wing, spilled loosely down her shoulders. Her face was slightly oval, her lips perfectly formed. When she smiled dazzling white teeth were revealed. Startlingly blue eyes, the color of a tropical sea, were a perfect counterpoint to her dark features. A form fitting blue satin dress complemented her eyes perfectly.

"I'm also pleased to meet you, Miss Dubois," Sean added. "I beg your pardon if I seem abrupt, but time is running out on us. With your permission, I'd like to ask you a few questions."

"About Thaddeus," Martine broke in. "Hattie

told me why you were here. Of course I'll help any way I can, although I probably won't be able to tell you anything you don't already know. A man as handsome as yourself could hardly be impolite, Ranger Kennedy."

"Please, make that Sean."

"Certainly, and you must call me Martine."

"It's a deal." Sean agreed. "Martine, did Thad mention anyone to you?"

"No, he didn't. Thaddeus talked very little about himself and his work, but that was the extent of our conversation. I'm sure you realize, talk was the furthest thing from our minds."

Sean blushed.

"Indeed, only what about after Thad left? Did anyone come looking for him?"

"No one came at all."

"Did Thad say where he was headed when he left San Antonio?"

"No, just he had to return to Laredo and rejoin his Ranger Company."

"He didn't mention anyplace he might stop along the way, or anyone he might see?"

"Again, no, I'm sorry I can't be more helpful. As I said, we didn't talk much. We were too busy enjoying each other. Thaddeus made a woman feel special and when we made love . . ." Martine's voice trailed off. "I'm sorry, Sean."

"That's all right. I'm sure you'd give us any other information you had. Thank you."

"You're very welcome."

"What will you do now, Sean?" Hattie asked.

"Reckon we'll go to the Casa d'Plata," Sean answered. "Thad probably stopped by there."

"Are you sure we can't do something for you before you go?" Hattie offered. "I'm certain Martine would like to get to know you better."

"No. We'd better get movin'," Sean replied. Despite his loyalty to Amy, his fiancée, he could feel a stirring in his body at Hattie's invitation. Eight months ago he would have taken the opportunity to sample the obvious pleasures Martine could offer, but that was before Amy. Amy, with the laughter in her eyes and the ready smile. Amy, with the long soft hair and perfectly formed figure. Amy, who made Sean feel alive like no other woman could. Now, he only lived for one woman . . . Amy.

"Sean, maybe I could stay with Martine for a bit, while you head over to the Casa d'Plata. There's no need for two of us to go there," Levi suggested. "Perhaps Martine will recall something which isn't coming to mind at the moment."

"I dunno," Sean hesitated.

"I think Levi has a wonderful idea," Hattie interjected. "Possibly he could help Martine remember."

"I still don't know," Sean replied. "What about you, Martine? What do you think?"

Martine ran her gaze up and down Levi's rugged

frame, her deep blue eyes sparkling with anticipation.

"I believe I would like that, very much indeed," she answered. "After all, if you don't mind my saying so, Ranger Mallory, you are also a very handsome man. I would imagine you also know how to pleasure a woman."

Levi blushed at her boldness.

"I can't say as to that, ma'am, I mean, Martine," he spluttered, "but if you wouldn't mind my company."

"Not at all. I'm very much anticipating our visit."

"Then that's settled," Levi said. "Sean, I'll meet you back at the hotel."

"Reckon I'm outnumbered," Sean chuckled. "All right, Levi. I'll see you later. Try not to wake me up when you get in."

The Casa d'Plata was one of the larger cantinas in the Mexican quarter of San Antonio. The rambling adobe structure covered an entire block. A hammered silver sign in the image of a hacienda over the front doors marked the establishment. Torches in wall brackets placed ten feet apart illuminated the sidewalk and street out front.

Despite its location, the saloon attracted as many Anglos as Texicans. It was usually jam-packed, and was this night. There were no seats at the gaming tables, while the dance floor teemed with couples swirling to the music from a six-piece guitar and trumpet Mexican band. Sean had to push his way through men standing four deep to reach the bar, where he called to the nearest bartender.

"Antonio."

The saloon man hurried over.

"Sean Kennedy. By all that is holy, this is a pleasant surprise. You're one of the last people I'd expected to see. I thought you were stationed down in Laredo."

"I am, and I didn't expect to be here either."

"You want a drink, of course."

"Naturally."

"Tequila or cerveza?"

"Tequila."

"Certainly. I'll have it in a moment."

Tony pulled a bottle from the back shelf. He placed it and a clean glass in front of the Ranger.

Sean poured a full measure, then took a good swig of the clear, fiery liquor. One advantage of his size was that he could hold more liquor than most men.

"That's real good, Tony."

"Nothing but the best for my Ranger amigo."

"I appreciate that, and I wish I could spend all night enjoying this fine tequila. However, I'm here for another reason."

"I suspected as much," Tony said. "You don't

have the usual smile on your face, my friend. You look much troubled."

"I am," Sean admitted. "I have bad news. Thad Dutton is dead. He was murdered, and I'm trying to find his killer."

"Madre de Dios!" Tony made the Sign of the Cross. "Thad Dutton dead. That is tragic. A hazard of your occupation, Sean. Nonetheless, one is never really prepared for death. I will miss Thad. He was a fine man."

"That he was," Sean agreed, and took another swallow of his drink.

"How did it happen?" Tony asked.

"We don't really know. Thad was gunned down not all that far from Laredo. It appears he detoured on his way there from San Antonio. I'm hoping to find someone who can help me track down his killer. Did Thad stop in here?"

"He came by several times."

"Did he have anyone with him, did he mention anyone, or perhaps some reason he wouldn't have headed straight back to the Ranger post?"

"No one at all. He sure didn't say anything about not heading right back to Laredo. In fact, the last I talked to him he was getting ready to ride out for there. He did spend some time with Delores. Perhaps she can answer your questions. I'll get her."

"I appreciate that, Tony."

The bartender headed for a back corner, where several of the percentage girls congregated. He returned with a dark-eyed Mexican beauty. Delores Montalvo was in her late twenties, short and full figured, with dark brown eyes, thick black hair, and ruby red lips. She wore a white peasant blouse, trimmed with lace at the bosom, and a flowing multi-colored skirt.

"Buenas Noches, Ranger Kennedy," she greeted Sean.

"Why so formal, Delores?" Sean rejoined. "We've always been friends."

"Because you've kept your distance since your engagement," she retorted. "You've done your best to ignore me."

"That's because you're such a temptation, mi corazon. You are a very dangerous woman," Sean answered.

"So why do you want to see me now?"

"I'll explain. Is there somewhere we can talk privately?"

"Of course, in fact we can use my room, unless you're afraid."

"This is too important, so I'll chance it."

"Then bring that bottle with you, and another glass."

"All right."

Sean picked up the tequila, two glasses, and then followed Dolores upstairs to her corner room.

"Don't just stand there with your hat in your hands, Sean. Please, sit down and pour us a drink," Delores ordered once the door closed behind them.

"All right." Sean filled both glasses with tequila, handed one to the woman, then sat in the room's only chair.

Dolores threw back half the contents of her glass. She took the bottle from Sean and settled on her bed, leaning against the pillows.

"There. Now, what's so urgent you're willing to be alone with me?" she asked.

"It's about Thad Dutton."

"Thad? What about Thad?"

"He's dead. Someone gunned him down, and I'm after whoever it was."

"You might look for a jealous husband or boyfriend," Dolores replied. "Or half the women in Texas. I would imagine there were any number of those who wanted to see Thad dead."

"Would that include you?" Sean asked.

Dolores downed the remaining contents of her glass and then refilled it.

"Sometime in the past, perhaps," she admitted, "until I figured out Thad for what he really was, a liar, cheater, and all-around scoundrel. Once I realized the kind of man he was, I lost any feelings for him. Oh, I know he was a Texas Ranger, and a darn good one," she continued before Sean could protest, "but that still doesn't mean he wasn't a no-good skunk, who'd chase anything in a skirt."

"You still let him come visit you, even the last time he was in town," Sean pointed out.

"Because entertaining men is my job. I know what I am too," Delores responded. "Besides, Thad knew how to make a woman very happy. I can't say I didn't enjoy his visits, plus he always paid extra."

"All right. I'm looking for something more specific, anything at all which might lead me to Thad's killer."

"I might be able to help, but it'll cost you."

"Don't play games with me, Delores. We're talking about the murder of a Ranger here."

Once again Delores drained her glass, then placed it on the nightstand. She rose from the bed, crossed the room, and plopped down on Sean's lap. She started fumbling with the buttons of his shirt.

"Are you certain I no longer interest you?" she asked. "Just once more, for old time's sake?"

"Those days are gone," Sean objected.

"They don't have to be."

Dolores slipped her hand inside Sean's shirt and began massaging his chest. She let her fingers drift lightly over his left breast and begin toying with his nipple.

Sean wrapped his hands around Delores' firm waist, lifted her from his lap, and dumped her unceremoniously on the floor.

"I told you no!" he growled. "If you have some information you'd best tell me right quick."

Dolores leapt to her feet.

"You . . . !" she screamed, swinging at Sean's face. He grabbed her wrist before the blow could land.

"Settle down!" he ordered. "I'm not letting loose until you do."

"I'll scream," she snapped.

"Do you really think anyone'll care?" Sean shot back. "Now behave or I'll haul you down to the jail."

"All right, I guess you win," Dolores conceded. "But like I said, what I know will cost you. Now let go of me."

Once Sean released his grip, Dolores settled on the bed.

"Okay. I'll pay you for the information . . . if it's worth it."

"Thad took up with a newcomer to town," Delores explained. "She was a blonde woman, young, pretty in a backwoods kind of way, if you like that sort of thing."

"Do you have her name?"

"No, I sure don't, and I didn't care to find out. You can understand why. She was from some- where down Brooks County way and was in town with her father, who's a rancher."

"Where'd you hear all this?"

"You know how word gets around," Dolores said. "I saw Thad with her a couple of times. She and her father left town, but I heard Thad followed them a couple of days afterwards."

"Who told you that? I want to talk with whoever it was."

"Check with Arnold, the desk clerk at the Bon Ton Hotel, which is where they stayed. He can give you her name, I'm certain."

"I'll do just that." Sean dug a gold eagle out of his pocket and handed it to her. "You'd better be givin' it to me straight, Dolores."

"I've got no reason to lie to you," she responded.

"Good. Then I'll say thanks, Dolores. Take care of yourself."

"Sure. Get out of here and don't come back, ever."

Sean buttoned his shirt and left. He headed downstairs, nodded a quick farewell to Tony, and started for the Bon Ton.

Engrossed in reaching the hotel, Sean didn't notice the cowboy at a rear table nod to his three companions. They dropped their cards, gulped down the last bit of liquor in their glasses, and followed the Ranger out of the Casa d'Plata.

Sean had gone about seven blocks before his lawman's instinct warned him of trouble. He was now in a desolate area of town, a district of ramshackle warehouses and storage sheds which stood as a buffer between the Anglo and Mexican sections. He stopped and turned, peering into the darkness of the unlit street, attempting to discern what had alarmed him, when a voice called from a side alley.

"Hey, Ranger. Remember me?"

Sean's hand dropped to the butt of his Colt.

"Keep your hand away from that gun, Ranger," the voice warned. "There's four pistols aimed smack at your belly right now. Unless you want your guts filled with lead, just unbuckle your gun belt and let it drop."

Knowing to grab for his six-gun meant instant death, Sean complied. Carefully, he loosened his gun belt and let it fall at his feet.

"That's more like it." The owner of the voice stepped from the alley, followed by his three companions. He struck a match so Sean could glimpse his face.

"You recognize me now?"

"Bud Hanratty," Sean replied. "I see you've still got the same friends, too."

"That's right," Hanratty confirmed. "You had me sent to prison for rustlin'. I spent all my time in that rotten cell planning my revenge. I was released six months ago, and I've been waitin' for my chance to get even. I never expected it to come so quick."

"So what're you gonna do, talk me to death?" Sean challenged. "If you're gonna plug me, do it and get it over with."

"Gut-shootin' you would give me real pleasure," Hanratty sneered. "However, that's too easy a way for you to die. Me and my pards are gonna take you apart with our bare hands."

With that, Hanratty stepped forward and sank a fist into Sean's gut. To the rustler's dismay, Sean barely grunted, and his return blow to Hanratty's chin knocked him back into two of his companions, sending all three sprawling on the ground.

Sean's remaining assailant rushed him, launching a punch at the big Ranger's jaw. Sean side-stepped, and the man's fist merely grazed his cheek before Sean pummeled his ribs with a powerful left. Bone cracked with the impact of the Ranger's huge fist. Sean followed that with a right to the man's belly, doubling him into a left to the face. Cartilage crunched and blood spurted from the outlaw's flattened nose. Sean drove a knee to his chin and the man collapsed, out of the fight.

The other three men had regained their feet. More cautious now, they circled the Ranger warily, seeking an opening. Hanratty fcinted a shot to Sean's stomach and then landed an uppercut to his jaw. Sean stumbled backwards, shook off the punch, and slammed one of his own to Hanratty's chest. When Hanratty staggered, struggling for breath, Sean drove another blow to the side of his face, splitting open his cheek and spinning him around. Hanratty dropped to his knees.

The other two renegades came at Sean, one

swinging wildly, the other circling behind him and attempting to pin his arms. Sean flipped that one over his head and into his partner, toppling them both to the dirt. One attempted to rise, then collapsed to his face.

Hanratty regained his balance and the infuriated rustler, blood streaming down his torn-open cheek, his left eye swollen almost shut, charged Sean, seemingly oblivious to the punches Sean landed to his face and midsection. He wrapped his arms around the Ranger, buried his head in Sean's gut, and smashed him against a wall.

Sean brought a fist down on the back of Hanratty's neck, breaking the outlaw's hold, and shoved Hanratty aside.

The other man still in the fight rushed Sean, slamming a punch to his left ear that momentarily stunned him. Hanratty took advantage of the opening. Shaking his head to clear the cobwebs, Sean failed to react quickly enough to the onrushing rustler, who landed a right to his jaw. Sean recovered and drove a left to Hanratty's gut. His following punch was intended to be the finisher, but just as he swung he slipped on a blood-slicked rock, and he missed his target completely. Off-balance, the Ranger was defenseless against Hanratty's three vicious punches to his stomach. Sean's hands dropped to his sides and he doubled over, leaving the rustler a clean shot at his chin. The punch connected hard, snapping Sean's head back. Hanratty followed that with a solid blow, which took the Ranger low in his belly. Hanratty's fist sank almost wrist-deep in Sean's gut. Sean jackknifed, and when he stumbled forward, Hanratty kicked him hard in the groin. Paralyzed with pain, the Ranger grabbed his crotch, groaned, and dropped to his knees. Sean crumpled to his face, then rolled onto his back. He moaned once more, shuddered, and lay still.

Hanratty's partner pulled out his gun and aimed it at the Ranger's chest.

"I'll finish off him for good," he snarled.

Hanratty grabbed his wrist.

"Are you loco, Tom? A shot'll make too much noise. Put that thing away."

He drove the heel of his boot into Sean's temple. Sean's head lurched sideways, and blood flowed from his ears and nose. Hanratty dragged the Ranger into the alley with the man's head lolling limply.

"That finishes him, so let's pick up Duke and Boyle and get outta here." A few moments later the only sound from the alley was the rustling of several rats, their keen sense of smell following the scent of fresh blood.

Chapter 6

A weary Lieutenant Jim Blawcyzk led his company of worn-out Rangers into the yard of their temporary headquarters. He waved the column to a halt.

"All right, men. Dismount," he ordered. "Take care of your mounts. Make sure you rub 'em down real good. Check for any saddle sores or other injuries. Go over their feet real good. If you find any loose shoes get your horse to Bill right away so he can replace them. After that feed and water those broncs. Once that's done you can turn 'em loose, then take care of yourselves. Clean up and rest a spell. We'll have a good supper tonight. Remember, any man who just gives his horse a lick and a promise will have to answer to me."

"You heard the lieutenant. Get busy," Jim Huggins reiterated. To Blawcyzk he added with a chuckle, "That last order wasn't really necessary, Jim. The men know how you are about horses."

"It doesn't matter how I feel about horses," Blawcyzk answered. "You doggone know as well as I do that a man's life depends on his horse out here. A crippled-up mount's no good to anyone. A man out of action because of a hurt cayuse could make the difference between us winnin' or losin' a skirmish with those renegades we're

82

after. One horse injured because of neglect could end up costing the lives of several good Rangers."

"Gee, it seems to me I've heard that somewhere before a time or two. Let's see, when was that? Oh yeah, you've given that same lecture a couple hundred times, at least," Huggins laughed.

"That's not insubordination I'm hearing, is it, Sergeant?" Blawcyzk grinned.

"From me? Of course not," Huggins sarcastically replied.

"Then you'd best get outta here, before I have you brought up on charges and put in front of a firing squad," Blawcyzk retorted.

"So now you're El Commandante in the Mexican army, rather than a mere lieutenant in the Texas Rangers? Just have whoever disagrees with you shot!" Huggins snapped back.

"That's it. I'm finished with you undermining my authority, Huggins!" Blawcyzk shouted. He pulled his Colt from its holster and aimed it at Huggins' stomach.

"Bang!"

Huggins yelped, clutched his middle, and slumped over his horse's neck.

Bill Dundee, the company's black cook and farrier, who was also unofficially on the rolls as a Ranger, looked up from the bay gelding he was currying and chortled.

"Summarily executed the Sarge again, eh Lieutenant?"

Dundee had watched this scene replayed at least a dozen times since being assigned to Blawcyzk's company.

"Sure did," Blawcyzk laughed. He slid his Peacemaker, which had an empty chamber in the cylinder, back into its holster.

Huggins straightened himself in his saddle.

"Jim, if you're gonna execute me, least you could do is drill me through the chest, rather'n pluggin' me in my guts," he grumbled. "I'd sooner die quick."

"That could be arranged," Blawcyzk responded, chuckling. "Bet a hat on it."

"Then I'd best git before it is. You need anything before I go?" Huggins asked.

"No. Take care of Dusty, then rest awhile. We'll talk after supper."

"See you then."

Huggins reined Dusty, his chestnut gelding, into the nearest corral, where he dismounted, stripped his gear from the horse, dug a curry-comb from his saddlebags, and began grooming the mount.

Blawcyzk smiled while he watched Huggins ride away. He and Huggins' constant ribbing of each other was a standing joke in the company. They'd become fast friends the first time they'd ridden together as Rangers, and their friendship had only grown stronger over the years. Each had saved the other's life more than once. While he'd never admit it to anyone else, Blawcyzk couldn't imagine taking on a band of outlaws or renegade Comanches without the tough veteran sergeant by his side.

"C'mon, Sam. Time to get you cleaned up," Blawcyzk told his paint.

He walked the palomino and white splotched gelding over to the far corral, where several other Rangers were already rubbing down their mounts. Those men gave Blawcyzk's paint a wide berth. The ill-tempered animal was a one-man horse and would take a chunk of hide out of anyone, other than Blawcyzk, who got too close to him.

As soon as Blawcyzk swung out of the saddle, Sam nuzzled his shoulder, and then nosed at Jim's hip pocket for his expected treat.

"Of course I've got your candy. Just let me get the bit out of your mouth," Blawcyzk chided the gelding. He slid the bridle off Sam's head, hung it on the fence, then dug a peppermint out of his pocket and gave it to the horse, who crunched down happily on the treat.

Blawcyzk removed the saddle and blanket from Sam's back and placed these on the fence, blanket reversed and atop the saddle to air out. He removed a brush from the saddlebags and commenced grooming the big horse.

A wave of nausea overcame him, along with an urgent need to find the nearest outhouse. Blawcyzk leaned against Sam's side until the feeling passed.

"Thought I was over that. I sure hope it ain't comin' back, Sam. Dunno how soon I can get the men back out there," he confided to him. "None of us are in any shape to be ridin', plus you and your buddies need some time to rest and fatten up."

The grueling patrol they'd just returned from had been especially difficult for the Rangers. They failed to capture or kill any of the outlaws they'd been seeking, nor had they recovered any stolen livestock. The closest they had come was a running gun battle with several Mexican rustlers, in which two of the Rangers had been wounded, but apparently none of the rustlers had been hit. Under the cover of a sudden thunderstorm, the raiders had made the Rio Grande and crossed safely into Mexico. Once sheltered by the trees and brush across the river, they had dismounted and dug in on the bank, rifles at the ready, making any attempt for the Rangers to follow sheer insanity. Swimming their horses through the turbulent waters of the Rio, the lawmen would have been easy targets for those outlaw guns, so the frustrated Rangers had been forced to turn back.

The weather for most of their trip had only added to their misery. It had alternated between blazing hot or rainy and cool, so the men had spent most of the time either dripping with sweat or thoroughly chilled, soaked to the skin. After weeks in the brush, the Rangers were exhausted, and their horses were in even worse shape. The animals were gaunt from lack of feed and water, with several of them suffering strains or cuts. A few, including Sam, also had taken bullets, but fortunately none of the animals' wounds were incapacitating. Time was the only and necessary cure for men and mounts.

Worst of all, a particularly nasty intestinal bug had swept through the company. Its effect was a high fever and chills accompanied by an extremely queasy stomach, so its victims could keep nothing down. In addition, the virus brought on an extremely urgent diarrhea. When a man wasn't leaning over the side of his horse vomiting, he was searching desperately for any kind of shelter where he could leap from the saddle and empty his bowels.

"I know the men'd appreciate some time in Laredo, but I can't even think about letting 'em head for town until I'm positive they're over this grippe. Reckon we'll just take it easy and rest here a few days until we see if this thing's run its course, pard," Blawcyzk concluded.

Blawcyzk finished rubbing down his horse, smeared salve over the bullet slash on Sam's right shoulder, and then turned him loose. Sam rolled in the dirt and shook himself off before trotting over to join several other mounts already working on the hay which two men had forked into the corral.

"I'll grain you in a few minutes," Blawcyzk promised, at which Sam looked up, snorted, then went back to munching hay.

Blawcyzk headed for the barn, filled a bucket with oats and corn, and returned to the corral. Looking for any sign of lack of appetite, he waited while Sam devoured the ration of grain.

"Well, reckon at least your belly's feelin' okay, pal. Wish mine was," he said, once the bucket was emptied. "You take it easy. Time to get myself some rest, so I reckon I'll take a bath and a short nap."

Blawcyzk untied his saddlebags, shouldered them, and headed for the ranch house, where he went to his room and dropped the saddlebags on the bed. He removed a bar of yellow soap from the alforjas, then stepped over to the bureau and took his one spare shirt, socks, underwear, and a towel from the top drawer.

The Rangers were using an old horse trough in an abandoned back corral as a makeshift bathtub. Rick Johnston met Blawcyzk at the broken-down gate to the enclosure. Johnston was stripped to the waist, and had a ragged towel draped around his neck.

"Just finished my bath, Lieutenant. Sure felt good. Don't worry, I left plenty of water for you," Johnston assured him.

"Thanks, Rick, I appreciate that. I'll see you at supper."

"Which might be the first meal I'll be able to keep down in a coon's age," Johnston noted. "Man, I hope I'm never, ever this sick again. Even takin' a Comanche arrow in the gut couldn't hurt my belly as bad as whatever we caught. See you later, Lieutenant."

Blawcyzk noted to his satisfaction the trough was still more than half-full with murky, tepid water. A thin film of soap scum floated on the surface.

"Beggars can't be choosers," he told himself. "At least Rick left enough water so I'll be able to take a good soak."

Blawcyzk draped the towel over the fence, stripped out of his filthy clothes, and slid into the trough, letting the water rise almost to his neck. He soaked for a good bit before scrubbing the trail grime out of his skin and then settled back once again to relax a while longer.

In the warmth of the late afternoon sun, the weary Blawcyzk soon dozed off, until he was awakened by Sam's soft muzzle nuzzling insistently at his head. Always happier in Blawcyzk's presence, the gelding had jumped his corral fence and trotted over to where his rider lay sleeping in his bath. The startled Blawcyzk leapt up, but slipped and fell back with a splash.

"Sam! What in blue blazes are you doin', hoss? You tryin' to scare me half to death? Get outta here!"

Sam nipped playfully at Blawcyzk's ear.

"I said leave me alone, doggone it!" Blawcyzk shouted.

Sam's only response was to tug harder on the Ranger's ear, forcing him to his feet. Sam buried his nose in Blawcyzk's belly, his rider grunting with the impact.

"I'll get ya, you son of a gun!" Blawcyzk growled and splashed water in the horse's face. Sam snorted, shook his head, and shoved Blawcyzk hard in the chest, dumping him back into the water.

"I'm gonna feed you to the buzzards once I get my hands on you," Blawcyzk spluttered. He lunged for the horse, but Sam backed away, whinnying.

"Just wait, pal," Blawcyzk warned. He grabbed for his towel, but Sam snatched it in his teeth and galloped off, head and tail held high, the towel flapping. Blawcyzk jumped from the trough to pursue his horse. When his left foot landed on a sharp rock, the lieutenant yelped with pain and plunged to his face. He rolled over and then stood up, hopping in place while holding the bruised foot. Sam remained just out of reach, prancing, snorting, and tossing his head, with the towel still clamped between his teeth.

Blawcyzk suddenly became aware of raucous laughter coming from the direction of the house and barn. Most of the other Rangers had been watching the spectacle, thoroughly amused at their commanding officer's predicament.

"Hey Jim, now are you gonna have Sam shot for insubordination?" Jim Huggins called. The sergeant was practically doubled over with laughter, tears rolling down his cheeks.

"You'd best be careful, Lieutenant, or you're liable to turn red as an Injun, standin' out in the hot sun in your birthday suit like that," Seth Wooley warned, with a broad grin creasing his face.

"Yeah, but the gals at Miss Lulu's back in Austin sure would be enjoyin' the view," Pete Larson added.

"I dunno," Patrick O'Mara disagreed in his thick Irish brogue. "Shure and begorrah, I think seein' the lieutenant in the altogether would send those ladies screamin' with terror into the night. It's a pretty scary sight. Besides, as we all know Jim's happily married, and a church-goin' man to boot. He'd have to go to confession before Sunday Mass if he tarried with one of those gals. You'd never find him at Lulu's."

"Private O'Mara . . ." Blawcyzk started to form a reply, but hastily stopped. He glanced down, now realizing just how ridiculous he appeared. A smile crossed his face, and then he burst into a guffaw, his laughter joining that of his men.

Blawcyzk's laughter abruptly halted when a dust cloud appeared on the horizon. The dark smear grew rapidly larger against the sky.

"Rider comin' hard. We'd best see what that's

about. Pat, you go meet him, and bring whoever it is straight to me."

"Yessir, Lieutenant." O'Mara lifted the gun from his holster.

"Just in case," he explained.

No longer worrying about toweling off Blawcyzk hastily redressed. Just as he jammed his Stetson over his still-damp thatch of thick blonde hair, Sam drew closer.

"Game's over, pard." Blawcyzk stated firmly. He grabbed the towel, leapt onto the paint's bare back and nudged him in the ribs. "Let's go."

By the time Blawcyzk covered the short distance to the house Pat O'Mara was escorting the newcomer through the gate. He was a young man of no more than fourteen, skinny with the lankiness of early adolescence. Tow hair bleached the color of straw poked out from under his battered hat. The sorrel gelding under him was soaked with sweat, its sides heaving as it struggled for breath. The exhausted youth slid from his saddle when they reached the porch.

"Pat, take care of that horse. Cool him out and then rub him down," Blawcyzk ordered. He slid off Sam's back.

"Sure, Jim. C'mon, boy." O'Mara took the reins and led the horse away.

"Seth, get this boy some water."

"Right away, Lieutenant."

"Lieutenant Blaw . . . Bla . . . ?" the boy stumbled over Blawcyzk's Polish surname.

"It's Bluh-zhick. Just call me Jim, or lieutenant. It's easier."

"Sure, Lieutenant. I'm Boyd Wells from the Western Union in Laredo. Frank Harris of the Lazy FH saw you and your men ridin' past his place this morning. He came into town for supplies and mentioned that the Rangers had returned."

"All right, get to the point, son."

"I've got a couple of telegrams here for you. Figured they might be too important to wait until you got into town. One's pretty old, because it was misrouted. Somehow it went to Junction rather'n Laredo, and it sat there for quite some time before anyone noticed."

He passed two yellow flimsies to Blawcyzk, who hurriedly glanced over their contents. As he read, the Lieutenant's clear blue eyes darkened with anger, glittering like chips of ice.

"You were right, Boyd, these are urgent. Thanks for being so diligent."

"So . . . what, Lieutenant?"

"Faithful to your duties. Sign of a man who'll do to ride the river with . . . or one who'll make a good Ranger in a few years."

"Thanks, Lieutenant," the youngster grinned, clearly pleased with the praise.

Seth Wooley returned with a pail and dipper.

"Here's that water, Jim."

"Thanks, Seth. Take Boyd inside and let him rest. Find somethin' for him to chow down on. Boyd, you go with Ranger Wooley."

"Right away, Jim. Come with me, son," Wooley said.

"What about Grady, my horse?" the boy protested.

"Ranger O'Mara's takin' good care of him. Grady'll be just fine," Wooley assured him. "Now let's find you some chuck."

The messenger followed the Ranger into the house.

"What do those messages say, Jim?" Sergeant Huggins asked.

"First one's from Sean and Levi. They haven't had much luck trailin' Thad Dutton's killer. They found the spot where Thad was gunned down, but lost the sign further on, so they headed for San Antonio, hoping to pick up something there. That's where this wire's from."

"How about the other one?"

"That one was from Thad. It says he was headin' to Brooks County to check on some kind of trouble down there. States he'd wire us from Falfurrias once he got there."

"Which he never did."

"Right, which means he never reached Falfurrias."

"Or he got there, but was killed before he could send a wire," Pete Larson observed.

"You could be right, Pete." Blawcyzk agreed. "We've got no way of knowin', unless we get word from Sean or Levi, since their message didn't say where Thad was killed."

"So what's our next move, Jim?" Huggins asked.

"First thing, soon as Boyd's horse is rested enough, I'm gonna give the boy a message to send to Sean and Levi up in San Antone. I want to let them know about Thad's wire, and I've got to order them to head for Falfurrias as quick as possible."

"They might already have uncovered something and are on their way, or they might even be in Falfurrias by now," Huggins pointed out.

"I doubt it, since we haven't gotten another wire from them. If they are, we're that much ahead of the game. Where's Woodson?"

"He was gathcrin' up some firewood for Bill," Larson answered.

"Get him for mc. Dundee also."

"I'll have 'em here in a jiffy." Larson headed off at a lope.

"Jim, you have any idea why Thad might have gone to Brooks County?" Huggins asked.

"Not a one, since his wire didn't give a hint. It just said he was goin' there to check on some trouble. At least now we know he did try to let us know he wasn't ridin' straight back. It's not his fault Western Union didn't deliver his telegram."

"That mistake cost us a lot of valuable time," Huggins pointed out.

"It did, but we can't do anything about that now, except hope the mix-up didn't give Thad's killer enough time to get away."

"Here's Pete with Woody and Bill."

Accompanying Larson and Dundee, the burly company farrier and cook, was a tall, slim Ranger of nineteen. He had sandy hair, light brown eyes, and he'd recently grown a mustache in an attempt to appear older. Instead, the bristly growth only emphasized his youthful looks. The heavy Smith and Wesson .44 which hung at his waist appeared ready to drag the youngster's gun belt over his thin hips and down around his ankles at any moment.

"Pete said you wanted us, Lieutenant?" he asked.

"Yeah, Woody," Blawcyzk answered. "I'm sure he's already told you we got a wire from Thad."

"Yep, he did. Thad went to Brooks County?"

"Apparently, so that's where I want you to head."

"Me, Lieutenant? Why? There are plenty of men in this company with more experience," Woodson objected.

"I know that," Blawcyzk answered. It struck him that he'd heard pretty much the same argument from Sean Kennedy. He himself had similarly objected to his company commander back when he was a young Ranger. However, his captain had insisted Jim could handle the assignment, and he'd been proved right when Blawcyzk tracked down the five men he'd been sent after. In a vicious gunfight, Blawcyzk had been shot and badly wounded, but still was able to kill three outlaws and capture the other two, who were subsequently hanged. "But you and Bill are the only two men who haven't gotten sick, so you're the only ones in any shape for a long hard ride," he concluded.

"Then why not send Bill?"

"You know the first reason. Unfortunately, although Bill's as valuable to me as any man in this outfit, officially he's not a Ranger. Second, and more important, I need him here to take care of the blacksmithing. Once we rest for a few days, we're ridin' back after those Mexicans who shot us up and put slugs into Tarry and Monahan. I'll need the best riflemen I can get for that and since Bill's a crack shot with that old Sharps of his, I'm plannin' on those .50 caliber slugs blowin' holes clean through some of those rustlers. Truthfully, I'd rather send both of you to Falfurrias, but I just can't spare two men."

"Why'd you send for me then, Jim?" Dundee asked.

"I want you to double-check Woody's horse's shoes," Blawcyzk explained. "Don't take any chances with 'em. Replace all four if you need to.

I'd also appreciate your makin' up a sack of grub for Woody. Spare as much as you can for him until you can get into Laredo and re-supply."

"I'll get right on that," Dundee promised.

"Good." Blawcyzk turned back to Woodson.

"Woody, you rest for two hours. Then I want you to ride for Falfurrias and get there as fast as you can without killin' your horse."

"What should I do when I get there?"

"I'm comin' to that. With any luck, Kennedy and Mallory are already there. The other telegram's from them. They were in San Antonio, but by now they might have found out Dutton headed for Brooks County and have followed him there, in which case you'll work with them."

"But if they haven't?"

"Then you'll have to try and do some detective work on your own. See if you can find out who killed Thad, or whatever else you can which might point in his direction. Be sure you wire me as soon as you hit town."

"I'll do my best, Lieutenant, count on that."

"I know you will. If I didn't think you could handle the job, I wouldn't have handed it to you," Blawcyzk answered. "Now get some rest. It might be the last you'll have for quite some time."

"All right. Is there anything else?"

"Just one more thing. Be careful, Woody."

"I will be. And thanks . . . Jim."

Chapter 7

In the deserted section of San Antonio where Sean had been attacked and left for dead, no one would stir until well after sunup. An hour passed, then two, while Sean lay unmoving, his breathing ragged, blood oozing from his wounds and trickling from his nose. He would have lain there until daybreak, slowly bleeding to death, had it not been for the rat, bolder than the rest of its fellows, which crawled across his face, then pushed its whiskered snout into his nostril, following the trail of half-dried blood. Sean awoke with a start. When his head jerked, the startled rodent scrambled over his chin and down his chest, squealing in fright as it scurried away.

Sean's eyes flickered open. The entire world seemed to be spinning crazily, so he closed his eyes again, attempting to quell the nausea which threatened to overcome him. Instinct warned him that if he threw up and passed out again he could choke to death on his own vomit.

Another quarter hour passed while the Ranger laid waiting for the vertigo to ease and the queasiness in his stomach to subside. Finally, realizing he could not last much longer, Sean rolled onto his belly. Immediately a swirling vortex of black threatened to swallow him.

Gotta . . . gotta get help . . . fast, he thought. *Have to try'n make . . . Hector's.*

Hector Melendez's livery stable was the nearest place he could count on for assistance.

Sean fumbled about the alleyway until he found his gun belt. Fortunately Hanratty had not bothered to take the belt and gun it held. Sean draped it around his neck.

Dragging himself along by hands and elbows, groping his way through the darkness, Sean inched his way toward the stable. Every movement sent almost unbearable pain through his battered body. His head throbbed, his ribs felt as if countless knives had been stuck in them, and waves of agony pulsed from his groin through his lower belly. Every few minutes, he had to stop to let the pain subside and catch his breath.

"Lord, help me," he whispered when the torment became almost too much to bear, but the determined Ranger found the willpower to struggle on.

Finally Sean reached the alley leading to Hector's stable, where somehow he managed to gain his feet and stumble toward the barn door. He stopped short just before sliding the door open, for angry voices were coming from inside.

"We're takin' these four horses," one insisted. "Try'n stop us and you'll get a bellyful of lead."

"You will not steal any animals in my care,

señores. I will not allow it. I wish to inform you that blue roan and the sorrel you are attempting to take are the caballos of two Texas Rangers."

"All the more reason I want this roan, then. This was Kennedy's horse and he won't be needin' it anymore. Besides, it's his fault none of us have been able to scrape together the cash to buy horses or saddles, because no rancher's willin' to give a job to a convicted rustler or his pards. Takin' the Ranger's horse'll make my revenge that much sweeter, so just stay out of our way, boy!"

The sound of a fist striking jaw followed.

"That's Bud Hanratty!" Sean hissed. He pulled his Colt out of the holster hanging from his neck and shoved open the door. Hector, stunned, was sprawled on the floor, while Amigo, his little pinto, was trembling in the corner. Four saddled and bridled horses, including Ghost and Monte, were waiting in their stalls.

"Hold it right there!" Sean's raspy voice cut through the aisle like a rusty hinge.

The four rustlers turned and stared in shock at the apparition before them. Sean's clothes were in tatters, his shirt torn open to reveal livid purple bruises across his chest, ribs, and abdomen. His right eye was blackened and swollen shut, his face scraped raw, and blood still dripped from his nose. The few areas of his flesh not smeared with blood and dirt were a deathly pale fish-belly white. But his dark eyes were still bright with determination and death glittered in their depths when he glared at Hanratty.

"Kennedy! It can't be. You're dead!" Hanratty shrieked. His voice rose in panic, seeing the big Ranger he'd thought he'd killed standing there with a Colt pointed straight at his belly.

Sean's voice was low and deadly in response.

"Not quite, Hanratty, no thanks to you and your pardners. I'd advise you to drop those guns. Right now!"

In response, Hanratty threw himself to the side and snapped a shot in Sean's direction. The hastily fired slug ripped past the Ranger's ear and out the door into the night.

Sean fired at the same moment, his bullet also missing its target and burying itself in a support post.

Duke Monroe whirled and pulled his Remington. He had just cleared leather when Sean put a bullet into his chest. Dust puffed from the outlaw's shirt, and the slug's impact slammed Monroe back into a stall door. He slid to a seated position and his chin dropped on his chest while his heart beat one final time.

Hanratty, Tom Shaw, and Hank Boyle concentrated their fire on the Ranger. One of Boyle's shots connected, striking Sean in the side, staggering him. Boyle drew a bead on Sean's chest, thumbed back the hammer of his pistol, and was ready to send a bullet through Sean's lungs. Just as he pulled back the trigger, Amigo, panicked by the gunfire, raced blindly for the exit. The tiny horse slammed into Boyle from behind and cut him down at the knees, causing Boyle to topple backwards into Hanratty, and then fall on his backside. His bullet plowed harmlessly into the hayloft. Before Boyle could recover, Sean shot him through the throat. Blood spurted from Boyle's severed jugular. Sean put another bullet into his chest and Boyle fell, leaving Sean a clear shot at Hanratty. The Ranger fired, his bullet taking the rustler high in the chest, just below his right shoulder. Hanratty spun into Ghost's open stall.

Overcome by pain and loss of blood, Sean slumped against the wall.

"Bud should'a let me put a slug in your brains back in that alley like I wanted," snarled Shaw, the remaining rustler. "No matter. I'll make sure you're dead this time, Ranger. I'm gonna blast you straight to Hell." He pointed his six-gun directly at Sean's forehead.

Shaw gave a strangled grunt, and his eyes widened with shock and pain.

Unnoticed behind the outlaw, Hector had recovered from Hanratty's blow. The young hostler had grabbed the only weapon handy, a long-handled pitchfork.

"Señor," he called to Shaw. When Shaw whirled to face this unexpected threat, Hector drew back with all the strength he could muster and flung the fork at Shaw. It struck the rustler in the belly, its tines driving deep into his intestines. Shaw clawed futilely at the pitchfork and jackknifed, jamming the handle of the fork into the dirt floor. It held him upright for a moment like some macabre scarecrow, until finally Shaw sagged, arms dropping as he toppled to the dirt.

Hanratty had had enough, seeing his three companions cut down and having taken a Ranger bullet himself. Despite his wound, he dragged himself onto Ghost's back and raked the horse with his spurs. Unused to such cruel treatment, the startled gelding leapt forward at a dead run. Sean could only watch helplessly through blurred vision while Hanratty and his horse disappeared out the back door.

A moment later, a loud splash, followed by a terrified scream, came from the San Antonio River, which ran just behind the stable.

"Help! I can't swim. Help me, somebody!"

Hanratty had made the mistake of whipping Ghost with the reins and viciously raking his spurs over the blue roan's flanks yet again. Ghost had never been subjected to any brutal treatment in his life. Rebelling against the rough handling, the big gelding reacted in a fit of bucking, his actions pitching Hanratty over his head and into the river.

"Please, help . . . plea . . ."

Hanratty's voice faded.

Hector crossed the aisle to where Sean lay against the wall.

"Ranger Sean? Are you all right, Ranger?"

"Not . . . too sure. Help me up, will you Hector?" Sean gasped.

"I must go for the doctor. You are hurt very badly."

"In a minute. Gotta . . . check those men."

"All right, but then I will go for him."

The liveryman helped Sean to his feet and the Ranger clamped a hand to the bullet wound in his side. They stopped alongside Tom Shaw, who lay curled up on his side, the pitchfork still protruding from his belly. The rustler looked at them through pain-glazed eyes.

"Warned . . . warned Hanratty . . . we should leave . . . town . . . without waitin' . . . for Duke and Hank . . . to . . . get patched up . . . ," he choked. "He wouldn't . . . listen . . . just like . . . wouldn't let me put . . . bullet in you . . . back in that alley . . . make sure you were . . . finished. Dumb bas . . ."

Shaw's voice trailed off as pain wracked his body. He shivered violently and coughed up blood.

"Reckon . . . I'm done for . . . ain't I?"

"I reckon," Sean replied. "Either you'll bleed to death or die of blood poisonin' from the prongs of that filthy pitchfork stickin' in your guts.

105

Don't look for sympathy from me, since you dealt your own cards. You might want to speak with your Maker, though, because you need His forgiveness, not mine."

"I . . ."

Shaw's voice faded. His eyes closed and his breathing became ragged.

"Is he dead?" Hector asked.

"Not yet. Just unconscious, but he can't last too long," Sean replied. "Guess you saved my life, Hector. I'm grateful."

"It was nothing. After all, they were trying to steal horses from my barn. Had you not come along, I'm afraid they might have succeeded. Now, you must let me get the doctor."

They turned at the sound of hoof beats from behind the barn. Soon Ghost appeared in the doorway, trailed by Amigo. The big blue roan trotted up to Sean, nuzzled his shoulder, and nickered.

Sean's eyes narrowed in anger at the raw gouges ripped in Ghost's flanks by Hanratty's spurs.

"Dumped Hanratty in the river, eh bud? Good work. Better'n he deserved, hurtin' you like that. Lemme find somethin' to fix those cuts."

"That is my job, Sean. You are going to lie on my bed until I get the doctor," Hector insisted. "I will take care of your horse."

"What about Amigo?"

"He's fine. My pequeno caballo pintado is much smarter than the two of us put together. When the bullets started flying, he knew enough to clear out, pronto."

"Don't make me laugh, Hector. It hurts too much," Sean pleaded.

"Then you will lie down, now."

Silvery spots were now glittering in Sean's vision and his knees threatened to give out at any moment.

"I reckon it's time to do . . . just that," Sean conceded. "While you're fetchin' the . . . doc, you'd better find Ranger Mallory . . . Levi. He's either at the . . . Alhambra or . . . or Miss Hattie's and one other thing. Soon as . . . it's light enough, check the . . . riverbanks for Hanratty's . . . body."

Sean never knew how Hector got him into bed and his boots off. The next thing he remembered was staring up from Hector's bunk at the face of Marshal Larry Kane.

"What the devil happened here, Sean?" Kane demanded. "There's two dead men in the barn and another with a pitchfork in his guts."

Sean managed a wry chuckle.

"There's another body to pull out of the river too, most likely. You got here a little too late, Larry."

"What do you mean, another body, Sean? Ranger? Ranger!"

Chapter 8

Woody Woodson stopped on a low rise, a somewhat unusual formation for this mostly flat, featureless part of the Texas south plains. Through the haze and heat waves rippling the atmosphere on this blistering hot afternoon, he could make out the buildings of a town in the distance.

"Didn't think I'd gotten this far," he muttered. "I calculated Falfurrias is still a day and a half ride further, but there ain't any other towns around here. That must be Falfurrias, unless the heat's addled my brains. 'Course, it could be a mirage. I might be lookin' at Falfurrias all right, but still have that day and a half's travel ahead of me."

Woodson dismounted, pulled off his Stetson, and wiped perspiration from the sweatband. He lifted his canteen from the saddle horn and poured half its contents into the hat. He held that in front of his horse's muzzle, giving the mount a short drink. That done, he took a long drink of his own, screwed the cap back on the canteen, and remounted.

"Well, let's see what's down there, horse."

He kicked the steeldust gray into a lope.

An hour later, Woodson reached the boundary of a small town. "Welcome to Mannionville" a large wooden sign proclaimed.

"This spot sure ain't on any map of Texas I've ever seen," Woodson stated, half-aloud. "Must be brand new. Well, let's give the place a look-see."

Ten minutes later, he was riding through the outskirts of town. Most of the buildings were indeed new, some made of raw, unpainted lumber, others more sturdily constructed, with fresh coats of paint or whitewash. The nearer Woodson came to the center of town the more impressive the structures became.

Woodson studied the buildings and Mannionville's inhabitants as he walked his horse down the dusty main street.

"Mannion's Mercantile" read the sign over the general store, in bold red and black lettering. "Mannion's Feed and Grain" stated another. "Mannion's Dry Goods, Sundries, and Notions" was lettered in gold leaf on the plate glass windows of another establishment. A barn down the lone side street was marked "Mannion's Livery Stable."

Whoever this here Mannion character is, he seems to be doin' right well for himself, Woodson thought. *Every storefront in town seems to have his name on it.*

A bit further on, he reached what passed for the center of Mannionville. A false-fronted building with a wooden awning shaded boardwalk was the Devil Dog Saloon, while next to that was

Josie's Dance Hall. Beside the dance hall was the Mannionville Manor Hotel and Cafe.

"Least there's a couple of places in town Mannion don't own," Woodson muttered. "Then again, on second thought . . ."

In fine print under the names of all three establishments was the phrase "Duncan Mannion, Proprietor."

Can't linger here too long if I'm gonna make Falfurrias before sundown tomorrow. Still, it won't hurt to have a beer or two. My throat's awful parched and my cayuse can stand a rest.

Woodson let his horse drink its fill at the trough in front of the town's only adobe structure, a small marshal's office and jail. While his gelding was sucking up water, the local lawman emerged from the office.

"Afternoon, stranger," he greeted Woodson. "Hot day, ain't it?"

"Tolerable hot," the Ranger agreed, studying the marshal. The man was built like a bulldog, shorter than average but blocky, without an ounce of fat on him. He was probably in his forties, balding under his black Stetson, which was decorated with a beaded hatband and an eagle feather. His features were even and not unpleasant, but his entire mien was that of a person who would not be trifled with. Unlike many small town lawmen, his appearance was decidedly neat. His black hat showed no trace of dust, a feat almost impossible to accomplish in this part of Texas. His boots were shined, his jeans and dark red shirt clean. A royal blue silk bandanna was wrapped around his neck, and his badge hung from a supple cowhide vest. His gun belt and holster were also black leather, and fancily tooled. The gun hanging at his right hip was a serviceable Colt Peacemaker, a model still fairly new to Texas.

"I'm the town marshal of Mannionville. John Spallone," he introduced himself. "Also the de facto mayor."

"I gathered that much from the star on your vest," Woodson smiled. "You the judge also?"

"Nope. That would be Mister Mannion himself."

"Somehow I'm not surprised," Woodson responded.

"You got a name?" Spallone pressed.

"Yup, Woody," the Ranger replied.

He decided not to let the local law know a Ranger was in Mannionville, preferring to stay incognito until he reached Falfurrias.

"Got more to attach to that?"

"Sure. Wood. Woody Wood."

Spallone glared, but relaxed.

"Reckon that'll do. What brings you to Mannionville?"

"Just passin' through. I'm headin' for Falfurrias. I didn't even realize this town was here, but it seems like a pleasant enough place."

"It is, for folks who don't stir up trouble, if you get my drift," Spallone answered.

"I'm not lookin' for trouble, Marshal. Just a beer or two, and some water for my horse, then I'll be on my way."

"Long as we understand each other. Now, it's about time for my siesta."

Spallone turned and disappeared back inside his office. There was a shaded hitchrail in the alley alongside the building where a flashy, long-legged sorrel horse, probably the marshal's, stood hipshot and dozing. Woodson also tied his horse there, out of the sun. He started across the street, heading for the Devil Dog.

Woodson was halfway across the street when a slim young Mexican emerged from the saloon. The Ranger stopped short, staring at the belt wrapped around the Mexican's slender waist.

"Hombre! What're you doin' wearin' Thad Dutton's belt?"

The Mexican answered by yanking his pistol in a lightning fast draw and firing once. The bullet struck Woodson low in his belly, two inches below his belt buckle. The young Ranger doubled over, clutching his middle. He stumbled forward for several steps, dropped to his knees, then pitched to his face, writhing in pain. He managed to push himself to his hands and knees once again, before toppling onto his side. Blood trickled between his fingers.

The few passersby barely glanced at the mortally wounded Ranger, then hurried on their way or disappeared into open doorways.

"My belly hurts . . . somethin' fierce. My . . . my guts . . . are on fire," Woodson moaned. "Help me. Please, somebody help me."

The Mexican approached, his gun still at the ready. He used the toe of his boot to roll the downed Ranger onto his back.

"Nobody in this town's gonna help you, hombre," he sneered. "You're gonna die right where you are, real slow and painful."

Woodson strained to look toward the marshal's office. The door was half-opened. When he started to call to the lawman for help the door slowly closed and the window shade was drawn.

Texas Ranger Matthias "Woody" Woodson would die alone in the middle of the dusty street. He would lie in agony and bleeding, for over twenty torturous hours, until his life ended at eleven o'clock the next morning. He was three days short of his twentieth birthday.

Chapter 9

When Sean next awakened, he opened his eyes to see a hammered tin ceiling overhead. He was in a soft bed, undressed, wrapped in clean sheets and covered with a blanket. He attempted a deep breath, however a sharp pain in his ribs and the bandages taped tightly around his middle prevented that. He could also feel the pressure of bandages on his scalp and face. The scents of soaps, medicines, and chemicals mingled in the air, while the only light came from a turned-low coal oil lamp.

Sean glanced around the room. Levi was dozing in a corner chair, Stetson tilted over his head, his long legs stretched out in front of him. A well-worn copy of *The Collected Works of Edgar Allan Poe* lay opened and face-down in his lap. His chest rose and fell with the regular breathing of a man in deep sleep.

Levi stirred a bit.

"Oh, Martine . . ." he moaned. "Yes . . . right there. Honey, that's so fine . . ."

There was a small blue glass bottle of smelling salts on the table next to Sean's bed. He picked up the bottle and tossed it feebly at Levi. It bounced off his partner's chest.

Levi jumped to his feet, yanking his Colt from

its holster as his hat flew off, the book slid from his lap, and the lanky Ranger dove to his belly \on the floor.

"Comanches! They've got us surrounded!" He yelled.

Sean's laughter came out more like a fit of coughing. Levi looked around in confusion.

"What the . . . ?"

"The only Comanches around here are the ones in your imagination, Levi," Sean grinned. "Lucky for you there aren't any live ones, since they'd have had you gutted and scalped before you even woke up."

"Kennedy, you son of a . . ."

"Careful," Sean warned, "you know Lieutenant Blawcyzk doesn't care for cussin'."

Levi pushed himself off the floor and slid his gun back in its holster.

"The lieutenant ain't within two hundred miles of here. He's not gonna hear anythin'."

Levi commenced a string of oaths that turned the air blue, until he finally ran out of breath.

"You about through?" Sean asked when Levi's tirade subsided.

"I'm just gettin' warmed up," Levi retorted. "When'd you wake up? And what d'ya mean by havin' Hector drag me out of a nice warm bed, tellin' me you were dyin' and I'd better come quick before you were gone?"

"Just now woke up, to answer your first

question. Were you in your bed at the hotel or Martine's?" Sean coughed, and then waited for his breath to return before continuing. "You seemed to be havin' a real fine time dreamin' about her before I woke you up."

"What?"

"You were talkin' in your sleep, pardner. 'Oh, Martine . . .' "

Levi glared at Sean.

"You would come to just in time to hear that. You ruined a perfectly good dream."

"Seems like you got the chance to read some Poe, too," Sean said. He nodded at the book on the floor.

Levi picked up the book, closed it, and placed it on the table.

"Yep, I did. Figured since I had time on my hands I'd take Bart up on his offer and borrow this book. That Poe was some character. He wrote a lot about death. Speakin' of death, it sure doesn't seem like you're dyin' to me."

"Hector must've exaggerated a trifle. I told him to find you and let you know what was goin' on."

Sean stopped, short of breath, and then coughed several times. The effort of speaking was proving taxing for the injured Ranger.

"Not accordin' to the Hector or the doc. Doctor Lambert said it was touch and go for a spell. Speakin' of the doc, I'd better fetch him."

"Just a minute, how long have I been unconscious?" Sean asked.

"Four days now."

"Four days, that can't be possible."

"It is and you were, pard. You were in pretty rough shape when Hector and I carried you here. You still are, for that matter. Now let me get the doc."

Levi left, returning a few minutes later with a man in his late twenties.

"I'm Doctor Roger Lambert," he introduced himself. "It's good to see you coming around, Ranger Kennedy. How are you feeling?" He picked up Sean's wrist to check his pulse rate.

Lambert was tall and blond, with piercing blue eyes and a precisely trimmed spade beard, which framed his square jaw. Lambert was unlike most of the frontier doctors Sean had run across in his Ranger career. Many of them were older, often having been cashiered from the United States Cavalry service for incompetency, and more than a few of them drank to excess. In contrast, Lambert seemed very precise and efficient.

"Not too bad, Doc, except I can't breathe because you've got me wrapped so tight."

"I'm sorry. I know it's uncomfortable, but that really is necessary. I took a bullet out of your side, and you have three cracked ribs, not to mention all the cuts and bruises, so you'll be wearing those bandages for quite some time."

"Sean, as long as the doc is here, I'm goin' to fetch Hector and Larry. I promised them both I'd let them know once you came around. I'll be back in a bit. Doc, if you know what's good for all of us you'll give my pardner there another dose of laudanum. In fact, you'd better make it a double."

"Get outta here, before I find a larger bottle and bounce it off your thick skull," Sean laughed. "Watch for Comanches out there."

"Why . . ." Levi started to say something, thought better of it, and left, slamming the door behind him.

"What's the verdict, Doc? My heart still tickin'?" Sean asked.

"Well, your pulse seems steady," Lambert replied, "and you're certainly in a good humor for a man who just came out of a coma. I need to check your other vital signs."

"Sure, Doc, I reckon I ain't goin' anywhere at the moment," Sean answered.

Lambert pulled back the covers to expose Sean's upper torso. He checked his temperature and then took out his stethoscope to listen to the Ranger's heart and lungs.

"Your vital signs are strong," he assured Sean, "unlike when you were first brought to me. You came closer to dying than you realize, Ranger."

"I appreciate you pullin' me through," Sean answered.

"That's part of my job," Lambert shrugged, "besides, I like a challenge. It keeps me on my toes. I'm going to change your bandages and re-dress your injuries now. This will hurt."

"I'm certain of that," Sean rejoined.

Sean had to grit his teeth against the pain while the physician pulled the bandages away from his flesh. Even at that he grimaced and let out a soft cry of pain more than once. Bits of dead skin and dried blood came away with the old dressings.

"I'm working as carefully as I possibly can, Ranger," Lambert reassured him. "The worst is over. All I have to do now is clean out the wounds, dress them, and re-bandage them."

"I know you're doing your best, Doc," Sean answered. "Don't worry about me. I'm doin' fine."

"Good, but tell me if there's any excessive pain."

"You'll be the first to know, Doc."

"Actually, I'll be the second, Ranger. You'll be the first," Lambert deadpanned.

"Point well taken," Sean chuckled.

Lambert efficiently cleaned and re-dressed Sean's wounds. Once the new bandages were taped in place, he drew the covers back over the Ranger.

"Ranger, you're doing quite well. There's no sign of any infection, most of the swelling is going down, and the abrasions are healing nicely. If you'd like, I'll have some food sent in for you later. Nothing too heavy, however, maybe some broth, tea, and perhaps some oatmeal."

"Anything will be fine, I'm starved," Sean answered.

"Good, food and rest are going to be your best healers."

"Food, yeah Doc, but not rest. I don't know if Levi told you, but we're after a killer, a low-down murderer who gunned a Ranger. I'll rest until tomorrow, but that's it. As soon as Levi returns, I'm gonna tell him to get our horses ready to travel."

"Perhaps I haven't made myself clear," Lambert replied. "You're in no shape to travel, since I removed a bullet from your side. You also have cracked ribs, and assorted bruises and cuts, some of which are fairly deep. You'll be confined to bed for at least two weeks."

"Maybe I haven't made *myself* clear, Doctor," Sean retorted. "There's nothing which can keep me in this bed." He started to swing his legs over the edge of the mattress, but let out a yelp when sharp pain stabbed through his groin. "Except this."

"Your groin, right?" Lambert said.

"Yeah, Doc. Feels like someone stuck a knife in it," Sean confirmed, gritting his teeth, as tears welled in his eyes.

"If you'd given me the time, I was about to explain that's a very sensitive area."

"Tell me somethin' I don't already know," Sean grunted.

"Sorry, anyway, as you are aware, you took a severe blow to that area. There is quite a bit of bruising and swelling of your . . ."

"I know what they are," Sean interrupted.

"Of course, only what I'm trying to tell you is there is no possible way you can sit a horse until that swelling lessens. Even sitting in a chair will be quite uncomfortable."

"Forget about it. I'm not worried about sittin' a horse. I'm engaged, Doctor Lambert. Amy and I are planning on bein' married in a year or so. That's what worries me."

"Don't be concerned. There should be no permanent damage."

"What about kids?"

"You'll be able to have as many as you and your wife want," Lambert assured him. "Just rest and everything will be fine."

"I'll try, Doc. Only one way or another, I'll be ridin' out of here in a week at the most."

Lambert looked at Sean thoughtfully.

"Ordinarily I would say that was impossible, but since you survived a beating that would have killed most men, plus taking a bullet, you may recuperate more quickly than I would think. In fact, with your determination I wouldn't be surprised if you did. Let's take things day by day and see how your recovery progresses."

"That's fair enough. I can't ask for more than that," Sean agreed.

"Fine, I'm going to let you rest some more. I'll have your meal brought to you in about an hour. I'll be back to check on you this evening."

"All right and thanks, Doc," Sean answered.

"Don't mention it. You just rest and get well."

Ten minutes after the doctor departed, Levi returned with Hector and Larry Kane.

"Hola, Sean, Ranger amigo mio," Hector exclaimed as soon as he entered the room. "Madre de Dios, I never expected to see you alive again. I have been praying to the Santisima Virgen and all the Santos Bendites for your recovery. Every night I go to the chapel and light candles to Nuestra Señora de Guadalupe for you. Gracias, Virgen Maria. Gracias, Santos Bendites."

"Sean needs all the prayers he can get, Hector, even when he's not hurt," Levi laughed.

"Just ignore him, Hector," Sean advised. "Your prayers seem to have worked. Muchas gracias, amigo mio. How's Ghost?"

"Espiritu is just fine and I have been washing the wounds to his flanks, which are healing rapidly. And yes, I have been giving him his licorice."

"I appreciate that," Sean answered.

"I'm glad to see you're back with us too, Sean," Kane added. "If you're up to it, I really need to find out what happened to you so I can finish my report on the incident. Levi didn't have much information."

"Of course he didn't," Sean grinned. "He was in a nice soft bed with a nice soft woman while I was gettin' myself beat up and shot."

"I left that bed soon as Hector told me what happened," Levi protested.

"That was good of you," Sean dryly answered.

"The report, Sean," Kane persisted. "I have to get back to my rounds. We did pull Bud Hanratty's body out of the river and the other bodies have been identified. Hector has already filled me in on what happened at his stable, so I just need your story on what occurred in the alley down off Robles Street."

"Sure, Larry, I was on my way back from the Gilded Cage."

Sean gave Levi a glance warning him not to speak and to hold any questions for later.

"Go on," Kane urged.

"Hanratty and his pards must've seen me in there. So, they followed me until we got to the warehouse district. Hanratty said he was gonna kill me for sendin' him to prison, and he came dang close to keepin' his word."

"Somehow you survived, made your way to Hector's, and ran into Hanratty and his bunch again."

"That's right. They were attempting to steal

horses to get out of town. I did try'n give 'em a chance to surrender. They wouldn't take it."

"So you drilled all four of 'em."

"No, three," Sean corrected. "Hector took care of Tom Shaw with his pitchfork. I also didn't finish off Hanratty. I nailed him, but my bullet didn't kill him, Ghost did that when he pitched him in the river. I can't blame my cayuse for doin' it, the way Hanratty took his spurs to him. Ghost was just fightin' back and Hanratty deserved what he got."

"You're right about Shaw," the marshal confirmed. "I just wanted to make sure you hadn't also shot him." Kane's stomach gurgled as bile rose in his throat. He still got nauseous every time the image of Shaw with that pitchfork stuck in his guts came to mind.

"I didn't kill him. You're lookin' a bit green, Larry."

"I need some air. Glad to see you awake, Sean and it's good to know you'll be fine. I'll be in touch if I have any more questions."

"I'll stop by your office before I leave town," Sean assured him.

"I must also be going," Hector added. "It's feeding time and my charges don't like to be kept waiting. Sean, I will come back tomorrow."

"Okay, Hector. Hasta la vista."

"Hasta la vista, Sean."

Levi closed the door behind them.

"All right, Sean, they're gone. What is it you've been bustin' a gut to tell me?" Levi demanded.

"It's that obvious, huh?"

"It sure is, so spill it."

"Dolores Montalvo at the Casa d'Plata told me where Thad went. He headed for Brooks County."

"Brooks County? Why the devil would he go there?"

"According to Delores, the reason involves a girl . . . blonde and pretty."

"That does sound like Thad all right, but there has to be more to the story. Dolores didn't give you anything else?"

"She claimed that's all she knew, other than the fact the girl was in town with her father. Dolores said the man is a rancher from somewhere in Brooks County."

"That's an awful lot of territory to cover, Sean," Levi pointed out. "Brooks is pretty spread out, and there's a whole bunch of ranches down that way. Dolores couldn't tell you who this gal was?"

"No, said she didn't want to find out, but she also said Arnold, the night front desk clerk over at the Bon Ton Hotel, should be able to tell us. Evidently that's where the girl and her father were stayin'. In fact, I was on my way there when I ran into Hanratty and his bunch."

"I reckon I've got a job then. I'll go talk to this Arnold."

"You've got a couple of jobs. You'll also need

to stop by the telegraph office and send another wire to Lieutenant Blawcyzk, unless you happened to already think of that."

"I sure didn't," Levi admitted. "I was too worried about you, pardner."

"Don't fret about it, it's not a problem. We wouldn't have wanted the lieutenant to know what's been goin' on the past few days anyway. Just tell him we've been followin' some leads here. Say we're waitin' on some more information and once we have it we'll be ridin' for Falfurrias."

"If he knows you're gonna be laid up awhile, he might send someone else."

"Which is why we're not gonna tell him I'm laid up. He probably will send someone anyway. My guess is once he gets our telegram he'll start a man for Falfurrias. He'll let us know if he does. Besides, we won't be hanging around here much longer."

"But I heard the doc say you can't ride for quite some time."

"That's the doc's opinion, not mine, which brings up another job I need you to do for me."

Levi sighed.

"You're wearing me to a frazzle. All right, what is it?"

"How much did Doc Lambert tell you about my injuries?"

"Just you were pretty badly beaten. He wasn't all that concerned about the slug you took. He was more worried about internal injuries and loss of blood, since you darn near bled out."

"Did he happen to mention I got kicked in the crotch?"

"No, he didn't, ouch." Levi winced. "What's that got to do with another job for me?"

"I'm still mighty sore."

"I can imagine, because I've gotten kneed a couple of times in a fight and it hurts plenty. I don't even want to think about what a boot can do to a man down there."

"You sure don't. What it does mean is it's gonna be tough for me to ride a horse for awhile. I need you to try and come up with some sort of pad for my saddle. Mebbe, I dunno, a sheepskin, or somethin' like that."

"I'll figure out something I can rig up. Sean, if there's nothing else, I'd better get movin'. It's getting late and I haven't slept much the past few days, unlike you," Levi grinned.

"Then you'd better get some shut-eye tonight. Once we start for Falfurrias, I have a feelin' neither one of us will be getting much sleep."

A soft knock came at the door.

"Ranger Kennedy? It's Mrs. Lambert with your supper. May I come in?"

"Of course," Sean replied.

"Wait just a minute, please, Mrs. Lambert," Levi requested. Turning to Sean he whispered, "Besides bein' the doc's wife, she's also his nurse, and real easy on the eyes." He raised his voice to call, "It's all right to come in now, Mrs. Lambert, Sean's decent."

Norma Lambert entered carrying a cloth-covered tray. She was petite, red-headed, and very pretty.

"I have beef broth, oatmeal, and black coffee for you, Ranger. The doctor wanted you to have tea, but I told him that's not a suitable beverage for a lawman."

She winked conspiratorially. "I added a dollop of good Tennessee bourbon to that coffee. You'll also find some apple crisp hidden under the napkin."

"You're a woman after my own heart. Thanks, Mrs. Lambert," Sean exclaimed. "You needn't have gone to all that trouble."

"Pshaw! It's not a bother at all," she replied as she placed the tray on the bedside table. "Food helps a body regain its strength, along with plenty of rest. Which means to say, Ranger Mallory, it's time for you to go."

"I can take a hint," Levi chuckled. "Sean, I'll be back in the morning, unless something real urgent comes up."

"See you then, Levi."

"Wait just a moment, Ranger Mallory," Mrs. Lambert ordered. "I insist you have supper before you leave. I made a lovely roast, along with boiled potatoes and green beans fresh from

128

my garden, along with that apple crisp, of course. There's way too much food for just the doctor and me to eat, so you'll join us."

"I can't say no to an order like that, ma'am," Levi said.

"Good. Now let's leave Ranger Kennedy to his meal."

Once Sean finished supper, he slid back under the blankets and dozed off. Two hours later, he was awakened by Levi.

"Sean? You awake?"

"I am now."

Sean sat up, painfully leaning against the headboard.

"Sorry to disturb your rest, but I figured this couldn't wait until morning."

"Don't worry about that. What'd you find out?"

"I've got a wire here from Lieutenant Blawcyzk. It's dated several days ago."

"What's it say?"

"He's already sent a man to Falfurrias, Woody Woodson. He wants us to meet up with him."

"How would he know about Falfurrias?" Sean wondered.

"Will you let me finish?" Levi answered. "It seems Thad Dutton didn't just take off without lettin' anyone know what he was up to. He sent a telegram to the lieutenant, but it was misrouted, so no one knew about it. Anyway, it seems the lieutenant got our first wire and Thad's at the same time. Thad's said he was headin' for Brooks County to look into some kind of trouble down there."

"So, Dolores gave me good information. Did Lieutenant Blawcyzk's wire mention what kind of trouble, or exactly where?"

"Nope. He didn't have a name for us either, but Arnold at the Bon Ton did. The lady we're lookin' for is a Susanna May Porter. Her dad is Ethan Allen Porter. Their ranch is somewhere outside Falfurrias. Arnold couldn't narrow it down further."

"That doesn't matter. With the names, we can check at the county land office, which'll have the records we need. That'll narrow our search considerably, although it looks like we're finally makin' some progress. Ethan Allen Porter, huh? Must be a Yankee," Sean speculated.

"Seems so, only it's about time we caught a break," Levi answered.

"You find out anything else?"

"No, that's all for right now."

"It's a lot more than we had. Thanks for not waitin' 'til morning to give me the information. Now, why don't you get that shut-eye?"

"That's exactly what I'm planning on doing, calling it a night. See you tomorrow."

"G'night, Levi. See you then."

Despite his injuries, Sean felt a sense of satisfaction for the first time since departing

Laredo. It appeared they might finally have a solid lead which would take them to Ranger Thad Dutton's killer.

Five days later, Sean was sitting on the edge of his bed while Doctor Lambert re-bandaged his ribs. Sean grunted when the physician pulled the bandages as tightly as possible.

"Doc, I can barely breathe. I thought you'd leave those a bit looser."

"If you're going to insist on leaving and spending the next week in a saddle, your ribs have to be kept as motionless as possible. I still wish you would reconsider your decision."

Lambert gave the strip of bandage he'd just wrapped around Sean's middle a rough yank, causing Sean to grunt again.

"You've already squashed my guts, Doc. Any tighter and you'll have my bellybutton pushed up against my backbone," Sean protested.

"Yeah," Levi agreed from where he stood across the room, watching the procedure. "You've got Sean wrapped up tighter'n a spinster in her corset."

"You're not helping the situation," Lambert told him, "especially since you're the one who came up with that device so your partner can ride more easily."

"Don't blame Levi, because I asked him to do that," Sean said. "There's no chance of me changin' my mind about leaving today. Every day I stay here gives Thad Dutton's murderer a better chance of gettin' away. Don't worry about me, Doc, I'll get by just fine."

"Well, I've given you my best advice, so I can't be responsible for anything that happens to you once you leave this room," Lambert warned.

"I understand that," Sean answered. "I'm not holdin' you to anything."

Lambert plastered the last piece of bandage in place. "There, that's done. You can get back into your shirt now."

"All right, Doc."

Sean shrugged into his shirt and then pulled on his boots. He tied a blue bandanna around his neck, rebuckled his gun belt around his waist, and jammed his Stetson over his dark hair, tilting it slightly to avoid rubbing the bandage still covering the right side of his forehead.

"You about ready to go, Levi?" he asked.

"Been ready, willin' and able, for quite a spell now," Levi answered.

"Then let's get goin'. Doc, how much do I owe you?"

"Fifteen dollars will cover everything."

"All right." Sean dug in his pocket and came up with a double eagle, which he handed to the physician.

"Thanks for everything, Doctor Lambert," he said.

Lambert opened a tin box on top of the bureau and pulled out five silver dollars. He placed those in Sean's hand as he said, "You're welcome. I just hope you don't undo all my good work with your insistence on leaving before you're almost completely healed. Since you are being so stubborn, at least check with another physician whenever you get the chance."

"I'll do that," Sean reassured him, "I promise I won't overdo it. We'll take it slow and easy the first couple of days, then after that we'll see. I have to get on that trail, so even ridin' slow is better than not ridin' at all."

"I understand. I wish you Godspeed, Ranger Kennedy. You also, Ranger Mallory."

"Appreciate that, Doc," Levi answered. "Hasta la vista."

After leaving Doctor Lambert, the Rangers headed to a nearby store to re-supply. From there, they went to Hector's livery to retrieve their horses.

"Sean, Levi, buenas dias," Hector enthusiastically greeted them. "I have your horses saddled and ready for you."

As usual, the tiny Amigo was at Hector's side.

Ghost poked his nose over his stall door and nickered to Sean. The Ranger rubbed his horse's velvety nose, then gave him a licorice.

"You missed me too, huh pal? I'm sure glad to see you again. You're lookin' good and I see your cuts are healing nicely. You've done a fine job with him, Hector, muchas gracias," Sean told the hostler.

"It was nothing, as always," Hector demurred.

Sean scratched Amigo behind his right ear and gave him a licorice. He then handed Hector the finely tooled leather lead he carried.

"This is for Amigo. He doesn't know it, but he saved my hide when he knocked Hank Boyle on his butt."

Sean scratched Amigo's ears again.

"Thanks, buddy," he told the little pinto.

"Sean, amigo mio, this is too fine a gift," Hector protested.

"Nonsense," Sean retorted. "If it hadn't been for Amigo here, I'd be lyin' six feet underground with a chunk of lead in my guts."

"All right, if you insist on giving us this gift, Amigo will wear it proudly. Muchas gracias."

"Sean, we'd better get movin' if we're gonna make Pleasanton by dark," Levi warned.

"All right."

"I'll get your horse, Sean," Hector said. "Here's a block of wood to help you mount. I thought that might be easier for you."

"I appreciate that," Sean answered.

Hector led Ghost from his stall. The big blue roan's saddle was thickly padded with a sheepskin, the skin rolled more thickly toward the pommel.

"What d'ya think, Sean?" Levi asked.

"It looks all right. I'll let you know once I'm in the saddle," Sean replied. "Let's find out."

Sean stepped onto the wooden block while Hector held Ghost's reins. He winced when the bandages around his ribs tugged as he swung his leg over Ghost's back. He lowered himself gingerly into the saddle, grimacing when pain shot through his still-tender groin. Sean sat for a moment until the pain subsided, then trotted Ghost up and down the aisle.

"You gonna be all right, pard?" Levi asked.

"Seems like it. This isn't all that bad," Sean replied. "Pretty clever on your part."

"Just tryin' to protect *your* parts," Levi retorted, grinning. "Well, since you're ready."

Levi swung into his own saddle and then took Toby's lead from Hector. "Hector, it was good to meet you. Next time I'm in San Antone, you can be sure I'll put Monte up here. Thanks for giving him such good care."

"I assure you, that is how I always treat my customers' caballos. The pleasure was all mine, Levi."

"Hector, thanks, as always," Sean said. "Take care of yourself."

"You also, and I will continue to pray for both of you."

"Thanks. Adios."

"Vaya con Dios."

Hector watched the Rangers until they reached the end of the alley and turned onto the street. He made the Sign of the Cross once they were out of sight.

Chapter 10

Despite Sean's injuries, the Rangers made steady progress en route to their destination. They spent the first night in Pleasanton, and the next evening settled for a campsite alongside a clear stream, where there was plenty of grass for the horses. Now, about two o'clock on the third day after departing San Antonio, they were passing through the small village of Hamiltonburg. The settlement was located at the confluence of the Atascosa, Nueces, and Frio Rivers. In later years, Hamiltonburg's name would be changed to Three Rivers to reflect its setting.

"You want to call it a day and find a room for the night, or keep on pushin' farther down the trail?" Levi asked Sean. "It's a good distance to the next town."

"It's still early, so I'd just as soon keep movin'," Sean replied. "How about you?"

"Makes no nevermind to me," Levi answered. "I only wanted to make sure you're not hurtin' too much to keep travelin'."

"I'm doin' all right," Sean replied. He stopped Ghost when the delicious scent of fresh-baked bread assailed his nostrils.

"However, something sure smells good. I reckon it wouldn't hurt to stop and get some grub."

"Right over there." Levi pointed to a newly painted building in the middle of the next block. "Betty's Bakery" proclaimed the sign hanging over the boardwalk out front.

They reined up in front of the shop, dismounted, and looped their horses' reins over the hitch rail. They ducked under the rail and stepped onto the walk. A bell attached to the bakery's door tinkled merrily when they stepped inside.

"I'll be right with you," a female voice called from the back room.

"Wow, if only Lieutenant Blawcyzk could see this place," Levi exclaimed. The shop's cases were filled with pies, cakes, and doughnuts of every size and flavor imaginable. On a stove behind the counter a coffee pot steamed, the aroma of the freshly brewed coffee mingling with that of the baked goods. There were four tables covered with red-checked tablecloths, and six stools at the counter. White lace curtains hung at the windows.

"With his sweet tooth, Jim'd buy the place out, that's for certain," Sean agreed. "It's sure got my mouth waterin'."

Not worried about being recognized as Rangers in this sleepy town, they took seats at the counter rather than a window table.

A grandmotherly woman in a blue gingham dress and flour-dusted white apron emerged from the back. A red bandanna wrapped around her head held her silver hair in place, and a bright smile creased her face.

"Howdy, boys," she greeted them. "I'm Betty, as in the Betty on the sign out front. This is my place. What can I get for you?"

"I'd like a piece of apple pie and a cup of coffee," Sean ordered.

"Make that two," Levi added.

"Coming right up." Betty glanced out the window, to where Ghost and Monte stood. "However, what about some water for your horses first? I have a bucket I can fill for them."

"That would be just fine, thank you," Sean answered. "If you'll give us that bucket and point us toward the pump we can fill it."

"Pshaw, don't bother, I'll take care of it. The pump is inside, in my back room," Betty explained.

"For sure the lieutenant would think he'd died and gone to Heaven if he ever set foot in this place, Sean," Levi chuckled. "Water for his horse and all these sweets."

"Boy howdy, that's for certain. He'd probably buy as much for that ornery Sam as for himself."

Betty reappeared with a full bucket of cool water. She waited while Levi watered the horses. When he returned, she sliced two huge pieces of pie and filled two mugs with black coffee, which she placed in front of the hungry pair.

"Anything else?"

"Not right now, but we will want something to take with us," Sean answered. He picked up his fork and dug into his pie.

The two men devoured their pie, as well as three cups of coffee each. Once he finished, Sean pushed back from the table, patting his belly in satisfaction.

"That was mighty fine pie, ma'am," he praised.

"Sure was," Levi added, "best I've had in a long time. So was the coffee."

Betty brandished the pot.

"Are you sure you wouldn't like some more?"

"No, ma'am," Sean answered. "We have to be moving, since we need to be in Falfurrias before the week's out. I would like half a dozen powdered doughnuts to take along."

"I'd like six cinnamon," Levi said, "plus a loaf of bread. The smell of your bread is what led us here."

"Of course," Betty replied. "I'll have those for you in a jiffy. Not the bread from the display case, either. I just took several loaves from the oven, so I'll get you one of those."

Betty soon had their doughnuts and bread wrapped and tied in brown paper.

"That will be a dollar and ten cents for everything," she smiled. "The next time you're passing through Hamiltonburg be sure and stop in again."

"We'll do just that," Sean assured her. He gave her a silver dollar and a quarter.

"The change is yours."

"Why, thank you."

"You're welcome. C'mon, Levi, let's get outta here before I sit down for more pie."

Once they reached their horses, they started to place their bread and doughnuts in their saddlebags.

"Sean," Levi suddenly whispered. "Take a look down the street. Anything seem suspicious to you?"

Sean turned slightly to get a better look.

"You mean that hombre leanin' against the bank kind of casual-like, too casual-like?"

"That's exactly what I mean," Levi confirmed. "His hat's pulled down real low, like he's tryin' to hide his face. Look at those four horses in front of the bank. Their reins aren't even looped over the rail."

"Let's mosey down that way, slow and easy," Sean said. "If nothing happens before we reach that bank, we'll leave our horses in front of the general store and go inside. We can watch the bank's front door from there real easy."

Staying out of sight alongside their horses, they placed bullets into the empty chambers under the hammers of their Colts, and then slid the guns back into their holsters. They untied the horses, backed them away from the rail, and led them toward the bank.

They were halfway between the bakery and store when shots rang out from inside the bank.

Instantly the man who'd been loitering in front of the bank raised his bandanna over his face, pulled out his six-gun, and grabbed the horses' reins. Three other masked men burst out of the bank, still firing at the tellers inside. Two of them carried canvas money sacks.

Sean and Levi pulled out their Colts. "Texas Rangers!" they shouted as one.

"Hold it right there!" Sean continued. "Drop those guns!"

The robbers whirled to face the Rangers and sent a fusillade of lead in their direction. One of the bullets tore through Levi's loaf of bread.

"My warm bread, you son of a . . . !" Levi shouted and then dove for cover behind a rain barrel. Another of the bullets struck Toby in the flank. The horse squealed in pain, reared up, yanking the reins from Levi's hands, and galloped off.

The town marshal raced out of his office with a rifle in his hands. Before he could get off a shot, one of the robbers shot him twice in the chest. After downing the marshal, the renegade attempted to jump into his saddle, but Sean, who had gone to one knee in the middle of the road, shot him through the stomach. The man dropped the moneybag he was carrying, then sagged over his horse, which spun and galloped off. The dying outlaw slid to the street, rolled over twice, and lay still. When another of the robbers' bullets ripped the air just over his head, Sean flattened himself on his belly.

Another of the men stepped into the middle of the street and started fanning his pistol, emptying his gun at the Rangers. Levi took precise aim, fired, and put a bullet into the center of the robber's chest, slamming him to the dirt.

"Never understood those hombres who fan a gun without aimin' careful," he muttered, punching the empties from his own gun and reloading.

The two surviving outlaws kept the Rangers pinned down while they mounted their horses and dashed out of town. Sean and Levi leapt into their saddles and raced off in pursuit.

One of the bank clerks, bleeding profusely from a wound in his chest, staggered out of the building and waved the Rangers down.

"They're probably headed for Choke Canyon," he gasped. "You'll have a hard time roustin' them out if they make it there."

"Thanks. We'll get them," Sean answered. He spurred Ghost into a dead run once again, Levi and Monte at their heels. Behind them, the clerk collapsed on the sidewalk.

The outlaws were rapidly pulling away, now merely a dust cloud in the distance.

"Let's slow up, Levi," Sean ordered. He pulled Ghost down to a brisk walk.

"I don't get it," Levi puzzled as he reined Monte alongside Sean's horse. "Why're we slowin' down? Ain't we gonna keep after those hombres?"

"We sure are," Sean told him, "but they're on fresh horses, while ours have been travelin' for days, so they're pretty tired. We wouldn't have a chance of runnin' those renegades down. However, we're gonna trail those snakes right to their hole. Once they think they've lost us, they'll probably slow down to spare their own horses."

"The clerk said if they got into Choke Canyon we'd never find them," Levi objected.

"That clerk didn't realize he was talkin' to a couple of Texas Rangers," Sean answered. "So he'd have no way of knowin' we can follow a trail most men can't. Besides, with any luck Choke Canyon's a box."

"Even if it is, there's most likely a lot of side canyons and draws for those jaspers to hide in," Levi pointed out.

"Which is another reason for us to take it easy for a spell," Sean explained. "Those hombres'll know every inch of that canyon. We don't, so it'd be real simple for them to hole up and arrange a nice little ambush for us. If we just go chargin' into that canyon after them, we'll only be inviting rifle bullets in our backs."

"That makes sense," Levi admitted. "I doubt they'll worry about hidin' their tracks. They're in too much of a hurry."

"Exactly," Sean replied, "so let's just play a bit of the tortoise and the hare."

They pushed their horses into a steady trot, a pace which they maintained until they reached the entrance to Choke Canyon. Levi pointed out two sets of fresh hoof prints on the narrow, dusty trail leading into the canyon.

"You were right, Sean. Those lobos didn't even bother to brush out those tracks, so they're either real certain of gettin' clean away or else they're sittin' behind some rocks waiting to put a slug through our guts."

"Let's make sure neither of those happens. We'll move slowly so the horses don't kick up much dust," Sean replied. He turned Ghost into the canyon trail.

For nearly three miles the Rangers followed the tracks of the outlaws' horses. The hoof prints twisted their way through brush-choked side trails, up talus slopes, and into dry washes. When they came upon a bend guarded by sheer rock walls and clusters of boulders, Sean called a halt.

"What d'ya think, Levi?"

"It's a perfect spot for a bushwhackin'."

"That's what I figured."

Sean and Levi studied the terrain for a few moments.

"You have any ideas?" Levi asked.

"Yep, I think Ghost and I can make it halfway up that slope on the right without bein' spotted, then I can go a bit further on foot. From up there

I should be able to spot those hombres, if they are waitin' to drygulch us."

"They'll be pretty dug in, most likely," Levi noted.

"I figure that. With luck, though, I'll be able to put a slug into at least one of 'em before they realize I've flanked 'em. Mebbe if I'm real lucky I'll nail 'em both. If I should get one the other will probably try to turn tail and run. Then I can drill him real easy."

"What if you can't get a clean shot?"

"I'll try to pin 'em down, so you can get to 'em, or I'll try and flush them out in the open for you."

"What about gettin' 'em to surrender?"

"Those boys ain't gonna surrender. They know the marshal was probably killed in that hold-up and most likely the bank clerk too. If you were cornered and facin' a rope, what would you do?"

"Go down shootin'."

"Exactly, so we're sure not takin' any chances with them. I personally am not ready to die from some renegade's bullet right yet."

"I've gotta agree with you there," Levi chuckled.

"All right, I'm gonna get started. Give me forty-five minutes. Either you'll hear shots by then or I'll be back."

Levi took his rifle from its scabbard and laid it across the pommel of his saddle.

"I'm gonna hole up in that nest of boulders just ahead on the left."

"That's as good a spot as any," Sean replied. "C'mon Ghost, once again it's time to prove you're worthy of your name." He heeled the gelding into a slow walk. The big blue roan could make his way through the thickest brush almost silently, only the occasional crackling of a dry branch or a hoof step on rock giving a hint of his presence. Sean rode five hundred feet up the trail and then turned toward the talus piled at the bottom of the two hundred foot high cliff. He worked the horse up the slope, picking their way up a path barely wide enough for Ghost to plant all four feet. Twenty-five minutes later, Sean reined to a stop at a cluster of stunted redberry juniper. The scraggly trees were clinging precariously to a relatively flat spot on the slope. Sean unshipped his Winchester and swung out of the saddle. He looped Ghost's reins around a dead juniper's trunk.

"This is as far as you go, boy," Sean told the horse with a pat to his nose. "You wait here for me."

After giving his horse a licorice, Sean removed his spurs and hung them from the saddle horn. The clinking of those spurs would carry a good distance in the confines of the canyon. He also removed his gun belt and hung that along with the spurs. A six-gun would be useless from the distance at which he expected to catch sight of the bank robbers.

Sean began his climb on foot, then after going two hundred yards, dropped to his belly to crawl the rest of the way, pushing his rifle in front of him. Ten minutes later he reached his destina-|tion, a flat shelf at the top of the slope, sheltered by the beetling cliff above. The shelf gave a clear view of the main canyon for a good distance, in both directions. Sean crept to the edge of the shelf and cautiously lifted his head to peer into the chasm.

"Got ya," he whispered in satisfaction. The two outlaws were perched in a nest of boulders on an outcropping below him, down-canyon and about three hundred yards distant. They had rifles settled on the rocks in front of them and were gazing intently down their back trail, waiting patiently to shoot their pursuers out of the saddle.

Prone, Sean put his rifle to his shoulder and squinted down the barrel to take aim at the man nearest him.

"Neither one of 'em's givin' me a clear shot," he muttered. "They're dug in real good."

He could only see the head and right shoulder of his target.

Sean squeezed the trigger. His bullet passed over the outlaw's head and ricocheted off the boulder in front of him, causing the man to jump up in surprise. Sean fired again and this time his aim was true, his bullet striking the outlaw in the middle of the back. The robber arched in pain before pitching over the edge of the shelf. He tumbled to the canyon floor, with a thin trail of dust marking his body's descent.

His companion swung around in an attempt to spot the source of the gunfire. When he sent two wild shots in Sean's direction, Sean returned fire, his bullet hitting the rock shelf just in front of the man's feet. The outlaw fired once more, scrambled down the rocks, and out of Sean's sight. A moment later the sound of rapidly fading hoof beats drifted to Sean's ears.

Levi heard the echo of the shots, and a few minutes later the hoof beats of a hard driven horse coming directly towards him. He left his rock shelter to stand in the middle of the trail, throwing his Winchester to his shoulder and pointing it straight up-canyon.

A moment later the horse appeared, his rider low over his neck, urging the animal on.

"Texas Ranger! Hold it!" Levi shouted.

The startled horse plunged to a stop. His rider struggled to control the pitching mount, at the same time attempting to draw his six-gun. Levi aimed at the renegade's chest. Just as he pulled the trigger the outlaw's horse reared, and the bullet Levi intended for the man's chest instead tore through his belly. The outlaw stiffened, still clinging to the saddle. Levi put his next bullet into the renegade's chest. The man fell to the trail, rolled over three times, and lay sprawled facedown, his gun still clutched in his hand.

Rifle still at the ready, Levi walked up to the downed outlaw. He pulled the man's pistol from his hand and then used the barrel of his rifle to roll him onto his back. The dead robber's eyes stared unblinkingly into the blazing afternoon sun.

"I told you to stop," Levi muttered. "You should have listened. Well, reckon there's nothin' to do now but wait for Sean."

Levi retrieved Monte from his hiding place. He tied his gelding and the outlaw's mount in a cluster of mesquite before settling against the trunk of one of the larger shrubs. He took out the makings and rolled a quirly.

"Hope you don't mind, but I'm not gonna offer you a smoke," he told the corpse.

A half-hour later, Sean returned.

"I see you got him," Sean noted, nodding at the dead outlaw.

"Yep, except I tried to stop him without shootin' him, but he didn't care to listen. The money sacks are still hangin' from his saddle. What about the other one?"

"I plugged him and knocked him off the cliff," Sean answered. "He's lyin' just off the trail about a quarter mile ahead. Soon as you're done with your smoke, we'll go retrieve the body."

"Sure." Levi took one last drag on his cigarette,

then tossed the butt to the dirt and ground it under his bootheel. He picked up the body of the man he'd killed, slung it belly down over the robber's horse's saddle, and tied it in place.

"Let's go get yours, pardner," he told Sean.

They found the other man's horse tied to a dead tree just below the hidden outcropping. Sean untied the animal and led it to where its rider lay dead. The horse shied at the smell of blood.

Sean used a soothing voice and soft touch to calm the nervous bay, "It'll be all right, boy. Just take it easy."

Once the horse quicted down, Sean tossed the last member of the gang over the saddle and lashed him in place. He picked up the horse's reins and swung into his own saddle.

"Let's head back to town," he ordered.

Sean and Levi kept a lookout for Toby on their way back to Hamiltonburg.

"Sure hope that bullet he took didn't kill or cripple him," Sean worried.

"I wouldn't worry about that," Levi tried to reassure his anxious partner. "I don't think he was hit that bad. He'll turn up, you'll see."

"I hope you're right," Sean answered. He pointed to a cloud of dust in the distance. "Company comin'."

"Probably a posse," Levi noted. "Well, they're a bit too late."

Several minutes later, the approaching riders met them, two miles outside of town.

"Howdy, men. I see you got those other two," the leader of the posse greeted them.

"We did," Sean replied, "and recovered the rest of the money, too. How about the two men we downed in town?"

"They're both dead. You hombres did good work. I'm Jed Hastings, the town mayor."

He proceeded to introduce the rest of the posse. Sean and Levi furnished their names.

"What made you two take a hand?" Hastings asked when the introductions were completed. "You men don't have any connection to Hamiltonburg, and you took a real chance of catchin' a slug."

"I guess we should explain," Sean said. "We're Texas Rangers."

"Rangers!" Hastings exclaimed. "That does explain things. It also explains how you were able to track them down."

"We're also tryin' to track down the extra horse we had with us," Sean answered. "Any of you seen a chestnut gelding with a star and strip on his face, and four white stockings, runnin' loose? He would've also had a bullet wound."

"I saw that horse tearin' south out of town like his tail was afire," Jeptha Murdock, the store-keeper, answered. "Haven't seen him since, though, sorry."

"That's all right," Sean replied. "We'll find him."

"In the meantime, how's that clerk doin', and the marshal?" Levi queried.

"Young Bob Nebbins? The doc says it's gonna be touch and go for him. He lost quite a bit of blood. Jeff Connors, the marshal, is dead. He took two bullets plumb center," Hastings answered.

"At least you took care of the men who killed him. We won't have to worry about a trial. Before sundown they'll be planted," Murdock stated.

"Do you know who any of them were, Ranger?" Hastings asked Sean.

"We didn't get a good look at the ones in town. We didn't recognize either of the two we shot it out with back in Choke Canyon, which means we also probably won't know the others," Sean replied.

"They're most likely drifters who thought they had easy pickin's, robbing a small town bank," Levi added. "Or outsiders who decided to see if the pastures were greener in Texas."

There were still a good number of people on the street when they reached town. They crowded around the Rangers and posse, shouting questions and jostling for a look at the two bodies.

"Tell these people to back off, mayor," Sean growled. "This ain't a circus."

"Keep back, everyone," Hastings ordered. "We'll take these bodies down to Lewis's store along with the others. You can look 'em over there."

A pudgy, balding man wearing a dark suit rushed up. He was gasping for breath as he said, "I see you killed those other two outlaws." He puffed, not bothering with the pleasantries and asked, "Did you recover my money?"

"Don't you mean your depositors' money, Jonah?" Hastings retorted.

"Of course, of course," the banker hastened to reply. "Was the money recovered?"

"These Rangers recovered the bank's money," Hastings answered and gave the banker a withering look.

"Rangers, this is Jonah Anson, the bank president. Notice he didn't mention his clerk who got shot trying to hold off those robbers. Jonah doesn't much care for anyone or anything, except his money. Don't bother to deny it, Jonah," Hastings snapped, when the banker opened his mouth to protest. "You'll get your money, once I'm certain we won't need it for evidence." He spurred his horse into a trot, leaving the banker staring after him with gaping jaw.

A moment later, Hastings pointed out a rambling structure, painted a dull green.

"That's Lewis's Hardware at the end of the block," he said. "The other bodies have already been brought here. Reckon Frank Lewis'll have two more coffins to build."

The store's proprietor had heard the commotion outside and was standing in front of his store, hammer in hand, when the posse rode up.

"The other two, I reckon?" he grunted. "Well, bring 'em inside."

The dead outlaws were taken off their horses and carried into the store. The first two were already in coffins, which were propped against the back wall. The dead men's shirts had been removed to reveal the bullet holes in their bodies. The murdered marshal was in another coffin, which was supported by two sawhorses. His shirt had also been opened to expose the bullet holes in his chest.

"Nice to see you respect your lawmen in this town, mayor," Levi said with disgust. "Your marshal was a brave man steppin' out into the street to face that gang. Right proper sendoff you're givin' him. Why don't you do the decent thing and close up his coffin? It's the least he deserves."

"It's also pretty ugly puttin' these outlaws on display like a carnival sideshow," Sean added. He was aware that in the past the Rangers had put outlaws they'd killed on public view, in one notable instance stacking a dozen or so like cordwood in the main street of Brownsville. The knowledge left a bitter taste in his mouth. That had not been one of the Texas Rangers' finest hours.

"Can't help what folks want. This is a small town and this is the biggest doin's we've ever had," Hastings shrugged, ignoring their jibes. "How about those two in the boxes? You recognize the hombres?"

"No," Sean answered.

"Bring the other two in back," Lewis ordered.

Once the bodies were placed in the back room, the Rangers and posse men went back outside.

"We're gonna head for the saloon and have a drink to celebrate our good fortune, gettin' the town's money back," Hastings told Sean and Levi. "We'd like you to join us. The drinks are on us, of course."

"No thanks, mayor," Sean declined. "We've still got to find our missin' cayuse, then be on our way."

"You're certain?" Hastings pressed. "We were gonna have a town meeting to ask if you boys could stay on until we appointed a new marshal."

"Sorry, but we couldn't do that in any event," Sean answered. "We've already got an assignment. We need to reach Falfurrias as soon as possible. We had to go after those bank robbers and it's cost us half a day or better. Once we find Toby, we're gonna move on."

"We can't change your minds?"

"Not a chance, mayor. So we'll say adios."

"Adios to you also, and good luck," Hastings replied.

The Rangers led their horses to the small plaza in Hamiltonburg's center and let them drink their fill from the trough. While the horses drank, Levi rolled and lit a quirly. Much to the Rangers' dismay Betty's Bakery was closed for the day. Besides Levi's bullet punctured bread their doughnuts had also not survived the pursuit of the bank robbers. With the bakery locked and shuttered, they would not be able to replace their ruined baked goods.

"I can almost taste that bread now," Levi mourned.

"At least it went down fightin'," Sean laughed. "Now let's try'n find Toby."

They mounted and rode slowly out of town.

"Toby did us one favor. He headed in the right direction, south," Levi noted. He studied the dusty road for any sign of dried blood.

"I don't see any blood stains in the dirt either," he continued. "Sure hope that means Toby wasn't hit too bad."

They plodded onward, working their way back and forth, checking any grove of trees or hidden draw where a frightened, wounded horse might seek shelter.

They had gone about two miles when they spotted an oncoming horse.

"That's Toby!" Sean exclaimed.

"It appears he's got a couple of riders, too," Levi added.

They waited for the horse to approach, not wishing to startle the already traumatized animal. However, Toby appeared calm enough under the guidance of his riders. They stopped just before reaching the Rangers.

"Howdy, boys," Sean softly called.

"Howdy yourself, mister," the youngster guiding Toby answered. "This your missin' horse?"

The two boys on Toby's back were clearly brothers, about eleven or twelve years old. The one in front had brown hair and blue eyes, the other hair of the same brown hue, but somewhat darker, and brown eyes. They were dressed in dusty shirts and jeans, bandannas looped around their necks, and were barefooted.

"He sure is," Sean smiled. "His name's Toby. We appreciate your findin' him for us. I'm Texas Ranger Sean Kennedy, and this is my ridin' pard Levi Mallory."

The boys' eyes grew wide.

"You're really honest to gosh Texas Rangers?" the second brother excitedly asked.

"We really are," Sean assured him. "I didn't catch your handles."

"I'm sorry, Mister . . . I mean, Ranger. We plumb forgot. I'm Christian Matney, and this is my brother Mark. We're right pleased to meet you."

"We're both pleased to make your acquaintances also," Levi answered. "How'd you happen to come across Toby?"

"You mean this horse? He was in our grandma's garden, pullin' up carrots and eatin' them," Mark answered. "That sure upset our grandma, until she saw he was hurt, so she had grandpa patch him up. Then Gramps said we'd better take him into town to see if anyone claimed him. I reckon you're gonna want him back. He's an awful nice horse. We were kinda hopin' we could keep him."

Mark's eyes were downcast.

"We knew someone would claim him, Mark," Christian said and then asked the Rangers, "How'd he get hurt, anyway?"

"Some bank robbers shot him," Sean answered.

"Bank robbers? Where?" Christian exclaimed.

"Right back there in Hamiltonburg," Sean told him. "Those hombres won't be botherin' anyone else. Tell you what, let's get you boys back to your grandma and grandpa. Once we get you home, we'll tell you all about that robbery. Please ride Toby slow, because we don't want his wound to get worse."

"All right." Christian reversed Toby. "It's not all that far to our grandma and grandpa's, mebbe a half-mile at the most," he explained.

A few minutes later they came to a small, neatly painted farmhouse. A wide front porch stretched the length of the house. A lone cottonwood shaded

159

the front yard, where a flock of hens and one rooster busily hunted insects. To the side of the house could be seen the wreckage of the garden, which had been trampled by Toby's hooves. A row of holes marked where the chestnut had pulled up most of the carrot crop. Beyond that was a small barn, springhouse, and chicken coop. A fat milk cow lay in a small enclosure, chewing her cud, while the corral held a pair of sturdy draft horses.

"Grandma! Grandpa!" Mark called. "Come outside! Hurry!"

The front door opened, and a middle-aged woman dressed in a blue gingham dress and white apron stepped onto the porch. Her hair was tied up neatly with a blue ribbon.

"My goodness, boys. What's all the fuss about?" she smiled.

"We found Toby's owners. Here they are. They're for sure Texas Rangers!" Christian answered.

He and Mark slid from Toby's back.

"Texas Rangers. Oh my," the woman exclaimed.

"Can they stay for supper, grandma?" Christian concluded.

"Yeah, grandma, can they stay for supper, please?" Mark pleaded. "There was a bank robbery in town. That's how Toby got hurt. The robbers shot him."

"Toby's the horse's name," Christian explained.

"The Rangers promised to tell us all about the robbery, so you have to let them stay for supper."

"I'm sorry, ma'am. The boys are a bit excited," Sean apologized. "We wouldn't want to impose on you."

"That's for certain," Levi added. "We're just mighty grateful they found our missin' cayuse."

Before the boys' grandmother could answer, their grandfather stepped from behind the barn, carrying an old Henry rifle. Clearly he had been covering the Rangers as they approached his farm.

"What's this I just heard? The Hamiltonburg bank was robbed?" he asked. "I had a good sum of money deposited in that bank."

"It was indeed robbed, sir," Sean confirmed, "but the money's safe. We took care of the robbers, and recovered all the stolen cash."

"You mean you killed those outlaws, don't you?"

"I reckon that's right," Levi answered. "All four of 'em. We didn't want to mention that in front of the boys."

"Then you did a fine job."

"You killed four outlaws! Golly!" Christian exclaimed.

"What about lettin' Ranger Sean and Ranger Levi stay for supper?" Mark again pleaded.

"Of course they'll stay for supper," his grandmother replied. "You gentlemen have me at a loss. The boys seem to know your names, but I don't."

"I'm sorry, ma'am," Sean apologized, touching two fingers to the brim of his hat in greeting. "I'm Sean Kennedy, and this is my pardner, Levi Mallory."

"Ma'am." Levi nodded a greeting.

"That's better. I'm Sherry Matney and this is my husband, Paul."

"Howdy, Mr. Matney," Sean said.

"Howdy yourselves. The name's Paul. Get down off your horses and make yourselves comfortable."

"We can't stay long," Sean responded. "We're in a hurry to reach Falfurrias. We'd just like to water our horses before we leave."

"Nonsense. You'll stay for supper, and you'll also spend the night," Sherry insisted. "There's not more than two hours of daylight left, so you can't travel much further tonight. We're having chicken and dumplings for supper, and there's more than enough for guests. There isn't enough room for you to sleep in the house, but you're more than welcome to spend the night in the hayloft. Don't argue," she added, when Sean started to object. "You'll feel much better after a good night's rest, so it's settled. Take care of your horses and clean up. I'll have the boys bring soap and towels out for you, and they'll show you where to wash up. Supper will be ready in just about an hour."

"There's no use arguin' with my wife once her mind's made up," Paul laughed. "Besides, she's right, you wouldn't get very much farther tonight. If you don't mind my sayin' so, you both look plumb tuckered out. Seems to me you could use that rest."

"I reckon we're stayin' then," Sean chuckled. "We're mighty grateful."

"Yay!" Christian and Mark shouted.

"You boys come with me and get those towels and soap for your new friends," Sherry ordered.

"You Rangers follow me," Paul instructed. "We'll put up your mounts, and I'll feed them for you. Then I'll show you where to find the wash bench." He glanced at Toby.

"That bronc's name is Toby, you say?"

"That's right," Sean confirmed.

"Just wanted to make sure, after all, Toby or not Toby, that is the question," Paul chuckled.

"Oh, no," Sean groaned.

"Too bad Dave Fox isn't here," Levi added, referring to a fellow Ranger notorious for his bad puns. "He'd appreciate that joke. As for me, it turned my stomach," he chortled.

"Perhaps it did, but don't forget old William Shakespeare himself was fond of the pun," Paul answered.

After the horses were fed and they had washed

up, the Rangers, Paul, and Christian and Mark sat on the front porch, where Sean and Levi related the tale of the bank robbery in Hamiltonburg. Sherry joined them just as the Rangers finished. Christian and Mark had paid rapt attention during the story and now stared in wonder at the lawmen.

"I reckon you must be the fastest men with a gun the Rangers have ever seen," Mark said.

"Yeah, Mark, they must be," Christian agreed. "Those gunslingers don't have a chance against Ranger Levi and Ranger Sean. Bet'cha they can outdraw any outlaw."

"You boys have been readin' too many dime novels," Sean grinned.

"You're just sayin' that, Ranger Sean," Christian protested. "You're real fast. Ain't he, Ranger Levi? You're real fast too, right?"

Levi came to his feet.

"Reckon we're gonna have to find out," he growled. "You two hombres think you can draw and shoot faster'n me?"

"You're challengin' these renegades to a showdown, pardner?" Sean broke in. "I don't know if I'd do that. They look mighty fast to me, and plenty tough. You might wind up in Boot Hill."

"They ain't so tough," Levi retorted. "I can plug both of 'em before they clear leather. Besides, they're yella. I ain't seen either one of 'em go for his guns yet."

"We're not yella, Ranger," Christian protested.

"Then where's your guns, Mister?" Levi demanded.

"We're goin' for them right now," Christian answered. "C'mon, Mark, let's get our pistols. We sure ain't gonna let a Texas Ranger call the Matney brothers, the toughest, meanest outlaws Texas ever saw, yella."

The boys headed inside the house.

"Looks like you started somethin', Levi," Sean noted.

"I just figure on lettin' those boys have a little fun," Levi grinned. "Me too."

Mark and Christian returned with hand-carved wooden six-guns stuck in their belts.

"Grandpa made these guns for us," Christian explained.

"Now let's see who's yella, Ranger!" Mark challenged.

"Then stop yammerin' and start shootin', hombres," Levi retorted. He emptied the bullets from his Colt and even though the gun was unloaded, for extra safety folded a cigarette paper and placed that under the hammer, preventing it from fully dropping. Unnoticed by the boys, whose attention was fully on Levi, Sean did the same.

The boys and Levi stepped into the middle of the yard. They stopped and faced each other, hands hovering over the butts of their guns.

"Draw, Ranger!" Christian shouted.

They grabbed for their guns. Levi's Colt was almost level when Mark "fired." Christian "shot" a split-second after Mark. Levi grunted, clutched at his stomach and chest, and then spun to the ground.

"We got'cha, Ranger!" Mark gloated.

"Yeah, I drilled ya right in your belly," Christian sneered. "Clean through your no-good guts, lawman."

"I nailed him plumb in the middle of his chest. Right through the heart, Christian," Mark said. "He's a goner. Guess we showed him, all right."

Sean leapt from the porch, hand on the butt of his pistol.

"You killed my pardner, ya no-good skunks," he snarled. "Now I'm gonna take care of the both of you. Go for your guns."

Mark and Christian grabbed for their wooden six-guns, but Sean "shot" first. Both boys pitched backwards, falling alongside Levi.

"That'll teach you not to kill a Ranger," Sean rumbled standing over the downed brothers.

When Sean turned back toward the house, Christian lifted his head, raised his pistol and "shot" Sean in the back. Sean yelped, grabbed his back, and fell to his face.

"You didn't make sure I was dead, Ranger," the youngster said. "I plugged you in your back, so you're finished too." He fell back. All four gunmen lay sprawled in the dirt.

Levi was the first to move. He slowly sat up, rubbing his chest. When he did, Mark jumped on his back.

"Wanna Injun wrestle, Ranger?" the youngster challenged.

"Yeah," Levi answered. He twisted and flipped Mark to the ground, pinning him under his chest.

"You're gonna have to take on both of us," Christian yelled, and also jumped on Levi. They wrestled furiously, arms and legs flailing, for several minutes. Sean merely remained where he'd fallen, watching their horseplay.

"That's enough, the three of you," Sherry finally called. "I'm about to put supper on the table."

"All right, grandma," Mark answered and the struggle ceased.

The brothers and Levi flopped on their backs, gasping for breath. Levi's shirt was half-open, and Mark's jeans were torn at one knee. Christian's bandanna was pulled over one ear. They lay there for several minutes before pushing themselves to their feet.

"Look at you three," Sherry scolded. "Now you'll have to wash all over again."

"I'm sorry," Levi apologized. "I just couldn't resist havin' a little fun with your grandsons. They remind me of my own brothers. I've got five of them, plus two sisters. My brothers and me were always roughhousin' and scrappin'. It's been quite some time since I've seen them."

"There's no harm done," Sherry reassured him. "It's just some dirt. I'm sure you must miss your family. What about you, Sean?" she asked, "do you have much family?"

Sean shook his head sadly.

"I'm afraid not, Sherry. I never really knew my pa and my ma died too young. She was a fine woman. She married again some years back, before we lost her. My step-pa's a real good man. He and my ma were real happy during the time they had together."

"You're a fine young man," Sherry answered. "You've had a decent upbringing, I can tell. Let's head inside for supper. Christian and Mark, and yes you, Levi, will need to scrub again. I'll hold supper for you."

"I'll help you set the table while we're waitin', Sherry," Sean offered.

"All right, if you'd like," she agreed.

"Here's the bullets from your gun, Sean," Paul said. He handed back the cartridges Sean had removed from his Colt before taking part in the imaginary gun battle.

After the boys and Levi had again washed, everyone sat down to supper. As Sherry had promised, there was chicken and dumplings, accompanied by black-eyed peas, homemade bread with molasses, freshly-churned butter, and plenty of milk for the boys and coffee for the adults.

"We always thank the Lord for our blessings before we eat," Paul noted. "As our guests, would you Rangers like to lead us in Grace?" he invited.

"Of course," Sean answered. Everyone bowed their heads while Sean prayed, "We thank Thee Lord, for this good food, and for our new friends. We ask for Your blessings on them. Amen."

"Amen."

"Now let's eat!" Mark exclaimed.

After weeks of bacon and beans wolfed down on the trail, or mediocre food in greasy cafes, the Rangers thoroughly enjoyed the home-cooked meal. Dessert was blackberry pie, and both men had two helpings.

"Are you sure you wouldn't like another piece of pie?" Sherry offered.

"No, thank you," Levi demurred. "Any more and I'd bust. Everything was sure tasty."

"Me neither," Sean said. "I can't hold another bite. Supper was delicious."

"Well, if you're certain, why don't you sit on the porch with Paul while the boys and I do the dishes?" Sherry suggested. "Then we'll join you."

"Aw Grandma, do we have to?" Christian complained.

"Christian, a good Ranger always helps out, especially his grandma," Sean told him.

"Yeah, he does. With you and your brother helpin', those dishes should be done right quick," Levi added.

"All right, I guess," Christian said. Reluctantly he and Mark began clearing the table. Their grandfather, Levi, and Sean headed outside, where Levi rolled and lit a cigarette.

Soon the boys and their grandmother joined them. Once they had settled, Sherry in her rocker, and the boys sprawled on the porch floor, Sean and Levi exchanged knowing glances. They grinned at Paul.

"You ready to tell the boys?" Sean asked.

Paul scratched his jaw.

"I don't rightly know. Maybe we should wait until morning," he mused.

"Tell us what, grandpa?" Christian urged.

"Yeah, grandpa. Don't keep us waitin'," Mark pleaded.

"Well, maybe it'll be all right, I'm not sure," Paul teased.

"Oh, come on, grandpa!" Mark again cried.

"All right, go ahead and tell them," Paul smiled.

"Boys, Levi and I have been doin' some serious thinkin'," Sean began, "and we talked our idea over with your grandpa while you were doin' the dishes."

"What idea?" Christian interrupted.

"Just let the Rangers talk or you won't find out until morning," Paul warned.

"Okay. I won't say another word," Christian promised.

"You see, the horse which you found, Toby, isn't exactly ours," Levi took up the story. "He belonged to another Ranger, Thad Dutton. Thad was killed in the line of duty. We're lookin' for Thad's murderer and we brought his horse along with us hopin' he might react if he recognized that hombre. He sure did that when we found the place where Thad was shot. Toby remembered what happened there, because he got real upset. We'd planned on keepin' him with us until we ran down the sidewinder who gunned Thad, then selling him."

"Now that Toby's hurt, we don't want to chance cripplin' him. So we decided, if it's all right with your grandma and grandpa, to give him to you boys. Once he's healed he'll make you a real fine saddle horse."

The brothers leapt to their feet.

"Gram! Gramps! Toby's ours! Can we keep him?" Mark pleaded.

"Yeah, please can we keep him?" Christian begged. "We'll take good care of him. He's a really nice horse. He loves us, too."

"Well, I think it's a good idea," Paul smiled, "but you'd better ask your grandma."

The boys climbed into their grandmother's lap.

"Grandma, please?"

171

"I'm not certain," Sherry said. "Will you clean his stall every day?"

"We sure will," Mark answered.

"And, we'll feed and water him, and brush him, and clean his corral too," Christian promised.

"We'll give him treats. Carrots and apples," Mark added.

"I dunno if I'd mention givin' Toby carrots right now," Sean laughed.

"Doesn't matter, since there don't seem to be many left in the garden anyway after he got done," Levi chuckled.

"We'll make sure Toby doesn't ever get in your garden again, grandma," Mark promised.

"Yeah, never again," Christian added.

"Well, then I guess it will be all right," Sherry answered.

"It will? Gee, thanks Grandma," both boys said at once. They kissed her on the cheek. "Thanks, Grandpa. Can we go play with Toby now?"

"In a minute," Paul replied. "Didn't you forget to thank someone?"

"Oh, gee, we're sorry," Mark said. "Thanks, Ranger Sean and Ranger Levi."

"Thank you both, Rangers," Christian added. "Don't worry about Toby, he'll be just fine."

"We know he will be," Sean answered. "Now go visit your new horse."

The boys raced down the steps, across the yard, and into the barn.

"Sean, Levi, I don't know how we can ever thank you," Sherry said, her eyes moist. "Giving our boys a horse . . ." Her voice trailed off.

"You already have thanked us, by feedin' us such a fine supper, and puttin' us up for the night," Levi answered. "Seeing the looks on those boys' faces when we told them Toby was theirs was thanks enough."

"Besides, Toby really does need to take it easy until that gunshot heals," Sean added. "Plus he was gonna need a home in any event. I can't think of a finer one than right here."

"Nevertheless, we're grateful," Paul answered.

Much to their surprise, the boys reappeared, running back to the house.

"Grandma, we thought of something. Can we sleep in the barn with Toby tonight?" Christian asked. "That way he won't be lonesome."

"And, with the Rangers?" Mark pleaded.

"I'm not sure that's a good idea," Sherry responded. "These men have been traveling for quite some time. They probably would like to get to bed early and have a good night's sleep."

"Toby won't be lonesome," Paul added. "He's got Max and Buck for company, as well as the Rangers' horses."

"But grandma, grandpa," Christian began.

"Sherry, Paul, if it's okay with you, we wouldn't mind lettin' the boys spend the night with us," Sean stated.

"Are you certain?" Sherry answered.

"Sure. Besides, Levi hasn't had the chance to tell any of his war stories for quite a spell," Sean said. "He'll put the boys to sleep right quick with those tales."

"They're all true, every one of them," Levi objected.

"Well, if you're positive you won't mind, then I guess it will be all right," Sherry conceded.

"Thanks, grandma!" the boys yelped joyfully.

"You're welcome. But don't you keep the Rangers up too late," She warned. "Once they say it's bedtime, there will be no arguing. Make sure you say your prayers."

"We promise," Christian answered.

"Then that's settled," Paul said. "Speaking of bedtime, it's just about here. It's been a long day. Dunno about the rest of you, but I'm ready to turn in."

The sun had already set, and dusk was rapidly descending.

"Same here," Sean answered. "We're gonna call it a night."

"Is there anything else you need?" Sherry asked.

"Not a thing. Thank you again for supper," Levi replied.

"All right then. Mark, Christian, come inside and fetch your nightshirts," Sherry ordered.

"Aw, grandma, Texas Rangers don't go to bed

in their nightshirts when they're in camp," Mark protested.

"Yeah and neither do tough outlaws," Christian said. "They sleep in their clothes. That's what we want to do."

"I was just teasing you," Sherry smiled. "Now come give your grandma and grandpa a kiss goodnight."

Once the boys had done so, Sean and Levi also bade their goodnights.

"Let's head for the barn," Sean said.

As they started across the yard, Levi began, "Boys, let me tell you about the time I fought off a whole horde of renegade Comanches, single-handed. I saved Sean's life, too. You see, there must've been a hundred of those Indians, and they'd captured Sean and were gonna scalp him . . ."

Chapter 11

The Rangers and the Matney family were all up with the sun the next morning. While Sherry prepared breakfast, Paul milked the cow and fed the horses. As Christian and Mark collected eggs and fed the chickens, Sean and Levi readied their mounts for travel. Once everyone's chores were completed, they headed inside for the morning meal. This time Levi led Grace.

"Lord, we thank Thee for Thy bounty, and for this glorious new day," he prayed. "Kindly bestow Your blessings on this family and also we ask for Your protection and guidance always. Amen."

"Amen!"

They dug into heaps of hotcakes with sorghum and butter, eggs, ham, and bacon, with plenty of black coffee for the adults and a pitcher of creamy milk for the boys. All too soon the meal was ended.

"We'd really like to stay a spell," Sean said, "but we've got to try'n make up some time. We'd like to thank you once again for your hospitality."

"It's us who need to thank you Rangers," Paul answered. "After all, you saved a lot of folks from ruin when you stopped that bank robbery, and you gave our grandsons a fine horse."

"That's right," Sherry added. "It was our pleasure to have you as our guests. You don't owe us anything."

"Yeah, but I had a lot of fun playin' with the boys and spinnin' some tales for 'em," Levi responded. "Made me feel like a kid back home in Stephenville again. I'm sure grateful for that." He glared at Mark and Christian. "If we ever get into a shootout again I'm gonna plug the both of you . . . right in your bellies like Christian drilled me," he warned, with a grin. "As our lieutenant would say, 'Bet a hat on it.' "

"Just try it, Ranger," Christian retorted. "Me and Mark'll get you before you can even draw your gun."

"And we'll shoot Ranger Sean right in the guts too," Mark added. "He won't beat us to the draw again."

"They'd do it, too, Levi," Sean laughed. "So pard, I reckon we'd better hit the trail before these boys decide to fill us full of lead."

They pushed back from the table and headed for the barn. Toby was in the corral with Max and Buck, the draft horses. He hung his head over the fence and nickered when he spotted Christian and Mark. Sean and Levi ambled to the corral along with the boys and their grandfather.

"Looks like Toby's already made friends with the boys," Levi observed.

"You'll do just fine here, Toby," Sean reassured

the horse, stroking his neck. "You'll have it a lot easier'n being a Ranger's mount."

"Boy howdy, that's for certain," Levi added. "No more tryin' to outrun Comanches or chase down outlaws, no more livin' for weeks at a time on whatever grass you can find, no more chance of gettin' hit by a bullet. Heck, you go with Sean, horse, I'll stay here."

"You're not gettin' off that easy, pardner," Sean said, "Besides, you eat a lot more'n that horse. You'd eat the Matneys out of house and home, so let's retrieve our horses and get movin'."

"I'll get them for you," Paul said. "That'll give you a couple more minutes with Toby and the boys."

While Paul retrieved their mounts, the Rangers and his grandsons stood by Toby, petting the horse and making their goodbyes. Sherry came from the house and joined them. She had two paper-wrapped bundles in her arms.

"These are for you," she explained. "I packed extra food for you. Levi, Sean told me how your loaf of bread gave its life for yours. I put a fresh loaf in here."

"Why, thank you," Levi answered. "I'll purely enjoy it and I'll remember you with every bite."

Paul emerged from the barn, leading Ghost and Monte.

"Thanks, Paul," Sean said. He and Levi took the reins of their horses. They shook hands with

Paul and the boys, hugged Sherry and kissed her on the cheek, then climbed into their saddles.

"If you are ever back this way, make sure you stop in," Paul told them.

"Yes. Make sure you do just that," Sherry added.

"Only if the boys promise not to shoot us," Levi grinned, "Besides, in a few years mebbe they'll join the Texas Rangers. They'd make good ones."

"You mean that, Ranger Levi?" Christian asked.

"Wouldn't have said it if I didn't," Levi answered.

"Gee, thanks, Ranger," Mark told him.

"Time to head out," Sean said. "We'll visit when we're in the area. Count on it."

"We will," Sherry replied. "Good luck to both of you."

"Thanks. Adios!"

"Vaya con Dios."

Sean and Levi turned their horses toward the road. Mark and Christian's shouts of "Goodbye" echoed in their ears as they headed out of the yard. Just before riding out of sight, the Rangers turned and waved farewell to the family, who stood watching until they could no longer see their newfound friends.

The eighty mile ride from Hamiltonburg to Falfurrias was uneventful. With the weather being dry and cool, Sean and Levi were able to push their horses right along. By mid-morning of the third day after leaving the Matney farm, the Rangers were riding down the main street of Falfurrias, the seat of Brooks County. The town was bustling with activity, so the two new-comers attracted little notice.

"You still planning on stoppin' at the county land office first, Sean?" Levi asked.

"No. That'll be our third stop," Sean answered. "I figure we'll drop by the telegraph office first, to see if there's a message from Lieutenant Blawcyzk. Then we'll stop at the sheriff's office. He should be able to help us locate the Porter place. Plus, if the lieutenant did send another man down here, he'll have checked in with the sheriff. Mebbe the sheriff will be able to tell us why Thad came down here, and who he might've tangled with."

"Then why stop at the land office at all?"

"Just to get a look at their records. We'll see if anyone's filed a lien on the Porter place recently and find out who holds their mortgage. Might give us an idea where to start diggin'," Sean explained.

"That makes sense," Levi agreed.

"Hey, son," Sean reined up and called to a boy of about ten, who was sitting on the boardwalk in front of a general store.

"Yessir, mister?" the youngster replied.

"Can you tell us where the telegraph office is at?"

"Sure," the boy answered. "Straight ahead about

five blocks. It's right across from the jailhouse."

"That's real handy," Levi chuckled.

"Thanks, son, go get yourself some candy," Sean told the boy as he tossed him a nickel.

"Gee, thanks, mister." The boy grabbed the coin and raced inside the store.

A moment later the Rangers reined up in front of the Western Union office. They dismounted and looped their horses' reins over a well-chewed hitch rail.

"You'll both get stalls, good feed, and a rub-down tonight," Sean promised the horses, with a pat to Monte's nose and a rub of Ghost's ears. He gave Ghost a licorice before climbing the steps to the Western Union offices.

The lone clerk in the office was hunched over his chattering key. He glanced up at the new-comers through his green eyeshade, neither pausing for a moment nor missing a stroke as he tapped out a message.

"Be with you fellers in a minute," he called.

"Sure," Sean agreed.

Two minutes later the operator tapped out his last letter. He pushed the eyeshade back over his gray hair.

"Sorry to keep you waitin', but I had to finish gettin' that wire out," he apologized. "Now, what can I do for you?"

"That's no problem," Sean answered. "We stopped by to see if there might be a message on file for us. I'm Texas Ranger Sean Kennedy, and this is my pardner, Levi Mallory. The message would be from Lieutenant Jim Blawcyzk."

"I sure do have one," the clerk answered. "Been wondering when you boys might show up. I've got that wire right here. Let me get it for you."

The clerk walked to a shelf behind a well-worn roll top desk. He reached into one of the pigeon-holes and pulled out a yellow paper, which he handed to Sean.

"Here it is. You want to read it over and mebbe send a reply?"

"Sure." Sean quickly skimmed the contents. "I do want to send an answer. Just say, 'Arrived. No other news. S and L.'."

"That's it?"

"That's it," Sean reiterated.

"Fine, it'll be thirty-six cents. You'll want a receipt, naturally."

"Of course," Sean confirmed. He dug in his pocket, came up with the exact amount, and handed it to the clerk, who scrawled out a receipt.

"Much obliged," Sean said. "We'll be in town for a spell. If we get any more wires, make sure and find us right away. Is that understood?"

"It sure is," the clerk replied. "Where'll you be stayin'?"

"We're not rightly sure," Sean admitted. "You have any suggestions?"

"The Heart of Texas Hotel is halfway decent. It

even has real bathtubs in some of the rooms. For your meals, the Bluebonnet Café has good grub," the clerk advised.

"Thanks. What about a stable for our horses?"

"The hotel has its own livery stable behind the place. They've got a young hostler there who'll take real good care of your broncs."

"Then that's where we'll stay," Sean decided. "How do we find the place?"

"Go down four blocks and the hotel's on the left. It's a big, three storied place, so you can't miss it."

"All right, thanks again."

"Don't mention it."

They stopped out front of the Western Union before remounting. Levi pulled out the makings and began building a smoke. "What's that wire say?"

"The lieutenant did send a man down here. Woody Woodson."

"Reckon that means our next step is to try and locate him," Levi said.

"I reckon so. Let's find the sheriff."

They remounted and walked their horses diagonally across the street to the Brooks County Sheriff's Office and Jail. Once again they tied their mounts to a rail in front of the building.

The young deputy on duty looked up from the newspaper he was reading when they entered the office.

"Howdy, gents, how can I help you?" he asked.

"Is the sheriff in?" Sean questioned.

"He sure is, but he hates to be disturbed without good cause. Unless you've got a powerful reason for seein' the sheriff, you'd better let me handle your problem. I'm Dan Devine."

"Sean Kennedy and Levi Mallory, Texas Rangers. We'd really like to see your boss right now," Sean snapped.

The young deputy swallowed, hard.

"You're Rangers? Why didn't you say so?"

"My pardner just did," Levi retorted.

"I'll take you to Sheriff Newton, if you'll follow me."

Devine rose from behind his desk and held open the wooden gate separating the waiting area from the rest of the office. He led the Rangers to an office at the end of the hall. The door was ajar, so Devine knocked on the frame.

"Sheriff?"

"What is it, Dan? It better be important. I'm trying to get this blasted paperwork caught up before it piles up so high it buries me."

"There's a couple of Texas Rangers here wantin' to see you."

"Rangers? Those hombres wouldn't be here without a reason, so send 'em in."

"Sure thing, Sheriff." To Sean and Levi the deputy said, "Go ahead."

The sheriff came from behind his desk when Sean and Levi entered his office. He waved at the files stacked haphazardly on the desk's surface and smiled.

"Howdy, I'm Dave Newton. You boys are givin' me an excellent excuse to get away from these papers."

Newton was a large man, in his middle forties, with the beginnings of a paunch starting to show. His dark hair was graying, his eyes brown. His badge was pinned to a leather vest, under which was a pale green shirt.

"Sean Kennedy and my pardner, Levi Mallory," Sean answered.

"I'm pleased to meet you. Now, what can I do for the Rangers?" Newton replied.

"We need a couple of things. Do you mind if we sit down?" Sean asked. "This will take a few minutes."

"Why no, of course not, take a seat," Newton waved them to two corner chairs and then settled into the one behind his desk. He pulled out the makings and started rolling a quirly. Levi did likewise. Sean waited until they finished building their smokes and lit up.

"Now, Sheriff, first question, there's supposed to be another Ranger, Woody Woodson, coming to Falfurrias. If I'm figuring correctly, he should have arrived here several days ago. Has he been in to see you?"

"No, there sure hasn't been any Ranger by. Not since that last one rode into town a few weeks back. You two are the first in quite a spell," Newton answered.

"Mebbe he was stayin' incognito for some reason," Sean speculated. "He's a young fella, not yet twenty. He's long and lanky, sandy hair and light brown eyes. Has a peach-fuzz mustache. Woody rides a steeldust gelding with a star on his forehead and one white sock on his right hind leg. Have you seen anyone answering that description?"

"I sure haven't," Newton stated. "No steeldust cayuse, either and I'm certain of that."

"Woody must've left Laredo later than we thought, or else he got delayed somewhere," Levi noted. "He'll turn up in a day or so."

"All right, Sheriff," Sean continued, "you mentioned another Ranger."

"Yeah, I did. His name was Thad, let me see, Thad Dutton, as I recall. He was a right nice feller."

"What brought him here?"

"You mean you don't know?" Dutton asked.

"Not really," Sean replied. "The only information we've been able to obtain is apparently Thad rode down here for somethin' involving a rancher named Ethan Allen Porter and his daughter Susanna May. That's all we know, so we're hopin' you'll be able to tell us something."

"I sure can, but it might not be much help. The Porters own a fair-to-middlin' sized ranch about sixteen miles southwest of here. They've done pretty well for themselves. The only problem is they settled on land right in the middle of Duncan Mannion's Lazy DM. Mannion's got the biggest spread in the county, but he's not happy with just that. He's building himself a boomtown and named it Mannionville, naturally. He owns just about all businesses in that town, plus he's been buying up all the smaller ranchers around him. Most of 'em were more'n happy to sell out, since Mannion offered them a fair price."

Newton paused to take a drag on his cigarette.

"However, there are a couple of holdouts. Jack Davies is an old bachelor cowboy, who's as stubborn as the day is long, and the Porters. Davies only has a couple of hundred hard-scrabble acres and some sorry cows, and so far he's had no problems. His land's pretty poor, so Mannion doesn't have any real need for it. However, the Porters' land also sits on Diablo Creek, which is one of the few reliable water sources in these parts. This means they control some important water rights. Mannion's tried to buy them out, like he did all the rest, but Porter said he wouldn't sell at any price. Claimed he'd set down his roots, his wife is buried on his land, and he wasn't movin'. Can't fault a man for that. Porter's a stubborn Yankee from Vermont. He says one of his ancestors was Ethan Allen, the Revolutionary War hero."

Again the sheriff paused, this time to shake the ashes from his quirly into an empty tin mug.

"To finish my story, ever since Porter refused Mannion's final offer he's been havin' all kinds of trouble, like fences cut, stock run off, several of his cowboys shot and a couple of them killed. He blames Mannion, of course, which makes sense, but there's no proof Mannion is behind all the shenanigans. Besides, Mannion's had rustler problems of his own, like all the ranchers down this way do. Mannion's got a pretty tough bunch of hands, but he's got real need for 'em, at least by his lights. I can't say I disagree with him."

"So Thad came down here to investigate Porter's complaints?" Levi questioned.

"That, and because he seemed to have a real interest in Susanna May. She's a looker, that gal, and can turn any man's head. Dutton was here for a couple of weeks or so."

"You said Porter *claimed* he wouldn't move," Sean interrupted. "Does that mean he changed his mind?"

"Evidently he has. Like I said, Dutton was here for a couple of weeks. He poked around for awhile, but said he couldn't come up with any evidence against Mannion or anyone else. He told me and Porter he had to return to his Ranger Company up in Laredo, but he'd file a report with Austin for follow-up. Porter said that was good enough for him and he'd keep on fightin'. He and

I both promised if we came up with anything solid we'd contact the Rangers pronto. Then last week, for some reason, Porter and Mannion unexpectedly came to an agreement of sorts. Mannion's supposed to buy Porter's Triangle VY, but apparently Porter will get to keep his house and a few acres. Makes no sense to me; however, it's really none of my business at this point. Why all the sudden interest in the Porters by the Texas Rangers? I also don't understand, why are you askin' about Dutton?"

"Because he never made it back to Laredo alive," Sean replied. "Somebody put a couple of bullets through him and his horse brought him into camp a few days later, dead. We've been tryin' to find Thad's killer, but haven't had much luck. The only clues we have are he came here, and was asked to do so by Susanna May Porter."

"Thad Dutton murdered!" Newton shook his head in disbelief. "I'm real sorry to hear that, but it's one of the hazards of being a lawman. You never know when you'll catch a slug. I'll help you any way I can, of course."

"We appreciate that, Sheriff," Sean answered. "First off I'll stop by the county land office to check the papers on the Porter spread and also the Lazy DM. Then I'll ride out to the Porters and talk with them. Mebbe even Duncan Mannion if we don't run out of daylight."

"Sure thing." Newton glanced at the clock on

the wall, which read quarter to twelve. "It's just about dinnertime. I'll bet you boys are plenty hungry, so I'll tell you what, why don't we head on over to the Bluebonnet Café? We can talk some more there and after we're done eating I'll take you over to the land office."

"That sounds reasonable," Sean agreed. "We'll need to care for our horses first. We've been travelin' for quite a ways and they need a good feedin' and rubdown. The clerk at the telegraph office recommended the Heart of Texas Hotel for us and our horses. He also mentioned that the Bluebonnet serves up some good chuck."

"Barney, at the Western Union," the sheriff chuckled, "he recommends the Heart of Texas to anyone who asks where to stay. He gets paid to do that by the hotel, I'm sure. They do provide decent rooms for people and clean stalls for broncs. I'll take you over there, you can settle your horses and reserve a room, then we'll eat."

"That's fine," Levi answered. "You're right, Sheriff, I'm so hungry I could eat an entire steer, horns, hooves, and all."

"Be careful what you order, because you might get just that," Newton laughed.

The food at the Bluebonnet Café was indeed as good as Barney and Sheriff Newton had claimed. After a hearty dinner of beef stew and homemade bread, the sheriff took Sean and Levi to the county land office. The clerk looked up from behind his desk when they entered.

"Howdy, Pres," the sheriff said.

"Howdy, yourself, Sheriff. I see you've brought some visitors," the clerk replied.

"I sure did. Pres, these two men are Texas Rangers Sean Kennedy and Levi Mallory and they'd like to look over some of your records. I assured them you'd cooperate as best you could. Rangers, Prescott Landis, the county land recorder. Just ask him for whatever you need."

"Sure, Sheriff," Landis replied, and then addressed the Rangers. "I'm glad to meet you gentlemen. Now, what can I do for you?"

"We'd like to look over the records for the Triangle VY and also the Lazy DM, especially any recent transactions or changes," Sean explained.

"Of course, and it will only take me few minutes to locate the files, so make yourselves comfortable."

Landis disappeared into the walk-in vault at the rear of his office. Sean reversed a ladder-back chair and straddled it, while Levi and the sheriff sat on a bench against the side wall.

"Thad Dutton's dead. I still have a hard time swallowin' that news," Newton remarked, "and the only lead you have is he came here with Susanna Porter and her father."

"That's it, Sheriff," Sean reiterated, "except

191

there is one other thing. Thad had a real fancy belt he'd had custom made. The leather was finely tooled and there was a Ranger badge on the buckle. His initials were on the keepers. He always wore that belt, but it wasn't on his body when we found him."

"I recall that belt and it sure was pretty," Newton said. He thumbed back his Stetson and scratched his head. "Sure seems like it wasn't on him when he rode out, however, I couldn't swear to it. More likely I just wasn't payin' attention. Mebbe whoever killed him took that belt."

"It's possible, Sheriff, but if he or she did take the belt they got it before they killed Thad. Thad was on his horse when he was shot. His foot hung up in the stirrup and the horse ran off with him. Plus, it appears Thad was able to get off at least one shot at his killer before they plugged him again and finished him. So, there's no way they took that belt after Thad was dead."

"I see what you mean. Well, I sure ain't seen anyone wearin' that belt around here and it wouldn't be too smart of 'em if they did. All the same, I'll keep my eyes peeled. You said he or she, Sean. Do you really think a woman might have done the killin'?"

"Anything's possible, Sheriff, you know that. Truthfully I doubt it, but we can't rule anything out."

"Reckon not," Newton conceded. "Here's Pres with the records."

Landis emerged from the vault, carrying several files.

"Here's your papers, gentlemen. You can use that side table to spread them out and look them over, not that you'll find anything. It's pretty much a moot point about the Triangle VY, because Duncan Mannion will be taking it over the next week or two, which is a pity, after all Ethan Porter's hard work."

"Sheriff Newton said Porter's gonna keep his house and a bit of land under their agreement," Levi pointed out.

"Oh sure, Mannion's a very generous man," Landis sarcastically retorted. "The sheriff knows as well as I do within a month after everything is finalized, Mannion will force Porter to give up what little he has left."

"We have no way of knowin' that for certain, Pres," Newton protested.

"Nothing we can prove, but mark my words it'll happen," Landis rejoined. "Well, you gentlemen take as long as you need going over those files. I'll be attending to my work. Just let me know when you're finished, please."

"Of course, and thank you for your assistance, Mister Landis," Sean replied.

Sean spread the papers out and for the next hour he and Levi scrutinized them, looking for any detail which might be out of the ordinary. Finally, satisfied the papers held no useful information, they returned them to the clerk.

"I told you they wouldn't be of much use. I wish they could have been," Landis apologized.

"Don't worry about it," Sean answered. "It was a long shot in any event. If we should need to see them later, we'll be in touch. Thank you again."

"They'll be available any time you need them, Ranger," Landis replied. "Good day to you both."

"Good day to you also."

After leaving the building, Sean, Levi, and Newton stopped on the boardwalk in front of the land office.

"What's your next step, Ranger?" Newton asked Sean.

"Sheriff, since we're gonna be workin' together, start callin' us Sean and Levi."

"Sure, as long as you call me Dave."

"It's a deal, now to answer your question, we're gonna head for the Porter ranch."

"You want me to ride along with you?"

"Not this time. Bein' strangers, we might be able to get something out of Porter you couldn't, Dave," Sean explained.

"I reckon you could be right," Newton agreed. "Porter and I are cordial enough, but we're not exactly friendly. I think he suspicion's I'm on Mannion's side, which ain't true. Unfortunately, I can't convince him of that. That might be why he asked your Ranger pard to come down here."

"All the more reason for you not to be with us then," Sean answered. "So if you can give us some directions to both the Porter and Mannion spreads we'll retrieve our horses and be on our way. Let's start for the hotel's stable."

"Sure," Newton said, as they began walking toward the Heart of Texas. "The Triangle VY's about sixteen miles southwest, like I said. You'll take the road toward Agua Nueva, which after about eight miles ain't much more than a cattle path. You'll see a sign for the Porter place nailed to an old fence post. Go left at the sign, and the main house is about a half-mile down. They're gonna be wary of strangers, so keep that in mind."

"We will," Sean assured him. "What about Mannion's place? How do we reach it from Porter's?"

"The Lazy DM's just about nine miles due west of Porter's. You'll leave the Triangle VY and at the sign for the place turn left and a quarter mile down the road, when the trail splits, you take the right fork. You'll head northwest for a bit, but then turn south and finally west. The trail will take you straight to Mannion's ranch."

"What about this here Mannionville?" Levi questioned.

"You'll retrace your trail from the Lazy DM, then head north at the first junction you come to," Newton answered. "Keep ridin' until you hit the main road to Laredo and ride toward Laredo. Mannionville straddles the road about six miles from the junction. You can't miss it."

"Thanks, Sheriff. We probably won't get back to town tonight or mebbe for a couple of days, dependin'," Sean said. "If Woody Woodson shows up, tell him where we went, and have him wait for us."

"Sure, I'll tell him," Newton agreed. "I'll keep my eyes and ears open, just in case someone lets something slip too."

"That's good. Here's the stable. We'll check in with you once we return, Dave," Sean said.

"All right and you two be careful."

"We will be," Sean assured him. "Hasta la Vista."

"Hasta la Vista."

Later that afternoon Sean and Levi approached the Triangle VY. On a small rise, they paused for just a moment to look over the ranch.

"Nice-lookin' spread," Levi noted.

"It sure is," Sean agreed.

The main ranch house was a low, rambling structure constructed of split cedar logs. A porch, which was decorated with an abundance of potted flowers and hanging ferns, ran the entire width of the front. Lace curtains at the windows were another feminine touch.

Across the yard, the bunkhouse was likewise solidly built of cedar, but was plain and unadorned.

Like the main house, it was shaded by several cottonwoods, which had evidently been planted as saplings, and were now good-sized specimens. A springhouse and smokehouse were to the rear of these two buildings. Beyond the bunkhouse were several sturdily built barns and corrals. Horses grazed in the pastures, while cattle dotted the distant fields.

"Let's get on down," Sean ordered. He put Ghost into a fast walk. A few moments later they were at the gate. Sean leaned from his saddle to lift the latch.

"Hold it right there, you two!" a voice rang out. "Keep your hands where I can see 'em, away from those guns."

"Sure thing, son, only we ain't lookin' for trouble," Sean answered. The speaker was a towheaded boy of sixteen or seventeen who had rounded the corner of the bunkhouse. His blue eyes and straw-colored hair made him seem even younger. The youngster had a brand-new Winchester leveled at the Rangers. Despite his youthful appearance, his face was set with grim determination, and the rifle was steady in his hands.

"We don't want strangers snoopin' around," the boy retorted. "What's your business?"

"We're here to see Ethan Porter and his daughter," Sean explained. "Could you let them know?"

"I'm Brad Porter, Ethan's son and Susanna's

brother," the youngster responded. "You can talk to me and I'll decide whether or not you can see my father."

"Bradley, what's that commotion out there?"

Sean and Levi glanced away from the boy to see a man of about fifty standing on the porch. He also had a rifle pointed at them. Unlike his son, Ethan Allen Porter had dark hair, eyes, and features. His dark eyes held a deep sadness, as if Porter had fought his last battle and knew he had lost. His voice still carried its distinctively clipped northern New England accent.

"These hombres claim to have business with you, Pa," the boy replied.

"Is that so?" the elder Porter said. "Would one of you mind statin' what it is?"

"Can we come in the yard and get off our horses first?" Sean asked.

"I reckon, but ride in slow and easy. One false move and we'll put bullets through you."

"Don't worry about that," Sean answered. "We're peaceable."

"Then come on in."

The Rangers passed through the gate, rode up to the porch, and dismounted. Ethan Porter remained on the porch, his rifle held at the level of their chests, while his son followed behind them, his Winchester trained at their backs. If Sean and Levi intended trouble, they would be cut down in an instant.

"Now, what's this all about?" Porter demanded.

"We're Texas Rangers," Sean answered. "Sean Kennedy and Levi Mallory. We'd like to talk to you."

"Rangers? Sure, come on in." Porter lowered his rifle, as did Brad.

"Rangers, Pop! Mebbe we can keep our home after all," Brad exclaimed.

"Brad, you need to get back to fixin' up that rear wall of the bunkhouse," Porter ordered. "Whatever the Rangers and I might have to discuss will be in private. Take their horses, care for them, and then get back to your job."

"All right," Brad replied. Levi and Sean handed him their horses' reins. The downcast youth slowly led the horses away, shuffling across the yard.

"You were a bit harsh on the boy, weren't you, Mister Porter?" Levi asked.

"I have to be. Brad's a good boy, but he just doesn't understand the way things are around here. He refuses to face reality, that it has become impossible for me to fight any longer. As for you men, I assume you're here to follow up for Thad Dutton."

"That's partially correct," Sean said.

"Fine, fine," Porter smiled. "Come inside. I'll call Susanna and have her make us some coffee. You did wish to speak with her also, did you not?"

"We did," Sean confirmed.

Porter took them through a sitting room

decorated with knick-knacks and china figurines. Lace doilies covered the tables, while the lamps' globes were done in a floral motif. They continued down a hallway to a room on the left. This one was far more masculine in tone, with heavy wooden furniture, Navajo rugs on the floors, and several sets of antlers on the walls. There were also several good-quality paintings of ranching and gun-fighting scenes. A portrait in oil of a fair-featured woman, clearly Porter's late wife, hung over the mantel, on which reposed a bronze sculpture of a cowboy roping a longhorn. The image in the painting bore a striking resemblance to young Bradley.

"This is my den and office," Porter said. "My late wife Libby always called it my cave. I suppose she was right, rest her soul. Make yourselves comfortable while I get Susanna. You may smoke if you wish."

Sean settled into a brown leather chair, while Levi found a spot on the leather sofa.

"Porter seems like a decent enough hombre," Levi noted.

"He does, only I can't figure why he jumped all over his kid like that," Sean said.

"It was a bit odd," Levi answered. "But I reckon it's none of our business." He pulled out his sack of Durham and packet of cigarette papers to begin building a smoke. He and Sean sat in silence while they awaited Porter's return.

The Triangle VY owner returned a few minutes later. With him was a young woman in her early twenties. Sean and Levi scrambled to their feet as she entered the room.

"Gentlemen, this is my daughter, Susanna May. Susanna, these are Rangers Kennedy and Mallory."

"I'm pleased to meet you, Ranger Kennedy, Ranger Mallory," Susanna smiled, her ruby-red lips parting to reveal perfect white teeth.

"The same here, Miss Porter, and the name's Sean."

"Mine's Levi."

"Then you must call me Susanna," she replied. "I have coffee on the stove and it will be ready shortly. Please, sit down. Father, have you offered our guests some whiskey or brandy? We will have no discussion of business matters until I return with your coffee and I mean it, Father." With that, she flounced out of the room.

"You must forgive my daughter," Porter apologized, as he took a seat in the chair opposite Sean and pulled a cigar from his shirt pocket. "Since my wife passed away she has taken over running the household. I can't win an argument with her, just like I could never win one with Libby."

Porter stuck the cigar in his mouth, struck a match, and lit the smoke.

"There's no apology necessary," Sean assured the rancher.

It was apparent to Sean why Thad Dutton had agreed to help this young woman. Susanna May Porter, like her younger brother, had blonde hair and blue eyes, only her eyes were a deeper shade, almost violet in hue. Her face was wholesomely pretty. She was slightly taller than average and her figure filled out the conservative gingham dress she wore perfectly. All in all, Susanna would be a prize for any man.

"Have you been traveling for a long while?" Porter asked.

"We've been on the trail for quite a spell," Sean answered.

The Rangers and Porter passed the time talking about cattle, raiding Mexican outlaws, and rustlers until Susanna returned. She carried a tray with a silver coffee pot, four china cups, saucers, plates, and a platter of cookies.

"I just made these cookies this morning," she said as she placed the tray on a low table. "I hope you like them. I also hope the coffee isn't too strong."

"It'd be real hard to make coffee too strong for us, ma'am," Sean replied.

Susanna poured each man a cup of the steaming black coffee, passed several cookies to each, and then poured coffee for herself. She sat alongside Levi.

"Now that we have our refreshments, you may discuss why you came here," she said. "I would assume it's about the investigation Ranger Dutton started, since he promised to have Austin follow through."

"It is," Sean hedged. "However, we need a bit more information from you, Mister Porter. Could you briefly recount exactly why you asked Thad, I mean Ranger Dutton, to come down here?"

"Of course," Porter agreed, "although I have to admit it was Susanna who convinced him of our need for Ranger assistance. You see, for the past several months, we have had all sorts of trouble. Fences have been cut, cattle and horses rustled, fields burned. Some of our men have been shot from ambush, with two of them killed. Yes, I realize all ranchers have similar problems to some extent, but this seems to be a determined effort to bankrupt the Triangle VY."

"Do you have any particular person in mind who might want to drive you off your ranch?"

"Certainly we do!" Susanna broke in. "Duncan Mannion. He's been after our property for a long time and when father absolutely refused to sell, he was furious. Shortly afterwards, the rustling started."

"We have no proof of that, Susanna," Porter pointed out. "Even Ranger Dutton could find none."

"I don't need any proof," Susanna insisted. "Duncan Mannion will stop at absolutely nothing to get what he wants. The man's a scoundrel and a rapscallion. He's also a lot of other things a lady can't call him."

"That still doesn't prove anything," Porter answered. "Rangers, I might as well tell you, I was at the end of my rope. So when Mannion offered to buy out my spread, except for this house and a few acres, I took him up on it. The transaction will be completed in two weeks."

"Unless these Rangers have come here prepared to stop Mannion," Susanna answered. "Have you? Did Ranger Dutton manage to come up with something that will prove Mannion is behind the raids on our home?"

"I'm afraid not," Sean replied. "You see, he never made it back to Laredo. Someone killed him and we're trying to track down the murderer. We were hoping you might be able to help us."

"Thad . . . Ranger Dutton . . . he's . . . dead?" Susanna dropped her coffee cup, which shattered on the floor. Her eyes welled with tears and she fled the room, sobbing.

"I'd better go with her," Porter said.

"It might be best if you give her a few moments alone," Sean advised.

"You may be right." Porter's shoulders slumped in defeat. "Ranger Dutton killed, well, I'm shocked, I must say. He was a fine young man."

"That he was," Levi concurred.

"Mister Porter . . ."

"Ethan."

"Of course, Ethan," Sean pressed. "What exactly did Thad find out, if anything?"

Porter shook his head. "Not much, I'm afraid. He certainly found no proof against Duncan Mannion or anyone else. He did follow the tracks of one of my missing herds, but they were too old, and the trail eventually petered out. So when Thad, Ranger Dutton, told us all he could do was make a report to Austin once he returned to Laredo, I knew there was no possibility of holding onto the Triangle VY. I thought I would lose everything. Frankly, all the fight's drained out of me. When Mannion offered me the chance to keep this house, I took it. It seemed best for everyone involved."

"Except possibly Brad?" Levi questioned.

"Yes, except Bradley," Porter sighed. "I can't blame the boy, because he was born here, and his mother's buried here. This is the only home he's ever known."

Susanna came back into the room, carrying a broom, dustpan, and towel.

"I need to clean the mess I made," she said.

"Why don't you let that go for now?" Porter suggested. "Are you feeling a bit better?"

"Father, I'm sorry," Susanna answered. "I apologize to both of you, Sean, Levi. I don't ordinarily lose my composure so easily; however, the news Ranger Dutton is dead came as quite a shock."

"We understand," Sean replied.

"Thank you, but perhaps I should explain further. Yes, Father and I were hoping Ranger Dutton would find out who is behind our problems. If he had, perhaps we could have kept our home. However, there's more than that. You see, I had grown quite fond of Thad . . . Ranger Dutton."

"Go ahead and use Thad's name, Susanna," Sean urged.

"Thank you. As I was saying, I had grown quite fond of Thad. We were becoming more than just friends."

Susanna stopped and pulled a lace handkerchief from her sleeve. She dabbed it at the corners of her eyes.

"I'm sorry," she sniffled.

"There's no need to apologize," Sean reassured her. "I know this may be difficult, but I do need to ask you one or two questions."

"I understand and I'll answer as well as I can."

"Thank you. Did Thad give you or your father any inkling at all of what he might have found?"

"Not a thing," Susanna answered. "As I'm sure Father has told you, there was nothing at all which could be used as evidence against Duncan Mannion or anyone else."

"All right," Sean continued. "Thad had a very distinctive belt, which he always wore. However, it wasn't on his body when we discovered him.

206

Do you recall if he was wearing it during his time here?"

"Oh, yes," Susanna answered. "It was quite handsome. You remember Thad's belt, don't you, Father?"

"I surely do," Porter answered. "It had a real fancy buckle with a Ranger badge engraved on it and his initials, as I recollect."

"That's right," Sean answered.

"Perhaps his murderer stole the belt after he shot Thad," Susanna suggested.

"No, that wasn't possible." Sean answered, without further explanation. "I have a feelin' if we can locate that belt, it'll lead us to Thad's killer."

"I certainly hope you're right, Sean," Susanna said.

Levi glanced at the rays of the lowering sun streaming through the west-facing windows.

"Sean, it's gettin' a bit late," he noted.

"I know," Sean answered. "Mister Porter, Miss Porter, thank you for all your assistance. If there's nothing else you can think of, Levi and I will be on our way."

"Why don't you stay for supper? In fact, why don't you spend the night here?" Susanna invited.

"That's a fine idea," Porter agreed. "We have plenty of room and you'll get a good night's sleep. You can start for Falfurrias in the morning."

"Thank you for the offer, but we're not going

back to town tonight," Sean explained. "We'll be stopping at the Lazy DM to speak with Duncan Mannion. If we don't get there before dark, we'll camp along the trail, and finish the trip at first light."

"You're wasting your time if you believe talking to Mannion will accomplish anything," Susanna declared.

"I'm afraid I have to agree with my daughter," Porter added.

"Nonetheless, we do have to talk with him, especially if what you say about Mannion is true, he might well be behind Thad's murder," Sean replied. "So we do have to leave now. If you think of something you might have forgotten you can reach us at the Heart of Texas Hotel in Falfurrias. If we're not there leave a message with Sheriff Newton."

"We'll do that," Porter promised. "We'll see you out, of course."

When they reached the porch, Porter called his son, "Bradley!"

The boy appeared from behind the bunkhouse.

"Yeah, Pa?"

"The Rangers are leaving now, so would you please get their horses?"

"Sure, Pa."

Brad went inside the main barn, returning a few moments later, leading an already saddled and bridled Ghost and Monte.

"Here's your horses, Rangers. I brushed them for you, and gave them some hay and water."

"We appreciate that, son," Sean thanked him. "Our names are Sean and Levi."

Brad gazed at the pair for a moment, then burst out, "Hey, mind if I ask you something? When I'm old enough, how would I join up with the Rangers?"

"Bradley, don't bother these men about that. They're pressed for time," Porter admonished.

"It's no bother," Sean answered. "Brad, once you're ready, you could either ride to Austin, stop at Ranger Headquarters, and ask to sign up, or you could find the nearest Ranger company and see if you can join them."

"That's nonsense," Susanna said.

"Besides, you wouldn't want to leave home, son," Porter added.

"Why not? We won't have a home much longer. There won't be any reason for me to stay here, once Mannion takes over our ranch," Brad retorted.

"That's not true," Porter objected. "We'll still have the house and some land. We can keep raisin' a few head of cattle, and you can always punch cows for Mister Mannion."

"I'd rather turn outlaw than work for that sidewinder," the boy vehemently replied.

"Bradley!" Susanna exclaimed. To Sean and Levi she added, "You'll have to forgive my brother. He's still very much a boy. There are many things he doesn't comprehend."

"I comprehend a lot more'n you might imagine, Sis," Brad shot back.

Susanna's eyes flashed angrily. She started to reply, but then abruptly changed her mind. She stood, frowning.

Sean shifted uneasily, wanting to get away from this awkward situation as quickly as possible.

"Well, if the choice is between turnin' outlaw or Rangerin', I'd recommend joinin' the Rangers, Brad," he stated. "We can always use another good man."

"Boy howdy, that's for certain," Levi agreed. "Only right now we'd better get movin', Sean."

"I'm ready."

Sean and Levi swung into their saddles.

"Remember, if you think of anything at all, even if you don't feel it's important, let us know," he told the Porters.

"We'll do that," Porter assured him. "Good day. And good luck."

"Thank you. Adios."

"I'll get the gate," Bradley offered.

"We appreciate that," Sean answered.

They turned their horses and headed for Duncan Mannion's Lazy DM.

After letting the horses warm up by setting their own pace for the first mile, Sean and Levi pushed their mounts into an easy, but ground-covering, lope. Levi looked up at the lowering sun.

"I dunno if we'll make Mannion's spread before dark," he observed. "There's not all that much daylight left."

"We're not headin' for Mannion's place, at least not tonight," Sean answered. "We're ridin' for Mannionville. I figure if we ride in there posin' as chuckline ridin' cowpunchers lookin' for work, we might be able to pick up some information. We'll spend the night and then head for the Lazy DM tomorrow."

"That makes a lot of sense, pardner," Levi agreed. "Someone might let something slip to a couple of cowpokes they'd never mention in front of a Ranger. And I wouldn't mind relaxin' with a few drinks and mebbe a game of poker in the local saloon."

"Just don't get too relaxed," Sean warned him. "By the way, did you happen to notice the look Brad Porter gave us when we rode away from the Triangle VY?"

"I sure did," Levi asserted. "That boy knows somethin'."

"More than that, he not only knows somethin', he wanted to tell us what it is, but he didn't dare."

"Maybe we should go back and try and talk to him, alone."

"He's not quite ready. He'd probably clam up if we pressed too hard and then we'd never get anything out of him. We'll leave him be for now. If necessary, we can always question him later."

"That's reasonable," Levi conceded. "Mebbe, with any luck, we won't have to bother the boy at all. Of course it's possible we're wrong about that kid. Perhaps he just wanted to ask if he could come with us and join up with the Rangers right now."

"Could be. Here's hopin' we get to the bottom of this without draggin' Brad into it," Sean replied. "C'mon, Ghost, get on up there." He pushed the blue roan into a faster lope.

Twilight had enveloped Mannionville by the time the Rangers reached its outskirts. They studied the boomtown while they rode down its main street.

"Dave Newton wasn't kiddin' when he said Mannion owned everything in this town," Levi muttered to Sean.

"Seems so," Sean agreed. He nodded toward the Devil Dog Saloon. "Let's put up our horses and head on over. If we're gonna pick up any information, it'll be in there."

Frontier saloons were notorious for gossip. Sooner or later, any and all news passed through them.

They left their horses in the care of a taciturn oldster at the livery stable and then walked the single block to the saloon. They pushed through the batwings and into the barroom.

It being midweek, the Devil Dog was not particularly crowded. The few patrons glanced up at the newcomers, then returned to their drinks. Only one card game was in progress, and the percentage girls were huddled in one corner, looking bored. Sean and Levi found a place at one end of the bar.

"Howdy, strangers," the bartender greeted them. His blue eyes held a friendly twinkle and a thick blond mustache graced his upper lip. "Welcome to Mannionville and the Devil Dog. What can I get for you?"

"Whiskey and bring the bottle," Sean ordered. He spun a coin onto the mahogany.

"Comin' right up."

The bartender produced a bottle of whiskey and two glasses. He set the glasses in front of the Rangers, filled them, and then placed the bottle alongside.

Sean lifted his glass and took a swallow of its amber contents.

"That's mighty fine red-eye," he told the bartender.

"Thanks, cowboy, Mister Mannion orders nothing but the best."

"You mean you don't own this place?"

"Not one stick of it. I work for Duncan Mannion, as does almost everyone in this town. My name's Curly Custis, by the way."

"Pleased to meet you, Curly, I'm Seamus Kean,

and this is my pard, Larry Malone." He used aliases he and Levi had employed in the past, just in case anyone eavesdropping might recognize their real names.

"Curly," Levi nodded.

"Hey, Curly," another patron shouted from the opposite end of the bar.

"Be right there, Carlos," Curly called back. "I've got to take care of another customer," he apologized. "If you need more whiskey just let me know."

Sean and Levi nursed their drinks while Curly tended to his other customers. After a short while, the bartender drifted back.

"You fellers doin' all right?" he asked.

"We're doin' just fine," Levi assured him.

"Sorry I had to leave you for a spell, but Carlos Delgado is one of my best customers, and he's ready to call it a night. He's also one of Mister Mannion's top hands."

Curly nodded toward the man who had summoned him. He was a good-looking young Mexican, or a Texan of Mexican descent. Delgado had a wiry frame, and appeared as if he could move with cat-like quickness. His features were even and pleasant, his skin somewhat lighter than most Mexicans. His eyes were deep brown, his dark hair closely-cropped. A neatly trimmed beard framed his jaw. He was dressed in plain cowboy garb, nothing fancy about any of his outfit except the bright red silk bandanna knotted around his throat, and the feathered band on his hat. The gun on his right hip was a well-worn .45 single-action Colt. He nodded back to Curly, picked up a full bottle, tucked it under his arm, and then turned and walked out of the Devil Dog.

"It's not a problem," Sean answered. "Your regular customers should come first. After all, we just drifted into town, and we'll most likely be driftin' on in a day or two."

"If you don't mind my askin', what brings you to Mannionville?" Curly questioned.

"We don't mind you askin'," Sean replied. "We're lookin' for work. We'd hoped to sign on with a cattle outfit, but so far haven't had much luck."

"You both look like you can punch cows," Curly observed. "I would think you'd be able to find something without too much trouble."

"We can punch cows, wrangle horses, even use our guns if we have to," Levi said.

Curly stared at Levi for a moment, and Sean guessed the bartender was about to ask whether his gun was the reason he and Sean were drifting, or more likely on the run from the law, then thought better of it. Men had been shot for asking questions like that.

"A lot of the ranchers aren't hirin', with this dry spell," Sean explained. "In fact, we just came from the Triangle VY. We didn't have any luck there either."

"I wouldn't imagine you did," Curly stated. "Ethan Porter's about to sell out to Mister Mannion, but I'd bet you could get a job on the Lazy DM. It's too bad Carlos just left, or I'd introduce you to him. Listen, why don't you ride out there in the morning? I can give you directions."

"That sounds like a fine idea," Sean replied. "What do you think, Larry? We can put up at the hotel for the night, and then take up Curly on his advice."

"Sure," Levi agreed. "Curly, any chance this Mannion hombre has a daughter as good-lookin' as Porter's? That gal's sure a sight to behold."

"He certainly does, but you'd better stay clear of Dorothea Mannion," Curly advised. "Her father wouldn't take kindly to a driftin' cowpoke messin' with his girl. The last man who tried that stirred up all sorts of trouble . . . and he was a Texas Ranger."

Sean stiffened, and had to stifle a gasp of surprise. He took another swallow of whiskey to steady his voice.

"A Texas Ranger, you said?"

"That's what I said," Curly confirmed. "Story goes that he came down here at the request of Ethan Porter, or more precisely Porter's daughter. That's more likely, bein' as she's so pretty she

216

can turn any man's head. Anyway, supposedly he was investigatin' Duncan Mannion. He was also spendin' a lot of time with Susanna May, until one day he happened to bump into Dorothea Mannion, literally. She was carryin' a bunch of packages out of the Mercantile and didn't see him. Next thing you know, that Ranger's goin' around town with Dorothea."

"Sounds like he didn't have much time for Rangerin'," Sean grunted.

"Seemed like it, but from what I understand he did do quite a bit of diggin'," Curly answered.

"So what happened then?" Levi urged.

"Darndest thing, because one day Susanna May came into town, spoilin' for a fight. She stayed at the hotel for three days, waiting for Dorothea to ride in from the ranch. When Dorothea showed up, Susanna May went after her and accused her of bein' a man-stealin' hussy, and a lot of other, less lady-like names. I wouldn't have thought Susanna could cuss like that. Then she took a swing at Dorothea. They had a knock-down, drag-out battle right in front of this here saloon. I'd never seen two females fight like that. It took John Spallone, the town marshal, and three other men to separate 'em. Neither one of those gals looked very pretty by the time that fight was done."

"Where was that Ranger when this happened?" Sean asked.

"He was down to Falfurrias at the time. From what I understand, he stayed around for a few more days, then headed back to Laredo. Word is he told Porter he couldn't help him, which is probably true, bein' as Porter's sellin' out to Mannion. He also probably figured if those gals got their hands on him they'd tear him to shreds," Curly laughed.

"I'd imagine you're right," Levi agreed. "I'd sure hightail it out of town if I found myself in that kind of situation."

"What kind of man is your boss?" Sean questioned.

"He's a decent enough person, I guess, long as you don't cross him. He's been more than fair to me, and most of the folks in this town would agree. Sure, he can be tough, but he's worked hard to get where he is, and he has to be tough to hold onto everything he's earned."

"He sounds like a lot of Texans," Levi noted.

"What about Mannionville?" Sean asked. "It seems like a pretty quiet town."

A flicker of doubt showed in Curly's eyes. He hesitated before he answered.

"It is. That catfight was the most excitement we've had in quite a spell. Other than the occasional drunk he has to toss in jail, our marshal's got it pretty easy. In fact, except for Friday and Saturday nights, he generally closes up his office by eight o'clock. By now he's fast asleep."

"It sure sounds like a nice place," Sean answered. "I reckon we'll take your advice and ride over to Mannion's spread tomorrow."

"You won't regret it," Curly assured him. "Tell him I sent you. The next drinks are on me, for luck."

"Why, thanks, Curly," Sean said.

Sean and Levi remained for another hour. By then, there were only three other customers remaining in the saloon.

"We're gonna call it a night, Curly," Sean told the bartender. "We want to get an early start tomorrow."

"Of course and I have a feelin' you'll get those jobs, so I'll be seeing more of you," Curly answered.

"Here's hopin' you're right," Sean replied. "Good night, Curly."

"Good night, Seamus. 'Night, Larry."

"G'night," Levi mumbled.

They walked from the saloon and stepped into the muggy night air. It only took a moment to reach the Mannionville Manor and settle in their room. Sean opened the window in hopes of catching any faint breeze. Then, he and Levi quickly undressed and stretched out on their beds.

"Real nice place, this Mannionville," Levi murmured. "Purely heaven on earth right here in south Texas."

"Yeah, too good to be true, pard," Sean

answered. "I have the feelin' they're hidin' somethin'.""

"I've gotta agree with you. Curly was a bit too friendly. He sure went out of his way to make Duncan Mannion sound like a plaster saint."

"He kind of stumbled about this town bein' quiet when I brought that up, too," Sean said. "Too bad we didn't get to meet the town marshal. I think it would've been interesting to get his thoughts."

"We'll still have a chance," Levi pointed out.

"I reckon you're right. Tomorrow we'll get to meet Saint Duncan himself."

"Who'll be in for a real shock when we introduce ourselves as a couple of Texas Rangers," Levi chuckled.

"That's an understatement if I've ever heard one," Sean laughed. "Speakin' of shocks," he continued, "that was pretty surprising what Curly told us about those two girls and Thad. Susanna sure didn't mention it," Sean said.

"She was probably too embarrassed to say anything. Her feminine pride was most likely hurt when she discovered Thad with another woman. Clearly she didn't know Thad's reputation with the ladies. She must've gotten real mad when she found out he didn't care for her as much as she did for him," Levi speculated.

"That's as good a reason as any," Sean answered.

"Here's another bone to chew on," Levi said. "That Mexican fella in the bar."

"The one the bartender pointed out? Carlos Delgado, Curly said his name was."

"Yeah, the hombre who's supposed to be one of Mannion's top hands. He pretty much matches the description of the rider that old rancher and his wife told us about, the one who was followin' Thad to kill him."

"I'd say he's a dead ringer," Sean answered.

"Which would tie Mannion to Thad's murder," Levi replied.

"What we need now is some proof," Sean pointed out. "It's too bad there wasn't any report found on Thad's body. That would've helped. We know Thad's killer couldn't have taken it off him, since Toby ran off with Thad still in the saddle, dead or dyin'."

"I suppose it's possible this Delgado, if he is the killer, murdered Thad on his own. Mebbe he had designs on one of those girls and got jealous when Thad moved in. That'd be a motive right there," Levi said.

"Or it could be another man entirely," Sean noted.

"You don't really believe that, do you?"

"No, I don't, but we have to consider that."

"I still can't figure why there was nothing on Thad or in his saddlebags about what he might've found down here," Levi said.

"Mebbe he mailed a report to Austin," Sean

answered. "By now Lieutenant Blawcyzk might have heard somethin' from Headquarters. To make sure, when we get back to Falfurrias I'll wire Captain Trumbull myself, and ask if he'd received any kind of communication from Thad."

"That'd at least give us somethin'," Levi replied. "I'd give my eyeteeth to find out who has Thad's belt. It'd sure ease my mind."

"Right now, so would a good night's sleep," Sean answered. He rolled onto his stomach. "Well, good night, pardner."

"Good night, Sean. Try not to snore too loud."

"Sure," Sean muttered.

Soon, both men were sound asleep.

The Rangers made it a point to call upon John Spallone the next morning, before they left for the Lazy DM. After obtaining information from the front desk clerk that Spallone dined at the hotel every morning, they found the Mannionville marshal eating breakfast in the hotel's café.

"Howdy, Marshal," Sean greeted, his voice friendly. "Mind if we join you? I'm Seamus Kane and this is my pardner, Larry Malone."

Spallone looked up at the pair.

"Reckon it's all right, leastwise since you're strangers in town, I can keep an eye on you."

Sean and Levi took seats at the local lawman's table. A waitress hurried over to take their orders.

"Ham and eggs for both of us, and fried

potatoes," Sean requested. "Along with plenty of black coffee."

Once the waitress headed for the kitchen, Sean returned his attention to the marshal.

"We're not lookin' to cause trouble, Marshal, if that's what's botherin' you," he explained.

"My pard's right," Levi continued. "We're lookin' for work. Curly over at the Devil Dog suggested we try the Lazy DM. He said the owner's a right nice feller."

"We like what we've seen of your town," Sean added, "but we thought before ridin' all the way out to the Lazy DM, we'd get your opinion."

"Duncan Mannion is a decent man to work for, long as you work hard and don't question his authority," Spallone answered. "Same thing goes here in Mannionville. If an hombre keeps his nose clean, he won't have any problem with me. However, if he crosses me, well . . ."

Spallone pushed back his chair, just far enough so the Rangers could watch as he patted the butt of his six-gun.

"We get your meanin', Marshal," Sean said.

"Good. Mannionville's a nice, quiet town, like you said, and I intend to keep it that way, so as long as you understand, we'll get along just fine."

"I have just one more thing. When we tried for jobs out at the Triangle VY, the owner said he wasn't hirin' because he was sellin' out to

Mannion. We got the impression he was bein' forced out. Any truth to that?"

"None at all," Spallone answered. "Porter's just lookin' to blame someone else for his failin' as a rancher. Mannion's got the biggest ranch in the county and he's made something of himself, so he's the biggest target. Actually, Mannion was pretty generous letting Porter keep his house and a few acres."

"Sounds like it," Levi conceded.

Spallone finished the last of his meal and pushed back from the table. He stood and left payment for the meal next to his plate as he said, "If you don't have anything else you want to ask, I need to get started on my rounds."

"No, you've answered all our questions just fine, Marshal. Thanks," Sean said. "Reckon we'll be seein' you around."

"Sure, sure," Spallone replied, "if Mannion hires you." He pulled on his Stetson and walked out of the café.

The waitress appeared with the Rangers' meals. Having not eaten much the night previous, they made short work of their breakfast. Once they had finished their coffee and paid the bill, Sean and Levi went to retrieve their horses.

"That's gonna be one surprised local lawman when he finds out we're Rangers," Levi half-whispered once they reached the street.

"True," Sean agreed. "Once we see Mannion,

there'll be no reason to keep our identities hidden. By tonight everyone in town will know there's a couple of Rangers lookin' for the sidewinder who killed their pardner."

They made the ride to Mannion's ranch at a leisurely pace, letting the horses choose their own gaits. The morning was hot, so Ghost and Monte were content to walk, only occasionally breaking into a slow jogtrot. It was midmorning when they reined up a short distance from the Lazy DM. Discretion dictated they take a few minutes to look the spread over before riding in.

Levi gave a low whistle.

"Boy howdy, that's some place," he exclaimed.

"It sure is," Sean agreed.

Duncan Mannion's residence was a large adobe structure built Mexican style. An arched veranda surrounded the house, which itself was centered around an enclosed courtyard. Bougainvillea vines climbed up the arches and over the tile roof. Their vividly colored flowers of purple, red, and magenta offered a counterpoint to the subtle tan of the house's adobe walls. Poinsettias, grown as large as small shrubs, added their brilliant red blossoms at the base of each pillar. The windows were few, up high, and narrow, affording both defense against attackers and protection from the summer heat and winter chill.

Beyond the house were several barns and the

bunkhouse, also constructed of adobe. There was a number of smaller structures of three or four rooms each, evidently homes for married servants or cowboys and their families. A springhouse and a smokehouse were located behind these. The sounds of a hammer ringing on metal came from a smithy. A low adobe wall, punctuated with wrought iron gates, enclosed the entire compound.

"Nice lookin' horses and cattle, too," Levi noted, studying the animals grazing in the distance. "You'd think Mannion would be happy with what he has."

"Some men never are," Sean observed. "Let's head on down there."

They put their horses into a trot. Two men, carrying rifles in the crooks of their elbows, watched the Rangers approach.

One challenged them when they reached the gate, "Do you two hombres have any particular business here?"

"We'd like to see Mister Mannion, if he's home," Sean answered.

"He is, but he didn't mention expectin' any visitors this mornin'," the guard retorted.

"He wasn't expectin' us, but he'll see us," Sean calmly replied.

"Why would he want to see two saddlebums?"

"Suppose we're lookin' for jobs?" Levi said.

"Then you'd want to see Bill Hollister, the foreman. He does all the hirin' for the ranch, but he wouldn't hire the likes of you two," the guard said, making no effort to hide his contempt for the dust-covered men facing him. Besides being coated with trail grime, Sean and Levi hadn't shaved for several days, nor had haircuts for weeks, adding to their shabby appearances.

"Well, instead of claimin' we want cow-puncher's work, how about telling Mannion we're Texas Rangers?" Sean asked.

"You two? Texas Rangers? Hah!" the guard sneered.

"Take a look."

Carefully, Sean slid his hand into his vest pocket and removed his Ranger credentials. He passed them to the guard.

"Rangers Sean Kennedy and Levi Mallory, and we want to see Mister Mannion now!" Sean snapped.

"Just a minute, you two. Look at these, Red." The guard passed Sean's papers to his partner, who also scrutinized them.

"I reckon they're who they claim to be all right, Clete," the second guard stated. "Better let 'em in. I'll tell Julio they're comin'." He handed the credentials back to Sean, and then started for the main house.

"All right, c'mon in. But, don't try anythin'," Clete grumbled.

"There a reason we should?" Sean asked. He sat lazily in the saddle, but his hand rested on the butt of his Colt.

"I guess not," the guard conceded.

When Sean and Levi reached the house, a young Mexican boy and an elderly Mexican servant awaited them.

"I am Javier," the boy introduced himself, smiling broadly. "I will take your horses. Por favor, be assured your fine caballos will receive the most excellent care."

"We're certain they will," Sean answered. "Gracias." He and Levi dismounted and then handed their reins to the young hostler. Javier led Ghost and Monte toward the horse barn, speaking softly to the mounts.

"Buenas Dias," the servant greeted them. "I am Julio, Señor Mannion's personal servant, follow me to the courtyard, por favor. Señor Mannion will be ready for you shortly. May I have your names again? Red was not exactly clear on those."

"Certainly," Sean replied. "Texas Rangers Sean Kennedy and Levi Mallory."

"Gracias," Julio said. He led them into the inner courtyard, which was lavishly landscaped with potted flowers of every hue imaginable. Shrubs provided added shelter, and a fountain gurgled in the center of the gardens. Caged songbirds trilled from their wicker enclosures.

Julio took Sean and Levi to a wrought iron table and chairs, shaded by a large palm tree.

"Please, make yourselves comfortable,

señores. I will have Francesca bring out refreshments while you await Señor Mannion."

Once the Rangers were seated, he disappeared inside the house. Sean and Levi looked around in amazement at the lush plantings and elegant setting.

"This is almost like an alcalde's hacienda in Sonora," Levi said.

"More like the governor's palacio," Sean answered.

Soon a beautiful young Mexican woman appeared, carrying a heavy silver tray. Her white linen blouse and dark skirt did little to conceal her lithe figure.

"I am Francesca," she announced. "I have brought you food and drinks. Please, enjoy yourselves."

She placed the tray on the Rangers' table and then poured chilled wine from a silver pitcher into two silver goblets. That done, she set two silver plates in front of Sean and Levi, and placed lemon slices, along with small, sugar-dusted cakes, on the plates. Alongside the plates she positioned thick, burgundy-hued linen napkins.

Francesca indicated a small silver bell on the tray.

"I will be waiting just inside the kitchen doorway. If you have need of anything further, please ring this bell."

"Gracias, Francesca," Sean said. "This will be more than plenty."

"Of course." The servant girl retreated to the kitchen.

Levi picked up a cake, took a bite, and then washed that down with a swallow of wine.

"Pard, this is the life," he said.

"I wouldn't get too used to it," Sean advised, grinning.

They relaxed for a half-hour, eating the moist cakes and lemon slices, enjoying the wine.

"I wonder how long Mannion's gonna keep us coolin' our heels, pardner," Levi wondered, using his napkin to wipe powdered sugar from his upper lip.

"I'd say not much longer. Here comes Julio now."

The manservant crossed the courtyard and signaled to the Rangers.

"Señor Mannion will see you now. This way, por favor."

Julio led them into the house. They went down a long corridor lined with oil paintings and sculptures, then into a parlor richly furnished with dark green velvet sofas and chairs. Matching tapestries covered most of the adobe walls in this room. A piano stood in one corner, and dark, heavily carved Spanish tables held artwork and bric-a-brac. The globes on the lamps were hand-painted in soft pastels, and crystals dangled from their bases. The thick adobe walls were doing their job. This room, like the rest of the house, was at least fifteen degrees cooler than outside.

"Down this hallway, Señor Mannion awaits in his office," Julio ordered.

He led them to a room half-way down on the left and said, "In there, señores."

"Gentlemen, welcome to the Lazy DM," Mannion greeted the Rangers as they entered the room. He stood behind a massive oaken desk. "Mi casa, su casa, as our Mexican friends say."

Mannion's appearance was not at all what Sean had expected. Judging from the house and its décor, he had thought Mannion would be well-dressed, in expensive clothes, possibly a transplanted Easterner. Instead, the Lazy DM owner looked more like a typical Texas cattleman. Mannion was in his middle forties, tall, and still lean. His dark brown hair was thick, with not a trace of gray, and carefully combed. He sported a bushy mustache which matched his hair, and his eyes were also brown. Mannion was dressed in well-worn jeans and a dark gray shirt, over which was a black cowhide vest. His boots, while shined, were not fancy, and the blue scarf knotted around his throat was cotton, not silk. The Stetson hanging on a hat rack next to the desk had once been white, but now was faded and stained with the dust of many days working cattle and horses. There was nothing extravagant about Mannion. Even his speech pattern was that of a native Texan. This room matched the man. While the furnishings were obviously of excellent quality, the office was cluttered with ranching tools and papers. The pictures on the walls were Texas landscapes, the objects scattered about were mostly Indian pottery and arrowheads. On the wall behind the desk hung a map of the region and an enormous set of horns from a longhorn steer.

The rancher picked up a rosewood humidor and opened it. He indicated a crystal decanter and tumblers on an oak sideboard.

"Cigars and some brandy, or perhaps whiskey?" Mannion offered.

"None for me, thank you," Sean answered. "The cakes and wine you provided were enough."

"I'll have a cigar and a brandy," Levi replied. He took one of the proffered cigars, then a match from the holder on Mannion's desk. He lit the cigar, drawing on it until it was burning steadily. That accomplished, he poured a full tumbler of brandy and took a sip.

"These are both excellent, Mister Mannion," he praised.

"My wife has them imported specially for me," Mannion answered. He too had procured a cigar and lit up. He gestured at the sumptuous surroundings. "She's also the one who designed and decorated this house. It's way too fancy for a simple rancher like me. Georgia is from San Francisco originally, then Santa Fe, so she's used to the finer things. You Rangers didn't come here to discuss furnishings, tobacco, and liquor. Please, have a seat and let's get down to business."

"Of course," Sean answered. He chose a red leather chair, while Levi settled onto a burgundy velvet sofa.

"I'm guessing you're here because Ethan Porter is stirrin' up trouble again," Mannion said. "That's too bad; I thought we'd settled things between us. I hate to see you men wastin' your time. I assume you're aware there was another Ranger here already. He found nothing to tie me, or anyone else from the Lazy DM, to Porter's problems."

"We're not exactly here about that, Mister Mannion," Sean replied. "You see, that Ranger, Thad Dutton, was murdered on his way back to Laredo."

"That Ranger was murdered?" Mannion exclaimed.

"He was," Sean confirmed.

"You don't really believe I had anythin' to do with that."

"Right now we're just tryin' to figure out exactly what happened. We've been followin' Thad's back trail. The last place he was seen before he was killed was a ranch between here and Laredo. Before that it appears the last people to see Thad alive were here in Brooks County."

"Mebbe someone from that ranch killed Dutton," Mannion suggested.

"No, that's not it," Levi explained. "The owners are an old man and his wife. They fed Thad dinner and then sent him on his way."

"Rangers make lots of enemies. It's pretty likely Dutton ran across one of his and they plugged him," Mannion theorized.

"We never said he was shot," Levi pointed out.

"What?" Mannion stumbled, but quickly regained his composure. "That's right, you didn't. I just assumed he'd been gunned down."

"You assumed correctly," Sean told him. "Someone pumped two slugs into Thad. We're gonna find whoever did that. As our lieutenant would say, 'bet a hat on it.' "

"I hope you do," Mannion answered. "However, is there any real reason to believe Dutton's death is tied into this area or to his investigation of me?"

"None whatsoever," Sean conceded. "So far we're pretty much gropin' in the dark and shootin' blanks. Sooner or later though we'll figure this out. When we do Thad's killer will hang or die with a bellyful of Ranger lead."

"I'll help you any way I can, of course. You'll have full access to my books and records, and free rein to travel anywhere on this ranch. I'll also instruct John Spallone, the marshal in Mannionville, to cooperate fully with you."

"We've already met the marshal," Levi stated.

"You did? When?" Mannion asked.

"Last night," Sean explained. "We spent some

time in your town posin' as grubline ridin' cowpokes in search of a job. Had a few drinks at your saloon, and then spent the night at your hotel. So you see we did some checkin' up on you, before we rode out here."

"You had no right," Mannion spluttered.

"We're Texas Rangers investigatin' a killin' . . . the killin' of another Ranger," Levi snapped. "We had every right."

Mannion swallowed hard before replying, "Of course you did. I lost my head for a moment. You have to do whatever is necessary to track down that killer."

"Don't worry, everyone in town says you're the salt of the earth," Sean said. "Of course, they're pretty much in your back pocket. We've already spoken with Ethan Porter too, to answer your next question," he continued. "Porter's pretty much confirmed what you've told us."

"So you really have no reason to suspect me," Mannion stated.

"Nor Ethan Porter," Sean pointed out. "I do want to ask, however, why are you so dead set on taking over the Triangle VY?"

In answer, Mannion turned to the map behind his desk.

"You see this map? All the land shaded in blue belongs to me. That dot is Mannionville." He pointed to an area shaded in yellow, which was notched into the blue. "This yellow area belongs to an old cowboy named Jack Davies. I'd like to buy him out, but his spread really isn't that important to me. However," Mannion circled his fingertip around a large, pink-shaded area near the center of the map, which was completely surrounded by blue. "This pink segment is the Triangle VY. As you can see, it's practically in the middle of my range. Diablo Creek runs through Porter's land, so he controls the water rights. If he dammed the creek, that would dry up all my acreage downstream of his place. So you see I need his land, not only to complete my holdings, but to secure those water rights."

"That makes sense," Sean agreed.

"I'm glad you understand. As I said, I'll cooperate with your investigation. So, if you're finished right now, I do have work to get at."

"We're almost finished," Sean answered, "However, I do have to make one more request."

"As long as it's reasonable," Mannion answered.

"I need to ask your daughter a few questions."

"Dorothea? Why? Surely she's not involved in this."

"I didn't say she was. I understand she and Thad had seen each other a few times, so your daughter might have information she hasn't mentioned to anyone. Perhaps Thad said something to her."

"I'm not sure I can allow you to speak with her," Mannion said.

"I'll be discreet," Sean assured him. "You sure don't want me to have to obtain a judge's order, because that would cause all sorts of rumors to start flyin'."

"No, I reckon not," Mannion conceded. He picked up a bell from his desk, rang it, and a moment later Julio appeared at the door.

"Yes, Señor Mannion?"

"Julio, fetch Dorothea and bring her here. Also, bring Señora Mannion, if you would."

"Of course, sir."

"You don't mind if my wife is present, do you?" Mannion asked Sean. "Her presence would be a comfort to my daughter."

"Of course not," Sean agreed. "Do you have any other children?"

"Two sons, Michael and Charles. Mike has a small ranch of his own outside Uvalde and Chuck is out with a crew on the west side of my range, doctoring cattle. You don't plan on questioning them, do you?"

"I don't see any reason to, at least not right now," Sean answered.

"Good."

A woman, dressed in chef's clothing, appeared in the doorway. She held a tray of sugar-coated doughnuts.

"Excuse me," she said. "If I am not interrupting, I have Duncan's doughnuts for him."

"Of course you're not interrupting, Mary,"

237

Mannion told her. "Just bring them in and leave them on the desk."

"Certainly." Mary rushed across the room, placed the tray on the desk, and then scurried out.

"You'll have to forgive Mary. She's my wife's cousin. The rest of her family was murdered by a band of road agents during a stage robbery, so she's quite frightened of strangers," Mannion explained. "Since my wife is her only living relative, naturally we took her in. Mary's an excellent cook and baker. When I'm home, I have doughnuts at this time every day. Feel free to help yourselves."

"Thanks." Along with the rancher, Sean and Levi each took one of the pastries. They had just finished the snack when two extremely attractive women entered the den.

Sean and Levi came to their feet and removed their hats.

"Gentlemen, this is my wife, Georgia, and our daughter, Dorothea. Georgia, Dorothea, Rangers Sean Kennedy and Levi Mallory."

"I hope we'll be able to say we're pleased to meet you," Georgia sniffed. "Please, sit back down."

"We certainly agree," Sean answered. He settled back in his chair.

Sean and Levi could see why Thad Dutton would have wanted Dorothea Mannion. While Susanna May Porter was wholesomely pretty, even beautiful, Dorothea Mannion was a supremely magnificent woman. She was tall, like her father, but had deep red hair, almost auburn, its coppery highlights like smoldering flames. It was piled high on her head, and held in place with a mother-of-pearl comb. Her eyes were a deep green, her lips perfectly formed. She wore a light green velvet dress which complemented those eyes perfectly, and cut just low enough to give a glimpse of her full bosom. The dress seemed to flow over her gently curved hips and down to her ankles. Her perfume gave off the merest hint of lilacs and jasmine. Georgia Mannion was every bit as beautiful as her daughter, even though she was in her forties. Only the slightest of lines showed around her eyes, while her figure was still slim.

"You've disturbed our morning reading of Chaucer," Georgia complained, once everyone was seated. "We're in the midst of his *Canterbury Tales.*"

"In the original Middle English or a modern translation?" Sean asked.

"You know Chaucer, Ranger Kennedy?" Georgia asked, clearly surprised.

Sean grinned and replied, " 'Whan that Aprille, with his shoures soote, The droghte of Marche hath perced to the rote. And bathed every veyne in swich licuor, Of which vertu engendred is the floure . . .' Shall I go on?"

"No. You've proved your point," Georgia

conceded. "Most Texans aren't so well-read, so I was a bit taken back by your question."

"My mother believed in education and reading. Some of that rubbed off on me," Sean explained. "I'm also fond of Charles Dickens. For some reason those first lines of the *Canterbury Tales* have always stuck in my head."

"Indeed, then you certainly understand why we are anxious to get back to our reading," Georgia answered.

"We won't take up any more of your time than is absolutely necessary," Sean assured her. "I'll get right to the point. Miss Mannion, there was a Texas Ranger named Thad Dutton investigating your father. You and he were having a, shall we say, relationship. I'm sorry to have to tell you that Thad was murdered and we're trying to find his killer."

Dorothea drew in her breath, sharply. Tears welled in her eyes and her lower lip trembled. She struggled for a moment to retain control.

"Thaddeus murdered. That is terrible news," she quavered. "However, who insinuated he and I were . . ."

"Don't even utter that," Georgia ordered. "Ranger, how dare you say such things about my daughter?"

"I'm sorry, but let me remind all of you this is a murder investigation," Sean said. "I have to ask these questions, no matter how disturbing they might be. As far as who told us about you and Thad, Miss Mannion, that's not important. The fight between you and Susanna Porter was witnessed by quite a few folks, so it's common knowledge."

"Don't try and protect me, Mother, it's useless," Dorothea said. "There is nothing to hide because Thaddeus and I always met in public. Our relationship was open and aboveboard, so there was nothing at all improper about it." To Sean and Levi she continued, "I hope you both believe that."

"We don't have any reason not to," Sean assured her. "So will you answer our questions?"

"As best I can," Dorothea said.

"Thank you. I only have a few. Did Thad mention anything at all about why he suddenly gave up his inquiry into your father's affairs?"

"No, he gave no indication at all. The only thing I know for certain, as I am sure my father has told you, is he found no guilt on my father's part. He didn't end his investigation all that suddenly. Once Thaddeus was convinced my father had nothing to do with the raids on the Porter ranch, he really had no reason to remain here."

"All right, I have a question which may make you uncomfortable, but why do you think Susanna Porter was so upset about your meetings with Thad, in fact so upset she started a public fight?"

"I'm not quite certain," Dorothea replied. "At first I thought she was just jealous. On reflection I'm not so certain; however, I do have a theory. I have nothing to base this on except feminine intuition, but perhaps when Thad told Susanna there was nothing he could do to help her father, she became enraged. Of course she couldn't take her anger out on Thaddeus, at least not physically. So her resentment of me for seeing Thad made me the logical target. Susanna attacked me out of frustration and, of course, jealousy. Again, this is just rumor, but supposedly she thought Thaddeus would marry her."

"Seems like she was jumping the gun, since she hadn't known Thad all that long," Levi replied.

"That was my thought also," Dorothea agreed. "However, when a woman is in love, she often loses all sense of reason."

"The same can be said for a man," Sean responded. "I have one last question for you, and then you can go back to your reading."

"Certainly. What is it?"

"Thad always wore a real fancy belt with fine carvings on the leather, a Ranger badge engraved on the buckle, and his initials on the keepers. It wasn't on his body when we found him. Whoever killed Thad didn't have the chance to remove his belt, since Thad's horse ran off with him after he was shot. Do you recall that belt?"

"Of course, because it was wonderfully done."

"Was he was wearing it while you were meeting?"

"Yes, he did have it on the first several times we had supper. The last time, he did not."

"He didn't? That's very unusual. Thad never took that belt off," Sean explained. "You're certain he wasn't wearing it?"

"I'm absolutely positive," Dorothea insisted.

"He didn't mention where it was?"

"No he did not, and a lady certainly wouldn't ask about a man's missing belt."

"Thank you, I don't have anything else to ask," Sean said. "Can you think of anything, Levi?"

"No," Levi answered.

"Then if you have no further questions, you won't mind my asking you to leave," Mannion stated. "You've already taken up enough of our time and upset my daughter."

"Not at all," Sean answered. "We may take you up on your offer to let us examine your files or ride your land to see if we can come up with something. However, right now that doesn't seem necessary."

"Anything you need, just ask," Mannion replied. "I want to see whoever killed Ranger Dutton brought to justice as much as you men do."

"We appreciate that," Levi replied.

"Since our business is done, I'll have Julio see you out."

"Thank you. We're grateful to all of you for

your cooperation. If you should think of anything which may be helpful, we'll be at the Heart of Texas Hotel in Falfurrias for a few days. You can get in touch with us there; or leave a message with Sheriff Newton."

"We'll do that," Mannion assured him. He rang the bell on his desk, and Julio appeared a moment later.

"Yes, Señor Mannion?"

"Julio, the Rangers have the information they wanted. Please see them to the door and have Javier bring their horses around, and then return here. I have something which needs to be done."

"Of course Señor Mannion. Follow me, señores, por favor."

Once Sean and Levi were on the veranda, Dorothea broke down in tears. Weeping bitterly, she ran to her bedroom, slamming the door shut behind her.

Mannion waited until his servant returned.

"Are the Rangers gone?"

"Yes, they have ridden beyond the gate."

"Good. Julio, find Bill Hollister and tell him to send Carlos Delgado to me, pronto."

"Yes, Señor Mannion."

Mannion poured himself a full tumbler of whiskey and downed it in one swallow. He poured another, downed that, and then lit up a fresh cigar. He paced the room, smoking and having several more drinks, until he heard approaching footsteps and the clinking of spurs.

Carlos Delgado stepped into the room.

"You wanted to see me, Mister Duncan?"

"Yeah, Carlos, I thought I told you to make sure that Ranger's body could never be found. You assured me it wouldn't be."

"That's correct."

"Well, it was and two Rangers were just here. They're looking for whoever killed Dutton. Why wasn't his body buried or dropped into a ravine somewhere, and why did you lie to me about that?"

Delgado shrugged.

"Dutton's foot got hung up in the stirrup after I plugged him and his horse ran off with him. I tried to catch it, but it ran down a steep bank, and my cayuse slipped and fell goin' after it. Nearly rolled on me and broke my leg. I jumped clear in the nick of time. That Ranger's bronc must've been part mountain goat to go down that slope with him hangin' over its side. Since we were in the middle of nowhere when I shot Dutton, I figured his body'd fall off that horse before it was ever discovered, or if someone did find him, by then he wouldn't be able to be identified. Did those Rangers happen to say where Dutton was found?"

"No, they didn't, but someone did find him. Now we've got two more Texas Rangers snoopin' around."

"I wouldn't worry about them. They have no way to connect me to that killin'."

"You'd better hope they don't come up with something," Mannion warned him.

"If they do, then there'll be two more dead Rangers. This time their bodies won't be found."

"If it comes to that, they'd better not be. Now get outta here, Carlos. I've got work to do. If I need you later I'll let you know."

"Sure. Don't fret, boss, things'll be just fine."

Sean and Levi rode for two miles before pulling up.

"That sure didn't get us very far, pardner," Levi noted.

"We didn't get anything more to go on, but I'm convinced Thad's death is tied into his investigation of Duncan Mannion," Sean replied.

"I am too, more than ever. What's our next move?"

"For today, we're gonna head back to Mannionville. We'll let word spread that we're Rangers diggin' into Mannion's affairs, and see what kind of reaction we get."

"Should be interesting, to say the least," Levi laughed. "After that?"

"Tomorrow, I'm ridin' for Falfurrias. You're gonna stick with me for a few miles to make it appear as if we're both headed there," Sean explained. "Then, I want you to double back and keep your eyes on things around here. Mebbe you'll come up with somethin'."

"I'll concentrate on Mannion's spread," Levi decided. "I'll also try to talk with Brad Porter if I get the chance. What'll you be doin' in Falfurrias?"

"Woody Woodson should have arrived by now. I'll fill him in on everything we've found so far. Maybe he'll have more information for us. I've also got to send wires to Headquarters and Lieutenant Blawcyzk. With luck, Thad sent a report to Austin before he was killed."

"Here's hopin'. We need a break of some kind," Levi answered.

"Boy howdy, don't I know it," Sean agreed. "I also want to go over those land records once more. I have a feelin' we missed something."

"Anything in particular?"

"I can't quite put my thumb on it. I just have a gut feelin' there's something in those papers we should have spotted."

"All right, but how long you figurin' on bein' in Falfurrias?"

"I'll be back in a couple of days, three tops."

"Good. Well, since we've got nothing to do but eat, sleep, and visit the saloon for the rest of the day, let's head for town, pardner."

Sean and Levi spurred their horses into a gallop.

Chapter 12

Dan Devine was at his usual post when Sean strode into the Brooks County Sheriff's Office late the next morning. The deputy looked up from his desk and grinned when he recognized the big Ranger.

"Howdy, Ranger," he greeted Sean. "Welcome back."

"Howdy, Dan," Sean replied. "The sheriff in?"

"He's in his office," Devine confirmed. "Just head on back there. We've been wonderin' when you might return."

"Thanks." Sean headed down the hall to Dave Newton's office.

Newton was behind his desk, still half-hidden by a mound of unfinished paperwork.

"Howdy, Dave," Sean called. "Looks like you haven't gotten very far with those files."

Newton fairly leapt to his feet at Sean's greeting. A half-smoked cigarette dangled from his lips.

"Sean, glad to see you're back and you're right. These papers'll be the death of me yet. Is there any news? Have you made any progress findin' Thad Dutton's killer?"

"About as much as you have with that paperwork," Sean ruefully admitted. "It's a puzzle, all right. I'm hopin' you have some word for me. Is Woody Woodson here?"

Newton shook his head.

"I haven't seen hide nor hair of another Ranger, or anyone who even vaguely resembles your description of Woodson," he answered. "Nor a steeldust cayuse with a star on his forehead and one stocking, either. Sure wish I had better news. Sorry, Sean."

"Somethin' bad must have happened to Woody," Sean said. "That's the only logical explanation. There's no other reason he wouldn't be here by now."

"I hate to agree with that, but you're probably right," Newton conceded. "Speaking of missing persons, where's your pardner, Levi?"

"He's stickin' around Mannionville, keepin' an eye on things there, particularly the Lazy DM," Sean explained. "I'll be headin' back there tomorrow or the day after."

"Then you must have dug up somethin'," Newton observed.

"Not enough to prove anything," Sean answered. "So, what now?"

"I need to stop by the telegraph office. I'm going to send a message to Austin and see if Thad telegraphed a report to Headquarters before he was killed, and another to Lieutenant Blawcyzk to let him know what we've uncovered so far. I guess I'll also have to let him know Woody's turned up missin'."

"Mebbe Woodson had to turn back for some reason. He might be back in Laredo with your company," Newton responded.

"Maybe," Sean answered, although he didn't think Newton believed that any more than he did.

"Mind if I walk along with you?" the sheriff requested. "You can fill me in on what you've learned on the way."

"Not at all. I'll be glad for the company," Sean agreed. "Besides, I want to go to the land office again. I dunno why, but I can't help feelin' I missed something in those papers. I want to look them over once more."

Newton glanced at the regulator clock on his wall. "The land office'll be closed for dinner by the time we get there. Why don't you send your wires, we'll grab some chuck at the Bluebonnet, and after that we'll examine those papers again."

"That's as good a plan as any," Sean agreed. "Lead the way, Sheriff."

After they ate, Sean and Newton spent the afternoon poring over the records for the Triangle VY and the Lazy DM. Prescott Landis also scoured the documents for any inconsistencies. Sean finally pushed back from the counter in frustration.

"I still can't find anything that means much," he muttered. "It's mostly the usual legal mumbo-jumbo."

"I'm afraid you're right," Landis agreed, "but I'm certain Mannion will find some way to force Porter out of his home. It might be a hidden clause in the sales agreement. The problem is, those papers won't be filed with my office until after the transfer of the Triangle VY to Mannion is completed."

"I'll bet you've got something there, Pres," Newton exclaimed. "How about it, Sean?"

"That's gotta be it. Good thinkin', Pres," Sean agreed. "Those papers'll be on file with the attorneys handling the sale. You must know who they are, Dave."

"I do. Hiram Beckett is Mannion's lawyer and Hezekiah Trask is Porter's."

"Let's go talk to them."

"They may not want to cooperate," Landis pointed out.

"Pres is right," Newton agreed, "and it's too late in the day to get a court order. Judge Whittaker will have closed up shop. For that matter, Beckett and Trask have probably gone home by now, too. We won't be able to do anything further until the morning, Sean."

Sean muttered an oath.

"Then I guess that'll have to do. Meantime, I've got to head back to the Western Union and see if there's any replies to my messages. Pres, thanks for your help."

"Anytime, Ranger. Sure wish we could've found something."

"Same here. Good night, Pres."

" 'Night, Ranger. 'Night, Sheriff."

" 'Night, Pres. Appreciate everything," Newton said.

Sean's frustration continued when Barney at the telegraph office informed him there had been no reply to either of his messages.

"Is there a possibility a wire still might come in tonight?" Sean asked.

"It's possible, but there won't be anyone here to receive it. We're not a round-the-clock office like the ones at railroad depots or in the big cities," Barney explained. "In fact, Ranger, you caught me just as I was about to lock up. You'll have to come back first thing in the morning. I open at eight o'clock sharp and I check the overnight wires right off."

"All right, Barney," Sean answered. "I'll see you then."

Sean had supper at the Bluebonnet Café and then stopped by the livery stable to check on Ghost, rub him down, and give him a licorice.

"I just can't figure this one out, buddy," he told the blue roan, scratching Ghost's ears. "Sure wish Woody would turn up. That'd set my mind at ease some. Well, nothing for you to do but rest, horse. I'll see you in the morning." Sean fondly slapped Ghost on his neck.

After leaving the stable, Sean ambled along the streets. While he enjoyed a good drink, he rarely got drunk. However, with his irritation building at meeting nothing but dead ends in his investigation, he was seriously considering giving in to the temptation to get rip-roaring drunk. He reversed course to start for the nearest saloon, Rosita's Fandango.

Sean was two buildings away from Rosita's when the tolling of church bells caught his attention. Two Mexican women, dressed in colorful skirts and crisp white blouses, their shoulders enrobed with brilliantly hued shawls, hurried past him. Their heads were covered with black lace scarves.

"Señoras, wait, por favor," Sean called after them. They turned to face the big Ranger.

"Si, Señor. What is it?" the older of the two asked.

"Why are the church bells tolling? Is there a special service tonight?"

"Si, Señor. Tonight we are having a Novena in honor of San Francisco de Assisi," she answered. "He is the patron saint of our church. May we go now? We must hurry, or we will be late."

"Of course, Señora, gracias," Sean replied. He looked after the women as they hurried toward the church.

Sean stood in reflection for a few moments. *It's been a long time since I've been to church. Too long, in fact. I can't recall the last time I've been to Sunday Mass. My Irish grandmother would drag me to church by my ears if she knew how long it's been. Mebbe the Lord's tryin' to tell me something.*

The tolling of the church bell again intruded on his thoughts.

I reckon I'll head for church. Some prayers might help. Lord knows nothing else has so far.

Sean reversed course again and reached the church just as the service began. The warmth of the building's adobe walls and the soft glow from its stained glass windows seemed to comfort him when he entered. He removed his Stetson, genuflected, and took a seat in the rearmost pew. The women he had stopped on the street turned to him and smiled.

Sean bowed his head and made the Sign of the Cross.

While Sean was making little progress in Falfurrias, Levi was hardly having better luck. He had spent most of the day observing the comings and goings at the Lazy DM, seeing nothing but the usual activities of a working ranch. Early in the afternoon, Carlos Delgado and two other cowboys rode out in the direction of town. Levi considered following, but decided against it. The hours dragged on and while Levi desperately wanted a cigarette, he couldn't chance it. Someone might glimpse a wisp of smoke or catch the odor of burning tobacco. He had decided to return to Mannionville, when the approach of a rider on a high-spirited palomino changed his mind.

"That's Susanna Porter," he muttered. "What the devil is she doin' comin' here?"

Monte raised his head to whinny a greeting to Susanna's golden-hided mount. Quickly, Levi grabbed his horse's nose.

"Oh no, you don't, pal," he warned the gelding. "You're not gonna give us away."

Levi backed his mount even further into the brush.

"Now things are finally gettin' interesting, Monte. Let's just sit here awhile and see what happens."

Susanna rode up to the main house, Javier took her horse away, and Julio led her inside.

"Gotta admit, I never expected to see that," Levi whispered. "Sure wish I was a fly on the wall."

Susanna remained inside for the better part of two hours. When she emerged from the house, she was alone, to Levi's disappointment. Javier brought out her palomino. Susanna mounted and trotted off.

"We're gonna follow her, Monte," Levi decided.

"I'll have a few questions for that lady when we catch up to her." He climbed into his saddle and put Monte into a slow jog, intending to keep just out of Susanna's sight.

Levi had gone less than a quarter mile before another rider came out of the brush. Intent on Susanna, the rider didn't notice the Ranger approaching. Levi had to haul Monte up short to avoid a collision with the other man's wiry pinto. He grabbed the pinto's reins.

"Whoa, easy there, son."

"Let go of my horse. What're you doin', Mister?" the rider demanded.

"I was about to ask you the same thing . . . Brad," Levi answered.

The pinto's rider was Bradley Porter.

"Ranger!" Brad gasped as he recognized Levi.

"That's right. Now, do you want to tell me what's goin' on around here? We can start with why your sister's visitin' Duncan Mannion."

Brad started and his shoulders slumped. Levi's shot had hit its mark.

"I reckon we'd better talk," he said. "I've been wantin' to do that anyway, ever since the day you and your pardner came to our ranch."

"Good, let's find a place where we can set a spell," Levi answered. This was the opportunity he'd been seeking, to question young Porter. Following Susanna would have to wait.

The Ranger and youngster rode for about two

miles, until they reached a small break in the scrub.

"We'll stop here," Levi decided. "We can get back off the trail far enough so it's unlikely anyone'll spot us."

"All right," Brad agreed.

They led their horses off the trail and unsaddled. The mounts were picketed to crop at some sparse bunch grass. Levi built a small, almost smokeless fire and boiled some coffee. Once it was ready, he poured a mug for the boy and one for himself. He brought out the makings and offered them to the youngster.

"Smoke?" he offered.

"Thanks," Brad answered. He took a cigarette paper and some Durham, rolled a quirly, and lit it. He leaned back against a rock and took a long drag on the cigarette. He closed his eyes and exhaled, smoke trailing from his nostrils.

Levi studied the boy while he also built and lit a cigarette.

"Whenever you're ready, Brad."

"All right, see I'm pretty sure Carlos Delgado killed Thad Dutton. I think my sister's involved too."

"What?" Levi exclaimed. "Mebbe you'd better start from the beginning. Take your time and try not to leave anything out."

"Okay. You already know about Susanna and Thad, but you don't know about Dorothea Mannion and Thad."

"Actually, we do," Levi corrected him. "Dorothea told us all about that when we were at the Lazy DM."

"So you know about the fight my sister had with her?"

"Yes, we first heard about that from the bartender at the Devil Dog."

"Figures, Curly would enjoy spreadin' news like that. His tongue wags more'n an old spinster's at a church social," Brad muttered. "That set-to was nothin' compared to the fight Susanna had with Thad. Not a fistfight, of course, although Susanna slapped Thad a couple of times. Her shoutin' was loud enough to wake the dead. She told Thad to get out and never come back."

"Which he did?"

"He did, but he came back a couple of times tryin' to get his belt back. Then he returned one other time."

"You know we're lookin' for Thad's belt?" Levi questioned.

"Yeah, I was hidin' under the window while you were at our place. I heard every word of the conversation. My sister lied to your pardner. She has, or I should say had, Thad's belt."

"Thad never took that belt off, except when he was takin' a bath," Levi answered.

"Or when he was with a woman?" Brad asked.

"Yeah, I reckon so," Levi reluctantly answered.

He knew where this conversation was headed and it made him uncomfortable. A boy shouldn't have to divulge such things about his own sister.

"That's how Susanna got Thad's belt. He was with her, more than once," Brad said, matter-of-factly. "My dad didn't know that, or at least chose to ignore it, mebbe hopin' if Thad could help us keep our place it would be worth the price."

Brad took a swallow of his coffee, and another long drag on his cigarette. His voice began to quaver slightly when he continued.

"After Susanna found out about Thad and Dorothea, naturally she was furious. After a few days she calmed down or so it seemed. Then one day I was checkin' our fenceline along the Lazy DM boundary when I saw Susanna ridin' toward Mannion's place. She didn't see me. Naturally, I was curious, so I followed her. Sure enough, she went straight to the main house. She was there for quite some time."

"You think she went there to confront Dorothea?"

"I doubt it, since that was after their fight in Mannionville."

"So what reason would she have for goin' to the Lazy DM?"

"I wasn't sure at first, and I'm still not positive, except that wasn't her only visit. She went there several more times I know of and mebbe a few others when I wasn't around."

Brad hesitated. He finished his cigarette, ground it out, and tossed the butt aside.

"I'm sorry, Ranger. It ain't easy talkin' about this. After all, no matter what she might've done, Susanna is still my sister."

"I know, son," Levi sympathized. "I appreciate your tellin' me this. Why do you think Susanna did go to the Lazy DM? Could she have been seeing Duncan Mannion?"

"No, I have a feelin' she went there to hire someone to have Thad killed."

"Carlos Delgado?"

"Yeah, Carlos Delgado." Brad bitterly spit the name out. "If Carlos Delgado did kill Thad, you can bet Duncan Mannion was in on it, too. Delgado wouldn't make a move without Mannion's say-so."

"If Thad hadn't found any proof Mannion was behind the raids on your ranch, Mannion would have no reason to kill him," Levi pointed out. "Sean and I both suspect Mannion's behind Thad's killin' and Delgado matches the description we were given of an hombre trailin' Thad. However, so far we haven't come up with any solid evidence."

"I might have what you need," Brad answered. "Remember I told you Thad had come back to see Susanna a couple more times after she found out about him and Dorothea?"

"Yeah."

"Those visits were also *after* Susanna's first couple of trips to Mannion's place. The first time, Susanna got Thad drunk and I mean really drunk. She didn't realize I was home, because me and Pa were supposed to be out overnight with some of the men, keepin' guard over our cattle. There was a full Comanche moon that night and Pa thought the rustlers might make a raid. I'd twisted my ankle in a chuckhole, real bad. I could barely stand, let alone walk or climb into a saddle, so Pa sent me home to rest it."

Brad halted, clearly hesitant to continue.

"Could I have another cigarette, Ranger?"

"Sure."

Levi passed Brad his sack of Durham and his cigarette papers. Brad's hands trembled as he built the smoke and then lit it. He drew in a long puff of smoke.

"Thanks. Anyway, I heard everything that night. Susanna told Thad she wanted to be with him, despite his seein' Dorothea. Next thing I knew is they headed past my bedroom to Susanna's. I didn't want to know any more. Just the thought of what they were doin' made me sick to my stomach. I tossed and turned most of the night, but finally fell asleep, until I was woken up by a lot of shoutin'. Thad and Susanna were arguin' again. Thad wanted his belt and Susanna told him he couldn't have it."

"Thad let her keep his belt?" Levi questioned.

"Not willingly. She must've hidden it, then when he woke up lookin' for it told him she was keepin' it, for what he'd done to her. She said if he didn't leave right then, she'd go to the law and claim he'd had his way with her against her will. They argued some more, until he finally left. Of course, I never let Susanna know I'd heard everything. Thad came back a couple more times, like I told you, but she wouldn't give him his belt. Of course Thad couldn't make much of a fuss, especially with my pa around."

"All right, so Susanna kept Thad's belt, and she's been visitin' the Lazy DM," Levi said. "How does that tie in with Carlos Delgado and Thad's murder?"

"I'm comin' to that, Ranger," Brad answered. "A while back, I rode over to Mannionville. My pa doesn't want me goin' there and he'd whale the hide off me if he knew, but I'm sweet on a gal there. Her name's Jane Sue. Her ma's a widow who runs a dress shop. I hadn't seen Jane for almost two weeks, so I took a chance Pa wouldn't miss me for a few hours and headed to town. I was tyin' my horse up in a side alley when I spotted Carlos Delgado comin' out of the saloon. He was wearin' Thad's belt."

"Which means your sister must've given it to him," Levi said.

"Seems so, anyway, next thing I know this stranger is yellin' at Delgado, wantin' to know why he's wearin' Thad Dutton's belt. Delgado never said a word. He just pulled his gun and shot that hombre. Never gave him a chance. Plugged him right in the belly, left him lyin' there in the street gut-shot, and no one'd help that poor jasper. I wanted to, but didn't dare. Delgado would've drilled me too, for certain. If he hadn't the marshal would have. I saw John Spallone plug an hombre once just for gettin' dust on his boots. I just waited a spell until I was sure I wouldn't be spotted, and then lit out of there."

Levi felt as if he'd been punched in the gut, hard.

"That stranger, Brad. Was he young, tall and real lanky, with sandy hair and a thin mustache? Brown eyes?"

"I didn't see his eyes, but yeah, the rest sounds like him," Brad confirmed.

"That was Woody Woodson, another Ranger. He was supposed to meet up with me and Sean in Falfurrias," Levi answered. Finally he knew what had happened to Woodson. Delgado had the murders of two Rangers to answer for.

"I had a hunch that hombre was a Ranger. Otherwise why would he have known that belt was Thad's?" Brad replied.

"That's right. Now we can pin the murder of one Ranger on Delgado for certain, probably two. Brad, do you realize what this means for your sister? It appears Susanna's an accessory to murder. That's probably why she visited Mannion today; because she's gettin' worried they might be found out."

"I know. That's why I didn't say anything when you were at our place," Brad said. "I didn't want to believe Susanna could do somethin' like this. I sure didn't want my pa to find out. Once he does, it'll just about kill him. I couldn't keep quiet any longer, because I liked Thad, despite everything. Whatever happens to Susanna, she brought on herself. I'll stand by her, as best I can, but if she helped get Thad killed, I can't do much for her."

"That's still a puzzle. Do you really think your sister could be so jealous she'd have a man killed?" Levi asked.

"I dunno," Brad responded. "What about Mannion? Seems like he'd be takin' an awful chance, havin' Delgado kill a Ranger and for what? No one had anything on him, not even Thad."

"Not as long a chance as you'd think," Levi explained. "If anything went wrong, he'd just claim Delgado acted on his own. It'd be hard to prove otherwise. I'm bettin' Thad had dug something up, or at least Mannion is convinced he had. I'm guessin' he and your sister decided to throw in together. She wanted to get even with Thad and Mannion needed him out of the way, before he got back to Laredo."

"What about the belt? Why would Delgado want that?" Brad asked.

"It was probably part of his price for killin' Thad. It's a mighty fancy belt. If Delgado's like most gunmen, he's got a big ego. He'd want that belt for a trophy and he'd have to show it off, 'specially since he got it off a Texas Ranger he'd gunned down. Far as him wearin' it, he undoubtedly figured he was safe enough, long as he stuck to the ranch or Mannionville."

"You're right. The marshal in town sure ain't gonna buck Duncan Mannion," Brad said. "Spallone knows who butters his bread."

"Can you tell me anything more about that marshal?" Levi asked. "His name's kinda familiar, but I can't quite recollect where I've heard it."

"John Spallone? He keeps the lid on the town for Mannion," Brad answered. "No one dares cross the marshal, especially with Mannion backin' his every play. Word is Spallone's a gunslinger who drifted to Texas from Kansas way. He's supposed to have killed quite a few men back there. He takes care of Mannionville, while Delgado and a few of his pardners watch out for Mannion and his ranch. I'm certain Delgado's bunch is behind the rustlin' of our cattle, but there's been no way to prove that."

"That's where I know Spallone's name," Levi said. "I saw it on a wanted dodger quite some time ago. We don't need to pin a rustlin' charge on

Delgado now, because we've got him for murder. With your testimony, we can make sure he hangs. We just might have enough to hang Mannion too."

Levi stood up and kicked dirt over the fire. He picked up the coffee pot and cups to put them in his saddlebags, then tossed the blanket and saddle on Monte's back.

"What're you gonna do now, Ranger?" Brad asked.

"I saw Delgado and a couple other riders headin' for Mannionville earlier," Levi answered. "I'm goin' there to arrest Delgado for murder. I just hope he hasn't decided we're gettin' too close to him and has skipped town."

"He wouldn't," Brad replied, "as long as Mannion is backing him."

Is Mannion still backing him? Levi thought and then said, "If Mannion's gettin' worried, he might've cut Delgado loose." He tightened his cinches.

"What about me?" Brad asked.

"You head back home and act like nothing's happened, if you can," Levi ordered. "If you don't think you can pull it off, stay out on the range until I get back."

"I'll head home," Brad replied. "Pa'd wonder what had happened to me if I didn't. I've been keepin' quiet around Susanna for weeks now, so a few more hours won't matter."

"Bueno, Brad, thanks again. I know this wasn't easy for you," Levi said. He slipped the bridle over Monte's ears.

"It was even harder keepin' it inside," Brad answered. "It actually feels good gettin' this off my chest. I just hope it doesn't kill Pa. He always favored Susanna."

"Don't sell your pa short, son," Levi advised. "He'll get through it and mebbe he'll get to keep the Triangle VY after all. You wait here for fifteen or twenty minutes after I ride out, just in case anyone happens to be around. It wouldn't do to be seen together."

"All right," Brad agreed. "Good luck, Ranger."

"Thanks, son."

Levi swung into the saddle, wheeled his horse around, and disappeared into the brush.

Chapter 13

Levi realized he would have more than just Carlos Delgado to face, if the gunman was still in Mannionville. Duncan Mannion controlled the town and just about everyone in it. Levi had no doubt that Curly, the bartender at the Devil Dog, had seen Delgado gun down Woody Woodson, but knew better than to mention it to a couple of strangers who'd just ridden into town. Therefore, the saloon man never said a word about that killing to Sean and Levi. Levi was also positive that the marshal, John Spallone, had been there when Woodson was killed. If somehow Woody had shot Delgado instead of taking the gunman's fatal bullet, Spallone undoubtedly would have put a slug into the Ranger, then claimed he had just stopped a cold-blooded killer. Levi could count on no help from him. With the rest of the town either indebted to Duncan Mannion or just plain scared of him, there would be no assistance from the townsfolk either. Levi would be on his own when he attempted to bring in Delgado for the killings of Woody Woodson and Thad Dutton.

Wanting to reach town before Delgado left, Levi kept Monte at a hard lope most of the distance to Mannionville, before reining the horse to a walk on the outskirts of town. While the jaded gelding shuffled through the dust of the main street, Levi lifted his Colt from its holster, put a bullet into the empty chamber, then slid the gun loosely back in place.

"I'm gonna want to know where Spallone is at when I go after Delgado, Monte," he muttered to his horse. "I'll stop at his office first."

Levi heeled the gelding into a slightly faster pace. When he reached the hotel, he stopped to allow his horse a drink from the trough in front and then dismounted. He led Monte across the street and looped his reins over the hitch rail in the alleyway next to the marshal's office, alongside a flashy, long-legged sorrel. Satisfied his horse was in the shade and as safe as possible from any stray bullets, Levi left him there and climbed the stairs to the office. He pushed open the door and stepped inside. Spallone was seated behind his desk, leaning back in his chair, his feet propped up on the desktop. He dropped them to the floor with surprise when he saw Levi standing in the doorway.

"Afternoon, Marshal," Levi said, a thin smile on his lips. "My pardner and I missed you when we came back the other day. I thought I'd introduce myself properly this time. I'm a Texas Ranger. Levi Mallory."

"So I've been told," Spallone replied, returning Levi's thin smile with one of his own. He glared malevolently at the Ranger. "What brings you back to town?"

"I think you already know that, Marshal. I'm lookin' for Carlos Delgado. I'm gonna arrest him for the murders of Texas Rangers Woody Woodson and Thad Dutton."

"I know about Thad Dutton bein' killed, but who's that other Ranger . . . Woodson, you say? Don't know anything about him," Spallone sneered.

"I think you do," Levi growled. "He was gunned down in the middle of the road, right in front of your office."

"I don't recall any such shootin'," Spallone retorted. "You got any proof against Carlos?"

"I've got all the evidence I need," Levi stated. "I'm not gonna waste my breath askin' you where Delgado's at, Marshal. I know you wouldn't tell me. I'm not expectin' any help from you either, just stay out of my way. You try and interfere, and I'll see you in jail . . . or in Hell."

"I'm a duly appointed officer of the law. You're in my town, Ranger. I'd be mighty careful," Spallone warned.

"You mean Duncan Mannion's town, don't you, Marshal?" Levi snapped. "If I were you, I wouldn't try puttin' a bullet in my back. You might end up catchin' one instead."

"I've never plugged a man in the back yet, Ranger, and I'm not about to start," Spallone retorted. "It makes no never-mind to me about you and Delgado. He's your business. I'll stay right here in my office and finish my siesta."

"You do that. Just don't forget, I'll still be watchin' my back, Marshal."

Levi turned on his heel and stalked out of Spallone's office. He paused on the steps, carefully scanning the street. He studied windows and doorways, looking for any lurking gunman ready to put an ambush bullet into his chest. Seeing none, he started slowly toward the livery stable. When he reached the barn, he slid open the door, staying to one side, out of the way of any bullets from a drygulcher inside. He waited until his vision adjusted to the barn's gloomy interior, and then stepped inside. He stopped in front of the fourth stall down. It held a chunky roan gelding.

That's Delgado's horse, so at least he hasn't left town, Levi thought. The Lazy DM gunman's companions' horses were in two stalls on the opposite side of the aisle way.

Levi left the stable and headed for the Devil Dog Saloon. When he reached the establishment, he took out his gun, holding it at the ready. Again, he paused just outside the door, under the wooden awning sheltering the boardwalk, until his eyes adjusted somewhat to the dark barroom, then pushed open the batwings and stepped inside. Curly was behind the mahogany bar and a few patrons were scattered about. The percentage girls were clustered at the far end of the bar, sipping watered-down whiskey. There was no sign of Carlos Delgado or his two companions. Cautiously, Levi slid his gun back in its holster and stepped up to the bar, far enough down from the door to avoid a bushwhacker's bullet from the street.

"Howdy, Ranger," Curly called. "Hot enough, ain't it? I reckon you're after a beer? I'll pour you one right now."

"Don't worry about a beer. I'm lookin' for Carlos Delgado. Has he been in here?" Levi questioned.

"Ain't seen hide nor hair of Carlos all day," Curly said. "Why're you lookin' for him?"

"I'm going to place him under arrest for the murder of two Texas Rangers. He shot down one of 'em right in front of your saloon, Curly," Levi growled. "You sorta forgot to tell me and my pardner about that."

"My memory ain't what it used to be," Curly shrugged. "Not to mention a man could get in a whole heap of trouble by spreadin' tales like that."

"He could also find himself in jail for obstructin' justice," Levi retorted.

"I reckon he could at that," Curly conceded. "You want that beer? You might as well wait here for Delgado. If he's in town, he'll stop by sooner or later."

"I'm right here."

Levi turned to see Carlos Delgado framed in the doorway. The gunman's hand hovered over the gun on his right hip. Around Delgado's waist was the belt which had belonged to Thad Dutton. He glared maliciously at Levi. His two companions were behind him. They slid along the wall and sat at the nearest table.

"You're lookin' for me, Ranger?" Delgado challenged.

"That's right." Levi eased his own hand toward his Colt. Delgado had appeared so suddenly the Ranger couldn't get his gun out in time to cover the outlaw.

"What for?" Delgado asked.

"I think you know, but to make certain, I'm placin' you under arrest for the murders of Texas Rangers Thad Dutton and Woody Woodson. The belt you're wearin' belonged to Dutton. That's enough evidence to hang you, Delgado."

"A young lady gave me this fine belt," Delgado answered, an unctuous smile on his face. "As far as you takin' me in, that sure ain't gonna happen, Ranger. I'm gonna plug you right in your lousy guts."

Delgado's hand was a blur as it slashed downward for his Colt. He lifted the gun from its holster, leveled it, and fired.

Levi shot a split-second after Delgado. He staggered when the gunman's bullet struck him in the belly. His own bullet missed Delgado and shattered the saloon's front window. Before Levi could get off another shot, Delgado shot him in the belly again. Levi clutched one hand to his middle and folded at the waist.

His knees began to buckle. He was dropping to the floor, still struggling to lift his pistol and put a bullet into Delgado, when the gunman shot him a third time, sending yet another slug into Levi's belly. Levi fell and landed face-down on the sawdust-covered floor. He tried to push himself up, but then collapsed.

Delgado shoved the toe of his boot under Levi's ribs and rolled him onto his back. Levi stared up at the gunman through pain-glazed eyes.

"You might've . . . got . . . me, but I'm . . . takin' . . . you with me . . . Delgado," the Ranger gasped. He strained to center the Colt he still gripped on Delgado's chest.

Delgado thumbed back the hammer of his pistol, pulled the trigger, and sent one final bullet into Levi's gut. Levi's body jerked from the impact. He grunted, shuddered, and then lay unmoving. Blood began puddling around him.

"Told ya, Ranger, and I got you right in your belly," Delgado muttered. As he calmly began reloading his gun, he nodded at Levi's body.

"Somebody better get him outta here," Delgado muttered. "He ain't good for business."

Delgado whirled when several shots sounded from the street, followed by rapid hoof beats. He was halfway through the door when John Spallone burst through the batwings. The marshal's smoking six-gun was in his hand.

"Marshal!" Delgado shouted. "What the devil's goin' on out there?"

"Porter's kid," Spallone answered. "I saw him ride into town a few minutes after that Ranger. I didn't think anythin' of that at first, until I started over here once I heard the gunfire. The kid was in the alley alongside this saloon, runnin' for his horse." Spallone gestured toward Levi's body. "He must've seen you plug this Ranger."

"Did you stop him?" Delgado demanded.

"I winged him, just as he got on his horse. He kept goin', but from the way he was ridin', all slumped over in the saddle, I figure I hit him hard. He won't get far."

"We'd better make sure of that, Spallone. Get your horse. Meet us at the livery. Kansas, Joker, let's move, we've gotta stop that kid."

Two minutes later, they were pounding out of Mannionville on Brad Porter's trail. They rode for two miles without seeing any sign of the wounded youngster.

"That kid's gotta be tough, stayin' in the saddle for so long after gettin' shot," Spallone observed.

"Mebbe you didn't hit him," Delgado answered.

"Nah, I'm certain I got him," Spallone assured

the killer. "He yelped, and fell against his horse, so I know I plugged him. I shot him again, but somehow he still managed to drag himself onto that cayuse and take off. He can't last much longer."

They kept their horses at a dead run for another mile.

"Up ahead," Joker Henry said. He pointed at a dust cloud in the distance. "It has to be the kid."

"We've got him now," Delgado snarled. He dug his spurs deep into his horse's flanks. The tiring animal leapt forward at the pain of steel ripping into his hide.

In another quarter mile, Delgado and the others pulled their horses to a halt. Barely two hundred yards ahead Brad Porter was slumped over his pinto, as his exhausted mount wandered aimlessly along the trail. Delgado pulled out his Winchester. Before he could take aim and fire, Brad slipped off his horse and tumbled into a brush-choked ravine.

"Told you I got him," Spallone triumphantly stated.

"Let's just make sure of that," Delgado responded. Rifle still at the ready, he put his horse into a walk, the others following. When they reached the spot where Brad had fallen, they peered intently into the ravine. The youth's body was nowhere in sight, completely hidden by the dense scrub.

"There's no way he's still alive," Kansas Casey observed. "Even if he is somehow still breathin', he won't be for long. He'll never be able to climb outta there, 'specially not with a couple of slugs in him."

"I reckon you're right, Kansas," Delgado admitted. "It's a lucky break for us. Now we'll have the chance to get rid of that Ranger's body before his pardner comes lookin' for him. With no body, there's nothin' to connect any of us to his killin'."

"You know that other Ranger'll come lookin' for him anyhow. Those hombres don't give up, 'specially when it comes to one of their own," Casey protested.

"Let him show up. He'll get just what the other three got, a bellyful of lead," Delgado sneered. He started to slide his rifle back into its scabbard, but then stopped. He looked up the trail to where Brad's pinto had halted. The tired mount was nibbling at some buffalo grass.

"We'll make certain of that kid," Delgado said. He lifted the Winchester, aimed, and fired. Brad's pinto leapt into the air, screamed in pain and terror, and fell to its side, thrashing help- lessly. The horse's movements soon ceased. Delgado slid his rifle back in its boot.

"There, now even if that kid is somehow still alive, he can't go far without his bronc," Delgado said. "Let's go."

Chapter 14

The next morning, as usual, Sean awoke with the sun. He washed, shaved, dressed, and then headed for breakfast at a small restaurant and general store he'd discovered, The Horse's Mouth. It was a cozy establishment, a combination café and mercantile. The place also had a considerable number of books on its shelves. At Sean's first visit, the proprietors had explained their love for books, and their hopes to make them more widely available in the small towns of frontier Texas.

"Good morning, Ranger," Laura St. John, who owned the restaurant along with her husband, Glenn, greeted the Ranger. "Sit anywhere. It's rather early for us to be busy quite yet."

"Mornin', Laura," Sean smiled in return.

He settled at a corner table near the back wall. Laura, a perky blonde, who always seemed to be smiling, brought over a pot of coffee, a mug, and a week-old copy of a Corpus Christi newspaper. She set these on Sean's table.

"Here you go," she said. "What would you like for breakfast?"

"I'll have a half-dozen biscuits, scrambled eggs, ham, and corn bread," Sean ordered.

"Comin' right up."

When Laura headed for the kitchen, Sean poured himself a cup of steaming black coffee. He glanced at a display of dime western novels arrayed on a shelf and laughed softly. Those lurid tales greatly exaggerated the exploits of the Texas Rangers and many other Westerners. The problem Sean had with those cheap books was that many Easterners and Europeans believed every word of them as gospel. Sean smiled, shook his head, and opened the newspaper, which he read while awaiting his meal.

Shortly, Glenn emerged from the kitchen, with Sean's breakfast on several plates balanced along his right arm. St. John had curly brown hair, tending to gray, and a neat gray beard and mustache framed his face. A pair of spectacles dangled from a string around his neck.

"Howdy, Ranger. Heard your voice, but even if I hadn't, once Laura placed that order I knew it had to be yours," Glenn said. "You're the only man I know who can eat this much at one sitting."

He placed Sean's meal on the table.

"Howdy yourself, Glenn," Sean answered. "If your food weren't so doggone good, I wouldn't eat so much. It's a pleasant change from my own trail cookin'."

Glenn smiled at the compliment. "That's good to hear, we do our best."

"You keep feedin' folks like this and you'll be in business a long time," Sean assured him.

Laura had finished serving another customer and came over to join them.

"We sure hope so, Ranger," she said. "We weren't sure if movin' down here from Buffalo was a smart idea. We were doing well up there, but figured we might do even better in a larger town."

"We still miss Buffalo, though," Glenn added. "There are some fine people in that town."

"I have a feelin' if you decided to pack up and move back you'd still do well," Sean told them. "Folks are always lookin' for a decent meal."

Several more patrons entered the shop.

"More customers, so we'd better take care of them, Glenn," Laura said. "If you need more coffee, just let us know, Ranger."

"I sure will," Sean told her.

Sean lingered over his meal, killing time until Western Union opened. Shortly before eight, he paid his bill, said goodbye to Laura and Glenn, and headed for the telegraph office. Barney was just turning the key in the lock when he strode up.

"Mornin', Ranger. I see you're right on time."

"Howdy, Barney, so are you."

"Yup, always am," the elderly clerk grunted. He opened the door. "C'mon in."

Sean followed him into the cluttered office. Barney headed for his telegraph key and desk.

"Looks like some messages came in, all right,"

the clerk noted. "I'll have them in a couple of minutes."

Sean paced restlessly while the key clattered and Barney scrawled out the contents of the overnight wires.

"I only have one for you, Ranger," he finally called. "Here you are."

He passed Sean a sheet of thin yellow paper.

"Woodson not heard from since leaving Laredo. Whereabouts unknown. Your orders are to stay with present assignment. Advise if Woodson arrives. J.B."

"This is it?" Sean asked. "Nothing from Austin?"

"That's all, Ranger," Barney confirmed. "I'll let you know right away if anything else comes in. If I can't locate you, I'll leave word with the sheriff."

"I appreciate that, Barney, thanks."

Sean left the Western Union and went straight to the sheriff's office. Dave Newton was sitting on the front steps and smoking, already waiting for the Ranger.

"Good mornin', Sean. Any word from Austin or your lieutenant yet?" Newton asked.

"Mornin', Dave. Nothin' from Austin yet. Woody's not back at Laredo and Lieutenant Blawcyzk hasn't heard from him either, so it looks like our suspicions are right."

"I was afraid of that," Newton replied. "What now?"

"We keep on tryin' to prove Delgado and Mannion are behind Thad's killin'," Sean answered. "You ready to call on those lawyers?"

"Sure am," the sheriff said. "Their offices are in the building next to the courthouse, right across the hall from each other. We can talk to both of 'em at once, if they're agreeable. They should be gettin' there right about now."

Newton took a final drag on his cigarette and then threw the butt into the street. He pushed himself to his feet.

"Lead the way," Sean told him.

The county courthouse was a block away from Newton's office. The building opposite contained the town apothecary, a millinery shop, and several offices, including the law offices of Hiram Beckett and Hezekiah Trask. When Sean and Newton reached the building, the sheriff called to the bearded, bespectacled man opening the front door.

"Hiram, hold on a minute!"

Attorney Hiram Beckett turned at Newton's call and said, "Good morning, Sheriff. This is a surprise, seeing you here so early, especially since there's no court today."

"I know that, Hiram, only I've got some other business. This is Texas Ranger Sean Kennedy."

Beckett scrutinized Sean closely while they shook hands.

"Good morning, Mister Beckett," Sean replied.

"I assume this business involves you, Ranger," Beckett stated.

"It does," Sean confirmed.

"Why don't we step inside my office?" Beckett suggested. "This boardwalk is hardly the place for a confidential discussion."

"That's a good idea," Newton agreed. "We'd also like Hezekiah to be there."

"He's already in his office, Dave. You and Ranger Kennedy make yourselves comfortable while I go fetch him."

"We'll do just that," Newton replied.

Newton and Sean settled onto thick leather chairs in Beckett's office, while Beckett went after his fellow attorney. Newton built and lit a quirly while they waited.

"Let's hope both these shysters cooperate with us," he told Sean.

"It'd make things a lot easier," Sean agreed.

A moment later Beckett returned and with him was a young lawyer, carefully dressed. His mustache was combed and waxed, not a hair on his head out of place. Sean and Newton rose to greet the new arrival, whose dark eyes were somber as he was introduced.

"Hezekiah, this is Ranger Sean Kennedy. Ranger, Hezekiah Trask."

"Hiram tells me you have something to discuss with us, Ranger," Trask said, as they shook hands.

"That's right," Sean answered.

"I assume you have credentials . . . proper identification?"

"Of course I do."

While a few Rangers wore a silver star in circle badge, usually carved by themselves from a Mexican five or ten peso coin, Sean was not among their number. He merely carried his Ranger commission in his pocket. He dug out the paper and handed it to the attorney. Trask scrutinized it carefully and then passed it to Beckett.

"This seems to be in order. What do you think, Hiram?"

Beckett also studied the credentials.

"Yes, it appears genuine," he admitted. "If you'll all be seated we can get to the matter which has brought Ranger Kennedy here."

He handed Sean's commission back to him.

Beckett sat behind his heavy pine desk, while Trask took the chair alongside. Sean and Newton returned to their chairs. Both attorneys pulled cigars from their pockets and lit up, while Newton rolled and lit another cigarette.

"Ranger Kennedy, what did you wish to see us about?" Beckett questioned.

"I'm following up on an investigation another Ranger, Thad Dutton, was conducting into the affairs of the Triangle VY and Lazy DM ranches," Sean explained. "There were apparently some problems between the owners. There have been suggestions of irregularities in the dealings between Ethan Porter and Duncan Mannion, particularly in the recent agreement whereby Porter is to turn ownership and control over most of the Triangle VY to Mannion," Sean fibbed. "You gentlemen are the respective attorneys for Porter and Mannion. With your permission, I would like to examine the sales agreement."

Beckett pursed his lips, pressing his hands together and blowing softly through them.

"I was of the impression Ranger Dutton's investigation had concluded," he probed.

"Not entirely," Sean again bluffed. "Unfortunately, Ranger Dutton will not be able to finish his work, because was murdered. I have reason to believe his killing is tied into his investigation."

Trask tsked sympathetically. "It is really a shame about your fellow lawman, Ranger Kennedy," he stated. "However, I don't believe we can show you the agreement between my client and Mister Beckett's. What is your opinion, Hiram?"

"I agree," Beckett concurred. "That would quite probably violate attorney-client privilege."

"Those papers are going to be part of the public record in a few days," Newton pointed out. "Then they'll be available for anyone to see."

"True, in a few days," Beckett smirked.

"We can get a court order, especially since this is now a murder case, a murder case involving the killing of a Ranger," Sean said. "It'd be a lot easier for all concerned if we didn't have to. Once we request that court order, the entire county'll know we're looking at Porter and Mannion. It'd be better for your clients if we did this quietly. Both of you are present, so it can't be claimed we favored one party over the other."

"Perhaps," Trask conceded, "only I still don't believe we can grant you access to those files."

Sean sighed deeply, and came to his feet. The next thing the lawyers knew, they were staring down the barrel of his heavy Colt Peacemaker.

"Lock the door, Sheriff," he ordered.

"Sure."

Once Newton had locked the door, Sean continued, "I'd hoped it wouldn't come to this. I assure both of you this gun is fully loaded. Attorney Beckett, it's pointed right at your, shall we say, private parts," he threatened. "It'd be a real shame if this weapon accidentally discharged."

"You don't think you can get away with this, Ranger?" Beckett thundered.

"I believe I can. The sheriff will witness that my gun fell, hit the floor, and went off from the impact, unfortunately severely wounding a dedicated attorney. Isn't that so, Dave?"

"I'd have to testify that's exactly what happened," Newton answered.

"He's only bluffing, Hiram," Trask suggested.

"That's easy for you to say, Hezekiah," Beckett stammered. "That gun's not pointed at you."

"It is now."

Sean shifted the Colt just slightly, so it was now aimed squarely at Trask's belly.

"You see, Attorney Trask, after this gun fell and wounded Attorney Beckett, he collapsed to the floor, thrashing in utter agony. In his struggles, he reflexively grabbed my gun, but instead of shooting me, tragically he put a bullet right through your middle, cutting short the life and career of a brilliant young lawyer. It's your choice, gentlemen."

"You wouldn't dare. You're a Texas Ranger, sworn to uphold the law," Beckett warned.

Sean returned the Colt to cover Mannion's lawyer.

"Thad Dutton was my friend and ridin' pard. Now he's dead and another Ranger sent down here is missin'," he snarled. "You really want to take the chance I won't pull this trigger?"

Sean thumbed back the hammer of his pistol. His dark eyes seemed to bore clear through Beckett.

"I . . . all right. You win, Ranger," Beckett's shoulders slumped in defeat. "I'll get those papers."

"Now you're talking sense. Dave, go with him to make sure he doesn't try anything."

"Glad to, Sean."

Sean moved the gun once more, again pointing it at Trask's stomach.

"Just so you don't try anything foolish," he said.

Trask said nothing, merely glared at the Ranger.

It only took a moment for Beckett to remove the sales agreement between Mannion and Trask from his files, and place it on his desk. Once he had, Sean slid his gun back into its holster.

"There you are, Ranger. I assure you that you will not find anything irregular or illegal in those papers. It is merely a standard real estate transfer contract. Attorney Trask will confirm that."

"My colleague is speaking the truth, Ranger," Trask said.

"Let me and Sheriff Newton decide," Sean answered. "With both of you as witnesses we took nothing from this file, nor made any changes to the documents."

Sean began scrutinizing the agreement. He pored over the papers for nearly three-quarters of an hour. Suddenly he drew in a sharp breath.

"I've got it, Dave!" he exclaimed.

"You've found somethin'?"

"I sure have, right here. Take a look."

Sean pointed to a short segment of the agreement. Newton quickly scanned it, and then gave a low whistle.

"That's it, all right. Pretty much . . ."

"Don't say anythin' more," Sean cautioned, cutting the sheriff short. He gestured toward the two attorneys.

"Yeah, reckon you're right," Newton admitted.

"What's 'it', Ranger?" Beckett demanded. "What have you found?"

"I'm afraid I can't say right now," Sean answered.

"You have to tell us. We insist that you do so, immediately," Trask persisted.

"I wouldn't push your luck if I were you, Trask," Sean warned. "You haven't done your client any favors, the way this agreement is written. In fact, you might have left yourself open to a breach of duty charge, perhaps even disbarment."

"What . . . what do you mean, Ranger?" Trask spluttered.

"You're the smart lawyer. I'll let you figure that out," Sean retorted. "Now that I've found what I need, the sheriff and I will be leaving. I warn you both, don't let anything happen to those papers, either set," Sean advised. "They may well be evidence in a murder case."

Sean pushed back from the desk. He and Newton headed toward the door. When they reached it, Sean turned back to Beckett and Trask. He pulled his Colt from its holster and grinned wickedly at the lawyers.

"Just so you know, I wouldn't have used this gun."

He shoved the gun back in its holster, turned away, and stalked out the door.

Newton could barely contain himself until they had crossed the street and entered his office. Once the door was closed, he burst out laughing.

"Sean, that was the greatest job of bluffin' I've ever seen." He chortled, "Pullin' your gun on those two shiftless sidewinders. I'll never forget the expressions on their faces. Beckett looked like he'd swallowed a lemon!"

"I figured that was the only way to get what I wanted," Sean replied. "I had to stretch the truth a bit, too."

"A bit!" Newton could no longer control his mirth. "Tellin' Trask he might be disbarred! He fell for it too. Man, I'd sure hate to get into a poker game with you, Ranger."

"Well, what Trask let go by is undoubtedly legal, but any lawyer worth his salt wouldn't allow a client to sign something like that," Sean answered.

"That's for certain," Newton agreed. "Like I nearly let slip, that clause pretty much signs Ethan Porter's death warrant."

"Absolutely it does," Sean agreed. "I would have liked to have brought those papers with us for safekeepin', but that might've made them worthless as evidence."

The clause in question read: "Upon the death of Ethan Allen Porter, the ownership of the remaining portion of the Triangle VY Ranch, including all improvements and buildings thereupon, will become the property of Duncan Quincy Mannion or his heirs, with no further compensation or consideration whatsoever due any and all heirs of the aforesaid Ethan Allen Porter."

"I wonder if Porter understands what that clause means," Newton mused.

"I'm certain he does as far as the property reverting to Mannion," Sean answered. "I doubt he realizes once those papers are signed, it'll only be a few weeks or mebbe a couple of months at most, before he meets with an 'unfortunate accident.' "

"Or a drygulcher's bullet in his back," Newton added. "His kids'll be tossed off their land without bein' able to do anything about it. I don't think that would upset Susanna all that much, but it'd just about kill poor Brad."

"Who might then do something really foolish, like goin' after Mannion," Sean said.

"What do we do now?"

"I've got to head back to Mannionville. Once I reach there, I'll see if Levi has come up with somethin'. If he hasn't, at least I can caution Porter not to sign that sales agreement. If nothing else, I'll arrest Carlos Delgado on suspicion of murder. That could make him or Mannion nervous enough so one of 'em might crack."

"In the meantime, I'll keep close watch on Trask and Beckett," Newton stated.

"You might want to obtain a court order authorizin' you to take those papers from 'em and hold them in your custody," Sean advised.

"Good idea."

Newton started to say something further, but never got the chance. He was interrupted when the teenaged apprentice to blacksmith Gunnar Jorgenson threw open the office door. The youth was frantic.

"Sheriff! Come quick! Hurry!" he shouted.

"What's wrong, Johnny?" Newton asked.

"Don't waste time. Get out here, fast!"

Newton and Sean hurried outside. Johnny pointed up the street. Several other passersby were also staring in that direction.

"Look, Sheriff!"

An exhausted black and white pinto gelding, limping heavily, was weaving its way down the road. Blood streaked the horse's neck. His rider was slumped over in the saddle, hands wrapped into the pinto's thick mane.

"That's Brad Porter!" Sean exclaimed. "Somethin's gone wrong, Dave!"

The worn-out pinto stopped, head hanging and spraddle-legged. Sean and Newton ran to the horse. Just as they reached it, Brad lost his grip on the horse's mane, and slipped from the saddle to sprawl in the dusty street. Partially dried blood covered the back of his shirt. A bullet hole was apparent, just under his shoulder blade. Another slug had ripped through the youngster's upper left arm.

"Someone get the doc!" Newton ordered.

"I'll get him, Sheriff," Johnny offered. He raced for the physician's office.

Sean knelt beside the boy and rolled him onto his back. He removed Brad's bandanna and opened his shirt to ease his ragged breathing. Brad's eyes flickered open. He struggled to speak, "Ranger."

"Take it easy, son. Don't try to talk," Sean advised. "The doc's on his way."

"Have . . . have to," Brad insisted. "Your pardner's . . . dead. Carlos . . . Delgado . . . killed him."

Sean gasped as if he'd taken a Comanche lance in the gut. His head reeled. He couldn't believe what he'd just heard.

"Levi's . . . dead? Are you sure, son?"

"Yeah. Saw Delgado . . . plug him . . . more'n once. Didn't give him a chance. Delgado killed . . . Thad Dutton, too . . . and that other . . . Ranger."

"Woodson?"

"Yeah . . . that's the name . . . Levi said."

Johnny pushed his way through the crowd surrounding the wounded youth, with Doctor Horatio Green, the town physician, in tow.

"Move aside, please," Green ordered Sean.

"I've gotta talk . . . to the Ranger," Brad insisted.

"You let me be the judge of that, son," Green responded. He made a cursory examination of the boy's wounds.

"I can't do anything here. Some of you carry him to my office," he ordered.

"Freckles. My horse," Brad choked out. "He saved my life. Needs . . . tendin' to."

"I'll take care of your bronc," Johnny offered. He gathered Freckles' reins and led the pinto away.

Sean, Newton, Jorgenson, and Sal Bromley, the owner of the feed and grain store, lifted Brad and followed Doctor Green to his office. They carried the boy inside and placed him on a table in the back examination room.

"I need him on his stomach, so I can get at the bullet in his back," Green ordered.

"Not yet. Not until I . . . talk . . . with the Ranger," Brad pleaded.

"All right." Green gave into the boy's plea. "But, only for a moment, son. That bullet has to come out and quickly." To Sean he added, "Keep your questions short."

"I will, Doc," Sean assured him. "Brad, what happened?"

"I ran into . . . your pard . . . watchin' Mannion's . . . place," Brad answered. "I was followin' . . . my sister. She and Mannion . . . workin' together . . . I think . . . Levi agreed."

"Why?" Sean puzzled.

"Susanna . . . jealous about . . . Thad and . . . Dorothea. Watched her . . . go to Mannion's . . . several . . . times. Couldn't tell you that when you . . . were at our . . . ranch."

"You'd better get to the point, son," Doctor Green warned him. "You've lost a lot of blood. You could lose consciousness at any time."

"All right," Brad answered.

"Just tell me about the killin's, Brad," Sean told him.

"Susanna . . . had Thad's belt . . . took it from him. Wouldn't . . . give it back. Levi thought . . . it was part payment . . . to Delgado for . . . killin' Thad. Next time . . . I saw it was in . . . Mannionville. Delgado was . . . wearin' it. Stranger asked him why . . . he had that belt. Delgado gutshot him. I didn't know then . . . but had feelin' hombre . . . was Ranger. Levi told me . . . he was."

"So that's what happened to Woody," Sean gritted. "How'd Delgado get the drop on Levi?"

Sweat glistened on Brad's forehead, and his eyes were bright with pain. His voice was fading as he struggled to answer.

"Levi told me . . . to go home. Instead, I followed him . . . to Mannionville. Saw Delgado and him . . . shoot it out . . . in saloon. Delgado plugged Levi . . . in gut . . . three or four times. Even after . . . Levi was down . . . Delgado put . . . another slug into him."

"Who shot you, Brad?" Sean asked.

"John Spallone . . . town marshal . . . caught me watchin' . . . Delgado kill Levi. He drilled me . . . . I got out of town, but . . . the marshal and Delgado, couple others . . . followed me. They would've finished me, but I fell off . . . Freckles . . . into . . . gully. Reckon they figured I . . . was dead. . . . They must've shot . . . my horse. Good thing they . . . didn't kill . . . him. Dunno how Freckles found me. Lucky . . . for me . . . he did. . . . I managed to . . . get back in saddle . . . and head for here. Didn't dare . . . try for . . . home."

"That's enough, Ranger," Green ordered. "You've got the information you wanted. If I'm to keep this boy alive so you'll have his testimony when the time comes, I need to get to work right now."

"Okay, Doc." Sean placed a hand on Brad's shoulder. "Thanks, Brad. You just let the doc care for you now."

"Sure, Ranger." Brad smiled weakly, then his eyes closed.

"Everyone out," Green ordered.

Sean and Newton paused in the front room.

"What're you gonna do now, Sean?" Newton questioned.

"Do you really need to ask, Dave?" Sean answered. "I'm goin' after Carlos Delgado, and Marshal Spallone. Once I'm through with them,

296

I'm goin' after Duncan Mannion . . . and Susanna Porter."

"You'll have more than just Delgado and Mannion to contend with," the sheriff warned him.

"I know that. I'm askin' you to come with me, Dave, along with any deputies you can spare."

"I can have four or five men ready to ride in twenty minutes," Newton promised.

"Make that ten," Sean answered.

Dan Devine was hurrying up the boardwalk as Sean and Newton stepped outside.

"Sheriff, what happened? I heard there was a shootin'," the deputy questioned.

"There was, Dan. We're ridin' for Mannionville. Round up Jake Haley, Ed Manning, and Ken O'Dowd," Newton ordered. "Pete Dailey too, if you can find him. Meet us at the office, pronto."

"All right, Sheriff."

Fifteen minutes later, with Sean in the lead, the posse galloped out of Falfurrias.

Chapter 15

Sean and the posse kept their horses at a run for the first mile and then pulled the mounts down to a steady, ground-eating lope, occasionally slowing the pace to a trot or walk. Several times they stopped to allow the horses a breather. As anxious as Sean was to reach Mannionville, he would not kill the horses to do so.

"Do you think it's the right idea headin' for town, rather than the Lazy DM?" Newton asked Sean, during one of the breaks.

"I sure do. Delgado knows I'll be showin' up there sooner or later. Evidently he thinks Brad's dead, which means Delgado doesn't realize I know he killed Levi. He'll be waitin' to surprise me with that news, figurin' he can push me into a rash move. Plus, he'll have plenty of backing in town, including the marshal. He'll be countin' on that."

"He could just drill you in the back from an alley or window," Jake Haley noted.

"He could, but I doubt it," Sean answered. "He'll want to gloat about killin' Levi. Besides, I don't believe Delgado's the back-shootin' type. If he were, he would've just bushwhacked Thad Dutton, rather'n followin' him and pluggin' him from the front, close-up. Delgado wants to face whoever he's gunnin'. He needs to be sure they know who shot them. Now let's get movin'.""

Sean pushed Ghost into a lope once again. For the remaining miles, he would keep the big blue roan at that steady gait. An hour later they were approaching Mannionville.

"Whoa up a second," Sean ordered, when they reached the edge of town. The posse reined their horses to a halt.

"Just remember, Carlos Delgado is mine. You men are here to cover my back," Sean reminded them. "Be careful. We don't know how many of Delgado's compadres are with him."

"You don't need to say that twice," Ed Manning answered.

"Good, check your weapons," Sean ordered.

The men pulled out their pistols, checked the actions, and placed cartridges in the empty chambers. They gave their rifles a quick inspection and then shoved them back in their scabbards.

"Everybody's ready? Then let's go."

Sean put Ghost into a fast walk.

Most of the passersby on the street vanished as if by magic when the posse rode into Mannionville. A few stood, staring after the lawmen, but most disappeared behind closed doors.

"There's no sign of the marshal," Devine noted.

"No, but you can be sure he's watchin'," Newton replied.

"When we reach the saloon, Dave, you and Dan come inside with me," Sean ordered. "The rest of you watch the street."

"All right, Ranger," O'Dowd answered.

Sean led the posse to the Dog Devil. They dismounted, and looped their horses' reins over the front hitch rail. Sean ducked under the rail and onto the boardwalk. Newton and Devine followed closely behind. They paused for a moment to allow their vision to adjust to the dimmer light under the awning. It would be even darker inside.

"Ready?" Sean asked. Newton and Devine nodded. Sean pulled out his Colt and then pushed through the batwings and into the Dog Devil.

Carlos Delgado was seated at a rear table, along with Joker Henry and Kansas Casey. He was playing solitaire, while his companions nursed glasses of whiskey.

Sean leveled his gun at Delgado's chest as soon as he spotted the outlaw. He cocked the Peacemaker's hammer.

"You killed my pardner, Delgado," Sean snarled. "Now I'm takin' you in to hang!"

Delgado began to rise from his chair.

"Don't go for your gun, Delgado," Sean warned. "Or I'll drop you where you stand, with pleasure."

The outlaw didn't listen. He scrambled to his

feet, grabbing for his pistol. Sean shot him twice through the stomach. Delgado staggered backwards, folded slightly, and then straightened. Despite the bullets in his gut, Delgado managed to pull his Colt from its holster. Not giving Levi's killer a chance to aim that gun, Sean fired again, hitting Delgado in the left side of his chest, spinning him around. Delgado fell onto his side. His arm raised slightly, then dropped. The gunman who'd killed three Texas Rangers never moved again.

At the same moment Delgado fell, Joker Henry went for his gun. Dan Devine put a bullet into Henry's chest, and the outlaw crumpled to the floor.

"You want a part of this?" Newton challenged Kansas Casey. His Remington was pointed at Casey's belt buckle.

"No, I sure don't, Sheriff," the shaken outlaw replied, staring at the bodies of his partners.

"Shuck that gun belt and get your hands up. Then turn around, now!"

"All right." Casey unbuckled the belt and let it drop to the floor. He raised his hands shoulder high and turned his back to the sheriff.

Sean walked over to Delgado. He pulled the outlaw's gun from his hand and tossed it in the corner, then rolled Delgado onto his back. He bent over the dead gunman, unbuckled Thad's belt, and pulled it from around Delgado's waist.

For a moment, Sean considered wrapping Thad's belt around his own waist for safekeeping, but quickly discarded the idea. There was no way the lanky Dutton's belt would fit around the burly Sean's middle. Instead he tucked the belt behind his own, to put in his saddlebags.

"You died too quick, Delgado," Sean muttered. "I should've gut-shot you like you did Levi."

"Look out, Ranger!" Devine shouted. Curly had pulled a double-barreled sawed-off shotgun from under the bar and leveled it at Sean's back. Before he could fire, Devine shot him in the side. Curly's fingers tightened on the triggers as he stumbled back, and he discharged one barrel into the ceiling. The deputy shot him again, through his right breast. Curly twisted from the bullet's impact and pulled the other trigger of the scatter-gun as he fell. The closely bunched buckshot shattered the back-bar mirror. Shards of glass showered down on the dead bartender.

"You all right, Ranger?" Devine asked. "He was gonna plug you in the back. That scattergun would've made mincemeat of you."

"I'm fine. Thanks, Dan," Sean replied. "Let's get outta here."

Newton put the barrel of his Remington against Casey's back.

"I'll deposit this buzzard in jail and then be right back," he said.

"I'll come with you," Sean answered. "Funny

this shootin' didn't get the marshal's attention. Mebbe he's not in town after all."

"Could be," Newton agreed. "C'mon, you," he ordered Casey as he nudged the outlaw along with a jab of his pistol.

A flurry of gunshots sounded from the street, followed by rapidly fading hoof beats, then more shots. Sean and Devine rushed outside. The rest of the possemen were still shooting at a horse and rider who were already out of pistol range and rapidly fading from sight. Ed Manning was sprawled on his back in the middle of the street, a crimson stain spreading across his shirtfront.

"What happened?" Sean demanded.

"The marshal came out from behind his office, shootin'. He cut down Ed right off and kept the rest of us pinned down," O'Dowd answered, cursing. "Reckon he's hightailin' it for the border."

"I doubt it," Sean answered. "I figure he's goin' to warn Mannion to expect some company, now that Delgado's dead."

Newton emerged from the saloon with his prisoner. He quickly took in the situation and asked, "Spallone, right?"

"Right," Sean answered.

"What're we waitin' for?" Pete Dailey demanded. "Ed was my best friend, and Spallone killed him. He's gonna pay for that, but he's already got a good start on us. You're lettin' him get away, Ranger."

"Spallone's not goin' anywhere, except the gallows," Sean assured the distraught Dailey. "We've got no chance of catchin' him before he reaches the Lazy DM. He's on a fresh horse, while our mounts are plumb worn out. The main house and bunkhouse at Mannion's place are built like fortresses. We've got to figure out how to get inside without gettin' shot to pieces."

"The Ranger's right. That sorrel gelding of Spallone's is the fastest horse in the county," Devine pointed out. "We'd never catch him even on fresh cayuses, let alone our jaded broncs."

Newton gave Casey a shove.

"I'm gonna put this jasper in a cell," he said. "There's nothing we can do for Ed right now. A couple of you carry him over to the marshal's office. We'll leave him there until this is all over."

Haley and O'Dowd picked up Manning's body and followed Newton to the marshal's office and jail. Casey was locked in the single cell, while Manning's remains were placed on a cowhide sofa.

The posse had already untied their horses, and was ready when the three men returned. Once the sheriff and two deputies mounted, Sean headed them for the Lazy DM.

With their horses exhausted, Sean held the posse to a slow lope. He was reluctant even to maintain that steady pace, but did have to make as much time as possible without crippling the horses. It was over an hour later when he called a halt, just out of sight of the Lazy DM.

"Dave, you and I are gonna scout ahead for a bit. The rest of you stay here," he ordered. "Smoke if you want, while you've got the chance."

"How long you figurin' on bein' gone, Ranger?" Haley inquired.

"Half-an-hour at the most," Sean replied. "There's no point in tryin' to sneak up on Mannion, since I'm certain Spallone's already warned him we're comin'. In fact, I'd eat my boots if he hasn't. I just want to refresh my memory about the set-up at Mannion's place. It won't take long."

"All right, we'll be waitin' for you," Haley grinned.

The Ranger and sheriff dismounted. They handed their horses' reins to Haley.

"Let's go, Dave."

"Right with you, Sean."

It only took a few minutes for them to cover the short distance to the ranch. They bellied down behind a clump of scrub junipers.

"They're ready for us," Sean noted. "I count at least six men guardin' the place."

"Yeah, but there's plenty of cover for us," Newton observed. "We'll be able to get in close. We should be able to pick off some of those guards before they even spot us."

"That's true enough, but the place is a fort, like I said," Sean replied. "Just gettin' past those boundary walls'll take a lot of work."

"And quite a few bullets," Newton added. "You reckon mebbe you can talk Mannion into surrenderin'? He's a wealthy man, with a lot of influence. He could afford the best lawyers he can find, so he might want to take his chances in court. So far, the evidence you've got is pretty flimsy, Sean. With Delgado dead you've lost a prime witness."

"I'm gonna give him the chance, but I doubt he'll take it," Sean answered. "He's worried about what Thad Dutton might've dug up, despite what he says. Otherwise why would he have had Thad killed?"

"I guess you're right at that," Newton conceded. "It sure would make things a lot easier if he'd give up peaceably, though."

The horses in the nearest corral had been milling around. Suddenly they stopped, looking into the distance, heads high and ears pricked forward at some sound or scent they had caught.

"There's Spallone's sorrel. The marshal's here, all right," Sean said. He drew in a sharp breath and then muttered a curse. "No! It can't be!"

"What?" Newton asked.

"You recognize that palomino alongside Spallone's horse?"

"Sure. That's Susanna Porter's horse." Newton

306

also issued an oath. "Blast the luck! Why the devil does she have to be here now, of all times?"

"I dunno, but it sure complicates things," Sean answered. "Bad enough we've got to worry about not hurtin' Mannion's wife and daughter, not to mention the servants, but now Susanna too."

"Hopefully Mannion will keep them out of harm's way," Newton said. "Meanwhile, have you got any idea how to get inside that place?"

"One or two," Sean replied. "First off, we've got to get close enough to even try. Let's get back to the men." They wriggled their way out of the brush and then headed back to the waiting posse.

Ken O'Dowd was the first man to spot them as they approached.

"Here comes the Ranger and Sheriff Newton," he said. "Won't be long now until we find out what's up."

A moment later, Sean and Newton reached the men.

"Well, Ranger? What're we up against?" O'Dowd questioned.

"Quite a few guards and a house built to hold off any Indian attacks or Mexican raiders," Sean answered. "It's not gonna be easy gettin' to Mannion. Don't forget Spallone's also in there."

"What in blue blazes'll we do, then?" Devine asked.

"First, I'm gonna give Mannion and Spallone

the chance to turn themselves in," Sean explained.

"There's not a snowball's chance in Sonora of them doin' that," Dailey retorted.

"I figure that, too," Sean answered. "So here's what we'll need to do."

Sean picked up a dead twig to sketch a rough map of the Lazy DM's main house, bunkhouse, and outbuildings in the sand. He went over his plans twice to make sure they were clear.

"Any questions?" he asked. There was no response.

"Good. We won't need the horses, so we'll leave 'em here," Sean ordered. "Get your rifles and all the cartridges you can carry."

Ten minutes later, Sean had his men in position around the Lazy DM. He was in the spot he had chosen for himself, a hollow behind a downed cottonwood.

Once he was certain the others were ready, Sean cautiously peered over the tree trunk. He waited until one of the guards was directly in front of him and then fired a shot just over the man's head. The guard jerked around, startled.

"Don't move, any of you!" Sean called out. "This is Texas Ranger Sean Kennedy, along with Sheriff Newton of Brooks County and several deputies. We're here to place Duncan Mannion and John Spallone under arrest. To the best of my knowledge, there are no charges against the rest of you. If you don't resist, you will be free to leave. One of you, find your boss. I want to offer him the chance to give himself up, peaceably."

The front door opened and Duncan Mannion stepped onto the porch.

"I'm right here, Ranger, so's the marshal," he shouted. "We have no intention of surrendering. If you want me and John, come and get us."

He slammed the heavy oak door shut.

The guard opposite Sean leveled his rifle at the Ranger. Before he could fire, Sean shot him through the stomach. The man dropped his gun, doubled up, and draped himself over the wall.

Instantly, the air around the Lazy DM became a maelstrom of flying lead. Chunks of adobe flew when bullets struck the barrier walls and the house.

A bullet fired by Red Dover plucked at Dave Newton's sleeve. Newton's return shot plowed into Dover's chest. Dover fell, face-up and unmoving.

While the posse kept up a continual fire, Sean and Dan Devine crept toward the barn. Bill Hollister, the Lazy DM foreman, was in the loft. His precise shooting was keeping Jake Haley and Ken O'Dowd pinned down.

"I've got to get Hollister," Sean shouted to Devine. "Keep me covered."

As Devine maintained a steady fire, Sean zigzagged toward a large clay flowerpot. He dove behind the pot, steadied his Winchester, and pulled the trigger. His slug tore into Hollister's belly. The foreman half-rose, jackknifed, and then plunged from the loft. He thudded on the hard-packed dirt below.

The accurate fire of the posse had cut the number of guards by half. Several of them were dead, several more wounded, and a number had turned and fled to the shelter of the bunkhouse. One of those in the bunkhouse tied a white rag to his rifle and waved it from a window as a sign of surrender.

"Now's our chance, Dan!" Sean shouted. He left his empty Winchester, pulled out his Colt, and raced for the barn. He leapt through the|door in a rolling dive.

Devine was close behind him. Clete Fleming rose from cover behind a light wagon, to draw a bead on the deputy's back. Jake Haley dropped Fleming with a bullet through his neck before he could pull the trigger. Devine slid on his belly into the barn.

"Made it, Ranger," he grinned.

"Good. Let's hope we can find what we need."

Sean and Devine rapidly searched the barn.

"Got a sledgehammer right here," Devine called.

"Let's see what else we can come up with," Sean answered. He headed for the storage room at the far end of the structure. Once there, he opened a large toolbox.

"I've got an ax, Dan."

"That should do," Devine replied. "Let's get outta here."

The Ranger and deputy headed for the door. Sean halted there and caught Dave Newton's eye by waving the ax. Newton nodded and then dove behind cover just as a bullet ripped the air just over his head.

"Sean and Dan have what they need," he shouted. "Pour it into that house, men!"

The posse rained bullets on the main house. Under the protection of the barrage of lead, Sean and Devine dashed across the yard and onto the veranda. They halted at the front door. Once Sean and Dan were huddled against the front wall, the rest of the posse held their fire, except for a few occasional shots to keep the men inside away from the windows.

"Just keep clear of any bullets comin' through this door, Dan," Sean warned the deputy.

"You do the same, Ranger," Devine retorted.

While the rest of the posse maintained their fire, Sean and Devine pounded away at the thick oak door. It resisted their efforts for some minutes, but then finally splintered. Sean smashed his shoulder into the door and slammed it open.

Two Lazy DM gunmen were waiting. Sean shot one through the chest. The dying man toppled into his companion, spoiling his aim. Devine put a bullet into the second man's gut. The renegade screamed, clawed at his bullet-torn belly, and pitched to his face.

"Spallone and Mannion are probably in the office," Sean said. "Follow me, Dan and watch for any snakes hidin' in the woodpile."

Cautiously, they headed down the corridor. The house was eerily silent, the only sounds Sean's and Devine's gasping breaths, and their footsteps.

The Ranger and deputy neared the parlor. Just as they entered, another gunman rose up from behind one of the sofas, shot, and his bullet tore a chunk of flesh from Sean's thigh, dropping him to his knees. He and Devine returned fire at the same time, their bullets slamming the man back. He fell against the piano, knocking a candelabrum to the floor, and then rolled over the keyboard. With a jangle of discordant notes, the gunman collapsed.

Devine pulled Sean to his feet. "You all right, Ranger?"

"Yeah, I'll be fine, that's one more down," Sean stated. "Lemme just bandage my leg quick." He pulled the bandanna from his neck and tied it around his thigh. After reloading their pistols, they continued toward Mannion's office.

With Sean limping from his wound, Devine moved more quickly. He was several feet in front of the Ranger when John Spallone emerged from Mannion's office. The renegade marshal leveled his six-gun and fired. His bullet struck Devine in the hip. The deputy staggered sideways, at the same time shooting back at Spallone. His bullet tore along the marshal's ribs. Spallone fired again, twice, both slugs ripping into Devine's chest. As Devine crumpled, the marshal then turned his gun toward Sean. Before he could thumb back the hammer, Sean fired. Spallone winced when the bullet burned a path along his scalp, knocking the Stetson from his head. He sent a snap shot at Sean, which caught the Ranger high in his right side, spinning him half around. Before Sean could return fire, Spallone ducked back into the office.

Colt at the ready, Sean covered the remaining few feet to Mannion's office and stepped inside. Mannion was standing behind his desk, a short-barreled revolver on the desktop in front of him. John Spallone, blood darkening the side of his shirt and dripping from his scalp, was in the corner. He held his gun at his side. Seated next to Mannion's desk was Susanna Porter.

"So, Ranger Kennedy, you didn't take me at my word, did you? You just couldn't accept that your fellow Ranger, Dutton, had no evidence against me. Now it comes to this."

"It sure does, although I have to admit I never expected you and the lady there were in cahoots," Sean snapped.

"Who made that ridiculous accusation?" Susanna demanded. Her eyes were wide with indignation.

"No one other than your own brother, Miss Porter," Sean calmly replied. "He knew what happened between you and Thad Dutton. He's been followin' you, watching your visits with Mannion. He put two and two together and told Ranger Mallory the whole sordid story."

"That's impossible," Susanna protested. "My visits with Mister Mannion were strictly business. They were merely to assure that the transfer of my father's property to the Lazy DM went smoothly."

"Then how did Carlos Delgado get Thad's belt?" Sean growled. "Don't bother to answer . . . You gave it to him."

"That's absurd," Susanna retorted. "You should be ashamed, Ranger, dragging my brother's name into this. Once I speak with him, this matter will be cleared up."

"I'm afraid you may never speak with Brad again," Sean answered. "He's at the doctor's in Mannionville, gravely wounded. You see, he followed my pardner there, and he saw Delgado kill Levi. Of course, he couldn't be allowed to tell anyone that, so Marshal Spallone put a couple of bullets into him. But Brad didn't die, at least not yet, as far as I know. I was able to talk with him before he passed out."

"You killed my brother!" Susanna shouted and

then leapt for Spallone. She passed between Mannion and Sean, preventing the Ranger from getting a clear shot at the rancher until too late. Mannion grabbed his gun from the desk and shot Susanna in the back. She screamed and then collapsed at Spallone's feet.

Sean and Spallone stood motionless and in silence for a moment, stunned by what Mannion had just done, then Spallone turned his gun on the rancher.

"Mannion, you no-good . . . There was no call for you to do that," Spallone cursed.

"I had to," Mannion shrugged. "You saw how she reacted about her brother bein' shot. I couldn't trust her. She would've spilled the beans about our deal. I was plannin' on gettin' rid of her anyway, once everything was settled and I owned the Triangle VY."

"I don't mind killin', but back-shootin' a woman goes too far," Spallone snarled. He fired twice, both bullets tearing through Mannion's lungs. Mannion was slammed against the wall, his eyes wide with shock at the realization the marshal had shot him. He slid to the floor, his blood leaving a crimson trail down the oak paneling.

Spallone turned to face Sean, a thin smile playing across his lips. He held his six-gun at waist level, pointed at the floor.

"I guess it's you and me now, Ranger."

"Reckon so," Sean answered. "You can still surrender, Marshal. I'll testify you shot Mannion for killin' Susanna Porter. It might help at your trial."

Spallone shook his head. "I can't do that, Ranger. I still think I'm faster'n you, big man!"

He leveled his gun. Sean shot him twice in the belly. Spallone's gun spilled from his hand, he slumped over Mannion's desk, and then rolled to the floor.

"Thanks for . . . savin' me . . . from a noose, Ranger," Spallone choked out. His wry smile crossed his lips once more, then he sighed deeply, and his body went slack.

Sean turned away. He left the office and started back down the hallway, where Dave Newton appeared at the far end of the corridor. Blood trickled from a bullet slash along the sheriff's forehead.

"We've got everything under control outside, Sean," he called. "We took quite a few prisoners, so we'll have to sort 'em out later. Most of 'em are just cowhands, and didn't really want any part of this. They don't deserve bein' sent to prison. What about in here?"

"It's over," Sean replied. "Mannion, Spallone, and Susanna Porter are all dead. So's Dan, Spallone killed him. I'm sure sorry it happened, Dave."

"Dan's dead?" Newton echoed, an expression

of deep loss crossing his face. He rubbed the back of his hand across suddenly moist eyes.

"I'm afraid so," Sean answered. "He was a mighty good man, Dave."

"Yeah, he was," Newton answered, struggling to keep his emotions in check. "I'll miss him."

He paused. "You said Susanna Porter's dead?"

"I did," Sean confirmed. "Mannion killed her. We can clear everything up later. Right now I want to find Mannion's wife and daughter. They need to know what happened."

"O'Dowd already found them. They took cover in the springhouse, along with the son, Chuck, too," Newton added. "O'Dowd tells me he wanted in on the fight, but his mother and sister wouldn't let him go. The boy's only fourteen, so I'm certainly glad he wasn't involved in this."

"That's the truth," Sean agreed.

Newton stared at Sean. Blood was darkening the leg of the Ranger's jeans and spreading down the side of his shirt.

"Sean, you'd better let me patch you up. Everything else can wait."

"Not quite yet," Sean objected.

"Now, Ranger!" Newton insisted.

Sean began to protest again, but he sagged onto a side chair before he could speak.

"I guess you're right, Dave," he murmured.

Chapter 16

Sean had to remain in Falfurrias for several more days to recuperate and complete his investigation. He talked with Ethan Porter, Georgia and Dorothea Manning, and waited until Brad Porter was well enough to question. Once he was able to interview the young cowboy, he finished compiling evidence, tied up loose ends, and completed a final report. After all that work was done, he saddled up and headed back to Laredo.

However, Sean detoured on his trip, returning by way of Hamiltonburg to visit the Matney family and give them the news of Levi's death. He also brought Monte, Levi's horse, as another gift for the Matney boys. He knew Levi would approve.

The entire family, especially Mark and Christian, took the news of Levi's loss hard. However, the two boys, with the resilience of the young, bounced back quickly. Sean spent the night at the Matney farm, and by the time he left the next day, Mark and Christian were galloping around on Toby and Monte, engaged in a fierce game of cowboys and Indians.

Several days later, Sean returned to his Ranger Company, at its temporary headquarters outside of

Laredo. After caring for Ghost, giving him some licorice sticks, and turning him loose with the other mounts, he cleaned up a bit himself, and joined Lieutenant Blawcyzk and Sergeant Huggins in the lieutenant's makeshift office. Blawcyzk and Huggins spent considerable time going over Sean's summation of the events in Brooks County. Finally, Blawcyzk looked up from Sean's report.

"I do have one piece of news for you, Sean, which I didn't want to mention until after I read your report," he explained. "Austin did receive something from Thad Dutton, just a few days ago. Thad mailed the file to Headquarters, rather than telegraphing Austin, since it wasn't that urgent, at least in Thad's opinion. Basically, Thad said he did believe Duncan Mannion was behind the trouble, but had no proof. Thad did recommend Austin send another man to Falfurrias if one could be spared. He didn't say this, but putting together his request with the information you've provided, clearly Thad felt he could no longer be effective in that situation."

Blawcyzk paused a few seconds before he continued, "I always figured Thad's womanizing would get him in trouble sooner or later, but I never expected it would get him killed. It's too bad. Thad was a darn good lawman, except for that one vice. Of course, Thad's not alone, since everyone has at least one weakness. Most of us have quite a few."

"That's true, Lieutenant," Sean agreed. "Besides, I doubt Thad had ever dealt with a woman as clever as Susanna Porter. As you saw in my report, she had convinced her father, even before Thad left Falfurrias, to sell out to Mannion. I wouldn't be surprised she had been tellin' Thad her father was going to sell the Triangle VY. That could be the reason Thad didn't push Austin harder to send someone to replace him. Not only that, while she was conspiring with Mannion, Susanna kept tellin' anyone who'd listen it was Mannion who was tryin' to drive her and her family off of their ranch. She was smart, all right."

"It wasn't only Susanna who wanted Thad dead," Huggins pointed out.

"That's right," Sean agreed. "While Susanna wanted him dead for leavin' her for Dorothea, Mannion wanted him dead because he felt Thad was sure to come up with something against him, if he kept diggin'. Mannion also wanted to make sure Thad wouldn't see his daughter again. Dorothea told me she and Thad had even discussed runnin' off and gettin' married."

"I can't picture Thad ever settlin' down," Blawcyzk disagreed.

"You might if you saw Dorothea Mannion," Sean explained. "She's absolutely beautiful.

Don't forget, her father was wealthy and that's a difficult combination for any man to resist."

"So Susanna Porter and Duncan Mannion made a deal. Mannion would have Thad killed, and in exchange Susanna would talk her father into selling out," Blawcyzk summarized.

"That's right," Sean confirmed.

"There's one thing I can't figure," Huggins said. "Why in blue blazes did Mannion's wife and daughter tolerate Susanna comin' around their place so much? You'd think they'd get pretty upset by that."

"At first glance, yes," Sean answered. "But, Georgia Mannion didn't want her daughter marrying a driftin' Texas Ranger, any more than her husband did. Don't forget, her family's pretty high up in San Francisco society. She would want someone better, at least in her mind, for Dorothea than a lawman. So Georgia went along with Mannion and Susanna's plan, or at least didn't disapprove of it. As for Dorothea, she had no choice of buckin' her mother or father. She didn't dare say anything to me and Levi when we talked to the Mannions, and naturally she was never given the chance to see either of us later."

"Greed and lust, two of the seven deadly sins, started all this trouble and drove them to the crime. It seems like one of those is behind most of the offenses we deal with," Blawcyzk noted.

"At least Ethan Porter will be keepin' his ranch."

"Yep," Sean answered. "It's gonna take him a long time to get over Susanna's death, and he's got to mend fences with his son. I have a feelin' he and the boy will work things out. They both love their place. Interestin' tidbit about how Porter named his spread, by the way. You know he's a transplanted Yankee, from Vermont. He came up with the VY for Vermont Yankee. The Triangle came from Vermont's shape, because the state's kind of shaped like a triangle, except the bottom is cut off flat."

"What about Mannion's family?" Huggins asked.

"I dunno," Sean admitted. "I'm sure they'll try'n hang onto the place. Mannion's older son has a ranch near Uvalde. Mebbe he'll sell that and head back home. I'm certain the younger boy will want to keep the Lazy DM, too. Mostly what happens'll depend on Georgia, since she inherits the estate."

Blawcyzk closed the folder containing Sean's report.

"You did fine work, Ranger," he praised.

"Thanks, Lieutenant," Sean replied. "But if Thad hadn't owned that fancy belt of his, we might never have found out who killed him. Same way, if Delgado hadn't made the mistake of wearin' that belt, Woody would never have asked about it, and Brad Porter would never have seen it around Delgado's waist. We might never have gotten the break we needed to connect Delgado to both killin's. It's also lucky whoever shot Brad's horse didn't kill it. The bullet just creased its neck and stunned it, like the old-time mustangers used to do. If that horse had been killed, Brad would have died for sure. Without his warnin', I might've ridden right into a trap."

"Nonetheless, you did a fine job unravelin' this whole mess," the lieutenant reiterated.

Blawcyzk looked closely at Sean. The big Ranger's exhaustion was apparent, and his wounds had not yet completely healed. More importantly, it would take some time for Sean to get over the loss of his riding partner and friend, Levi Mallory.

"Sean, I'm puttin' you on furlough for seven days," he ordered. "I don't care what you do with the time off. Sleep for a week, go into town and get drunk, or just lie around doin' nothing, you need a good rest."

Sean looked at his lieutenant. A broad smile crossed his face.

"Jim, make that ten, and it'll give me enough time to get home and visit Amy. In fact, that'll give me enough time to marry her. After what I've just gone through, and seein' what happened to Levi, Woody, and Thad, I realize life's too short. I'm not puttin' off getting hitched any longer."

Blawcyzk laughed.

"Make it fourteen days, Sean," he answered. "Kiss the bride for me."

"And for me," Huggins added.

"Is that an order, Lieutenant?" Sean grinned.

"It is. One you'd better obey, or else!"

"Then I'm gone."

Sean headed out of the office at a trot.

About the Author

Jim Griffin developed an interest in the frontier west, particularly the Texas Rangers, at an early age. He grew to be an avid student and collector of Ranger artifacts, memorabilia, and other items. His collection is on display in the Texas Ranger Hall of Fame and Museum in Waco.

Jim's quest for authenticity in his writing has taken him to the famous Old West towns of Pecos, Deadwood, Cheyenne, Tombstone, and numerous others. While Jim's books are novels, he strives to keep his stories as accurate as possible within the realm of fiction. To that end, his good friend Texas Ranger Sergeant Jim Huggins, along with friends Karl Rehn and Penny Riggs, help him with the technical and historic aspects of his books.

A graduate of Southern Connecticut State University, Jim divides his time between Branford, Connecticut and Keene, New Hampshire when he isn't traveling through the western United States and Canada. A devoted and enthusiastic horseman, Jim bought his first horse when he was a junior in college. His favorite breed is the American Paint Horse. Jim is a member of the Connecticut Horse Council Volunteer Horse Patrol, an organization that assists state park rangers in patrolling state parks and forests.

Jim's books are traditional Westerns in the best sense of the term, portraying strong heroes with good character and moral values. His heroes and villains are clearly separated. No brooding anti-heroes will be found in the pages of a Griffin novel. He was initially inspired to write at the urging of friend and well-known author James Reasoner. After successful publication of his first book, *Trouble Rides the Texas Pacific*, released in 2005, he was encouraged to continue his writing.

Jim Griffin is a member of the Western Writers of America and Western Fictioneers.

Center Point Large Print
600 Brooks Road / PO Box 1
Thorndike, ME 04986-0001 USA

(207) 568-3717

US & Canada:
1 800 929-9108
www.centerpointlargeprint.com